Harp on the Willow

ALSO BY BJ HOFF

EMERALD BALLAD
Land of a Thousand Dreams
Dawn of the Golden Promise
Heart of the Lonely Exile
Sons of an Ancient Glory
Song of the Silent Harp

RIVERHAVEN YEARS
Rachel's Secret
Where Grace Abides
River of Mercy

MOUNTAIN SONG LEGACY
A Distant Music
The Wind Harp
The Song Weaver

STANDALONES
American Anthem*
Song of Erin**
Harp on the Willow

*American Anthem is a trilogy that includes: *Prelude, Cadence,* and *Jubilee.*
**Song of Erin includes two complete novels: *Cloth of Heaven* and *Ashes and Lace.*

Harp on the Willow

BJ HOFF

HARVEST HOUSE PUBLISHERS
EUGENE, OREGON

Scripture quotations are from the Contemporary English Version © 1991, 1992, 1995 by American Bible Society, used by permission, and from the King James Version of the Bible.

Cover by John Hamilton Design

Cover Image © givaga, Jon Bilous, v.gi, Josh Cornish / Shutterstock; Greg Komar

Published in association with the Books & Such Management, 52 Mission Circle, Suite 122, PMB 170, Santa Rosa, CA 95409-5370, www.booksandsuch.com.

HARP ON THE WILLOW

Copyright © 2018 by BJ Hoff
Published by Harvest House Publishers
Eugene, Oregon 97408
www.harvesthousepublishers.com

ISBN 978-0-7369-2067-4 (pbk.)
ISBN 978-0-7369-4299-7 (eBook)

Library of Congress Cataloging-in-Publication Data

Names: Hoff, BJ, author.
Title: Harp on the willow / BJ Hoff.
Description: Eugene, Oregon : Harvest House Publishers, [2018]
Identifiers: LCCN 2017035103 (print) | LCCN 2017040278 (ebook) | ISBN 9780736942997 (ebook) | ISBN 9780736920674 (paperback)
Subjects: | BISAC: FICTION / Christian / Historical. | FICTION / Christian / Romance. | GSAFD: Christian fiction. | Love stories.
Classification: LCC PS3558.O34395 (ebook) | LCC PS3558.O34395 H37 2018 (print) | DDC 813/.54 —dc23
LC record available at https://lccn.loc.gov/2017035103

Printed in the United States of America

17 18 19 20 21 22 23 24 25 26 / BP-GL / 10 9 8 7 6 5 4 3 2 1

For Jim, Dana, Jessie, and Eric
No writer ever had a better support team.

We hung our small harps on the willow trees.

<small>PSALM</small> 137:2

CONTENTS

ONE

A Doctor's Day

*Here is a task for all that a man has
of fortitude and delicacy.*
ROBERT LOUIS STEVENSON

*Potomac Highlands of West Virginia
July 1869*

Daniel Kavanagh, MD, was given to defining a good day as one when the elderly and somewhat eccentric Miss Gladys Piper had no more than one imaginary disease that required treatment during her office visit.

A good day got even better when not a single man from the hill folks came down and threatened to hurt him unless he accompanied him back up the hollow to "fix his woman."

And if he happened to meet Serena Norman on his way to lunch at Helen's Mountain Inn—well, Daniel figured that would serve to make any day just about perfect.

By eight thirty on this oppressively hot and muggy Monday morning in July, he had already resigned himself to the fact that it was not going to be a good day. To begin with, he had learned over the weekend that Serena was off to Buckhannon for a week, visiting an aunt. The fact that he had to hear this news second-hand rather than from Serena herself stung more than he cared to admit.

And now, as he and Sarge the Newfoundland walked into the waiting room of his office and found not only Miss Gladys Piper waiting for him, but also a hatchet-faced man with one black eye, badly swollen, and a long, dark beard that all manner of creatures could have nested in, Daniel submitted then and there that indeed, this was not going to be a good day. Not at all.

ᔡ

Miss Gladys, of course, did not have an appointment, and Daniel was fairly certain the man with the black eye was not in the book either. In truth, with Audrey, his receptionist, at home with a sprained ankle, he didn't actually know who was in the book. The patient log was solely Audrey's responsibility, which in her mind meant that neither Daniel nor anyone else was to touch its hallowed pages except in case of a genuine emergency.

Audrey Truman had let it be known in crystal clarity that if Daniel wanted her to stay on upon his predecessor's retirement and subsequent passing she would do so only on her own terms—and those terms meant that she would continue to manage the office precisely as she had under Dr. Franklin.

At the time, Daniel had thought he would not have it otherwise, for although Audrey might be something of a martinet, she did keep the office running with admirable efficiency. And even if he didn't always respond well to her autocratic and uncompromising way of doing things, he never failed to appreciate the headaches she saved him on a daily basis.

At times like these, when he knew next to nothing about the day's agenda—and when he was facing a surly looking mountain man in addition to an obviously impatient Gladys Piper—he found himself appreciating Audrey even more.

He left the Newfoundland in his customary place, in front of the waiting room counter, then proceeded to take Miss Gladys into the examining room. As he closed the door behind them, he heard the Newfie utter a low growl, which Daniel knew to be not so much a warning to the dangerous-looking man in the waiting room as a reminder to Daniel that he should not be taking all day with the business at hand.

⌒

"Sidney Franklin never kept me waiting."

Daniel turned from washing his hands and smiled at the feisty spinster lady who sat as far forward as possible on the end of the examining table, her slender, prominently veined hands folded primly in her lap.

"I do apologize, Miss Gladys. I didn't realize you had an early appointment."

She didn't exactly sniff her disapproval. She didn't have to. The doctor had seen that look before. Nor did she admit that she didn't have an appointment. Miss Gladys had never seemed to feel the need for such formalities.

"Well, now," he said cheerfully, "why don't you tell me what the problem is? Not the heart palpitations again, I hope."

She ignored his question. "Where is Audrey?"

"Unfortunately, Audrey tripped Friday evening over an exposed tree root in her backyard and sprained her ankle. I expect she'll be out until later in the week. So—how have you been since I saw you last, ah...last Monday, wasn't it?"

A week was about as long a time as Miss Gladys ever went between visits.

"Audrey was always a careless girl."

Audrey was sixty-two years old, and Daniel doubted very much that she even knew the meaning of the word *careless*. But he merely smiled and said, 'I'll be sure to mention to Audrey that you asked after her. Now, why don't you tell me what brings you out this morning? It's going to be another sizzler, isn't it?"

Although she had a fine buggy at her disposal, Miss Gladys almost always walked the short distance from her stately brick home on Laurel Street. She was fond of saying, to anyone who might inquire as to why she didn't use the buggy for excursions, that she did not believe in pampering herself.

"It's my ears," she said in reply to the doctor's question.

"Your ears?"

"They've been ringing. It's very annoying."

"I'm sure it is." Daniel paused, thinking. "I don't recall your mentioning this when you were in last week, Miss Gladys. Exactly how long have your ears been troubling you?"

Her answer came with no hesitation. "Since Friday. Four days now."

"Well, let's just have a look."

He checked her ears, being careful, as he had been instructed during previous examinations, not to "muss" her elaborately dressed red hair.

The blazing red hair was the one affectation—if it could be so termed—that Miss Gladys allowed herself. The only resident of Mount Laurel who knew just what it took to restore the crowning glory of a woman Gladys Piper's age, a style that featured a fiery cloud of waves and curlicues, was Hester Marshfield. Hester's self-proclaimed ministry was to the women of Mount Laurel who required assistance with "maintaining a comely appearance at any age."

It was widely held that Hester Marshfield was privy to all manner of ladies' secrets. And secrets they remained.

"Everything looks perfectly fine, Miss Gladys," he told her. "But let's check your pulse and listen to your heart, shall we?"

As he expected, nothing seemed amiss. Miss Gladys's heartbeat was strong and precise, her pulse that of someone half her age.

While Daniel wouldn't think of minimizing her symptoms, he was grateful that Sidney Franklin had volunteered his opinion on these "ailments" of Mount Laurel's wealthiest resident. Gladys Piper was, according to his predecessor, a thoroughly lonely woman. She had spent her entire life in Mount Laurel, living alone for many years with scarcely anything to occupy her interest or her time except her flower garden and her piano. She had never married, had no remaining family, and, at her advanced age, had seen most of her friends and acquaintances pass on before her.

Doctor Franklin had been convinced—and Daniel was coming to the same conclusion—that Miss Gladys's many maladies were most likely of her own invention. Sidney Franklin had contended that the doctor's office was the one place where Miss Gladys could count on receiving someone's undivided attention and a measure of concern for her well-being.

That being the case, Daniel almost always made it a point, as had Doctor Franklin before him, to spend a generous amount of time with her, even to fuss over her a bit—without, of course, engendering any undue alarm about the state of her health, which was, in his opinion, remarkably good.

In truth, he had grown rather fond of Miss Gladys, in spite of the fact that she was seldom anything but acerbic and often downright testy with him. He figured it would probably take more years than Gladys Piper might have left before she gained any real trust in him, but in the meantime he would do his best to take proper care of her.

To that end, he also prayed that his patience would not fail him.

After completing the examination, he considered carefully how to advise her. "Well, Miss Gladys," he finally said, "let me ask you some questions."

She looked at him, and Daniel wasn't sure whether it was eagerness or a trace of concern he saw in her eyes.

"How have you been sleeping lately?" he asked. "Any problems there?"

Her chin lifted slightly, the finely wrinkled but still elegant long neck tightening. "None at all. I have nothing to clutter my conscience and keep me awake. I sleep like a baby, if you must know."

"That's good," Daniel said, not doubting her for a moment. "Very good. And what about your appetite recently? Have you noticed any difference in your eating habits?"

One patrician eyebrow lifted in obvious disdain, as if she thought the question utterly foolish. "My appetite is exactly as it has always been. I adhere to a wholesome diet, and a moderate one."

Again, Daniel accepted her reply at face value. Gladys

Piper's militarily erect posture and unusually fine complexion and figure—for a woman of her years—seemed to confirm a lifetime of healthy habits.

"Yes, of course," he said somewhat lamely. "And I don't imagine you use spirits, do you?" he said, giving in for an instant to the streak of Irish mischief that seemed bound to assert itself at the most inopportune moments.

The look the woman turned on him would have withered a cactus.

Daniel continued his inquiries for a few more minutes, learning nothing surprising. Based on Miss Gladys's past history, he felt fairly safe in assuming that the recent ringing in her ears was merely another addition to her ever-expanding catalog of imaginary complaints.

Even so, it wouldn't do to take any symptom lightly. The woman was eighty-one years old, after all—a fact Daniel was fairly certain she had never divulged to anyone other than himself and the late Sidney Franklin.

"Well, I don't believe this is anything you should worry about, Miss Gladys," he said, meaning to reassure her while not minimizing her concern. "Here's what I'd like you to do. I want you to try taking more frequent rests throughout the day. A busy lady like yourself often tends to overdo. You may be taxing yourself too much. I want you to promise me that you'll have a rest regularly between activities from now on."

He paused. "Incidentally, do you still garden as much as you used to?"

"Why wouldn't I?"

Why indeed?

"Yes, well, I'm going to ask you to confine your gardening to the early morning hours. This kind of heat isn't good for anyone. And remember now—lots of rest."

After a few more minutes of conversation, during which Miss Gladys assured him that she would follow his instructions to the letter, Daniel escorted her from the office, reminding her that he wanted to see her in his office again the following Monday, or sooner if the ringing in her ears worsened.

He told himself that even if he was fostering her tendency to invent, he couldn't do otherwise than take her numerous ailments as seriously as those of any other patient.

Besides, he knew what it was like to be lonely, and he thought it would be an even harder thing to be old and lonely.

～

He spent the next fifteen minutes trying in vain to convince the tough-looking mountain man, who called himself simply Ratliff, that he was not able to pull his "thumping" tooth.

It was probably nothing but a kind of adolescent peevishness on his part that made Daniel bring the Newfie into the examining room, but there was a certain reassurance in having the large black dog nearby. Sarge seemed to have formed his own opinion of the man, and it wasn't looking good for Mr. Ratliff.

For his part, Daniel found it difficult to take his eyes off the man's beard. He couldn't be absolutely certain he had spotted movement in that matted brush, but he was suspicious all the same.

"It's as I told you, Mr. Ratliff, I'm not a dentist. I'm not in the least experienced at pulling teeth. You really don't want me working on your tooth."

Mr. Ratliff glared at him through the eye that wasn't swollen shut. "I told you, I don't care what kind of doctor you be, dentist or not. This here tooth needs yanked. I tried to pull it myself, but I couldn't get a good holt on it. That's why I come to you."

Some of these fellows from the hollow could be awfully hot-tempered, Daniel knew, though on closer inspection he decided that Ratliff didn't look as mean as he had first thought. Perhaps it was only the pain that caused him to screw up his face in such a way. All the same, you never could tell what one of these mountain men might do if provoked.

He stood there, taking stock of his options. "You're quite sure you want me to do this?"

The man winced and put a hand to his jaw. "Yank it," he said in a tone that brooked no further argument.

Daniel delayed only a moment. Then, in spite of his better judgment and with some trepidation, he yanked it.

He was rewarded with a gap-toothed, obviously pleased—if somewhat bloody—grin of satisfaction. "Why, you done real good, Doc! Yessir. Real good. Got 'er on the first try, and I felt nary a twinge."

Only then did Daniel release the breath he had been holding to draw a sigh of relief.

⌒

For the next three hours, he saw one patient after another, which was the way he liked his mornings to go. When the office finally emptied out, the gnawing in his stomach reminded him that it was almost noon.

He felt more than ready for some of Helen Platt's chicken stew and dumplings, regular Monday fare. There was a time when he would have preferred a lighter spread on such a blistering day, but Helen's Mountain Inn didn't cater to the individual tastes of Mount Laurel's residents. Certainly not to "city folks" like himself.

In truth, he was no longer "city folks," having made his home here for more than three years now. To the natives, however, Daniel suspected he would always be that "young doc from New York City."

In any case, he had eventually adapted to the local custom of hot and heavy meals in all kinds of weather, as had Sarge, who would eat just about anything that didn't talk back as it went down.

"Let's go, you great oaf," he said, going to the front door and waiting for the Newfie to follow. "If you promise not to drool all over me, I'll order a plate for you."

TWO

WALKING THROUGH MOUNT LAUREL

This is my Father's world
He abides in all that's fair...
MALTBIE D. BABCOCK

As he stepped outside, Daniel caught his breath. Surely this was the hottest and most humid day of summer so far. The heat was palpable, thick, and rising in ripples off the street. The weak shower that had fallen in the early hours before daylight had scarcely wet the dust and only added to the humidity.

He fell into rhythm with the big Newfoundland's ponderous gait. They met only half a dozen or so other pedestrians, but there were more carriages than usual this time of day. It seemed that everyone had either stayed indoors or sought refuge from the sun in their buggies.

As they started down tree-lined Tygart Street, a farm wagon rattled by at a treacherously high speed, a cloud of dust spraying the lathered horses. The children in back seemed to be having a heated quarrel. One was crying, the others yelling.

Daniel stopped a moment to watch, frowning at the perspiration-drenched driver who was half standing, slapping the reins and shouting at the horses.

He started walking again, taking in his surroundings as he went. Mount Laurel was, for the most part, a relatively prosperous farm community, engulfed by the Allegheny Mountains. Resting in the foothills, the town resembled an egg-shaped bowl plopped down in the middle of some giant loaves of bread.

Small but thriving farms dotted the countryside, which was lush and dense with great forests. Numerous species of wildlife, including black bears, wild turkeys, bobcats, and white-tailed deer roamed the hills. Rhododendron, or "great laurel," could be found just about everywhere, and according to the locals, six major river systems were located in the area, along with the best trout streams in the state. It was, pure and simple, a place of rare and spectacular beauty.

He believed himself fortunate indeed to live among such grandeur and richness of the earth. He had loved the town almost from the first time he'd seen it, after the war. On most days he took at least a brief time to simply pause and look out on the valley and let its lavish splendor fill his heart.

Today, however, should he allow it, could all too easily be dimmed by the shadows that sometimes swallowed up his hard-won contentment. Whether it was the oppressive heat, the ache from the old wound in his back, or a combination of the two, he found it difficult to escape the memory of another hot July day, in another scenic little town. Indeed, a town much like Mount Laurel, though not quite as large.

A town called Gettysburg.

He forced himself to dismiss the unwelcome memory, unwilling to give any quarter to the back pain, the wilting heat, or to what his friend Stephen Holliday sometimes called his "Irish gloom." Instead, he picked up his pace and began to whistle. At his side, the Newfie puffed a little as he kept stride with him.

His office was on the "high end," as the locals called it, of Tygart Street, the main thoroughfare. He was somewhat removed from the business section, but only by a few buildings. From his office, the town sloped gently downward. On the way to the inn, they passed the large sand-colored building that housed the Mount Laurel Historical Society and Museum, which served mainly as a depository for displays of local rock samples and military artifacts. A few doors down, the Methodist church, a clapboard building with the same kind of parched grounds and wilting flowers that could be seen all over town, rested snugly behind the privet hedges that always seemed to flourish, regardless of the heat.

Directly across the street, the Presbyterians worshiped in a moderate-size brownstone with a stately glass window at the front. To its left lay the town square, which was really more a diamond than a square. A few children were playing tag around the tarnished statue of a Shawnee Indian maiden who had supposedly, at much risk to herself, shown kindness to some of the early settlers.

Daniel could never quite shake the feeling that the "maiden" more aptly resembled a warrior, but in these matters, as in a number of others, he kept his opinion to himself.

A few of the children's mothers rested on benches nearby, fanning themselves as they watched their young ones play. The old-timers who usually congregated in the area were nowhere to be seen today. A good thing, to Daniel's way of thinking. This kind of heat could not only spell bad news for the elderly but would likely create a more crowded waiting room at his office.

Next came the bank, and then J.D. Broomhall's dry goods store, which also housed the post office. Farther on, just after Canaan Street intersected, they met up with Bernard Cottle, who was standing out front of his Good Sole Shoe store, leaning up against the front of the building as if he had nothing else to do.

"Not much going on today, Bernie?"

The tall, balding bachelor—one of the few in Mount Laurel— shook his head with a mournful look. "Might as well be a Sunday for all the business I've had this morning, Doc. Not that I blame folks for staying in on a day like this. Expect the heat doesn't slow things down much for you, though, does it?"

"Not today, it hasn't."

Daniel went on, with Sarge pulling slightly ahead. No doubt that supersensitive nose could already smell Helen's chicken stew on the air. On the other side of the street was the office of Mount Laurel's weekly newspaper, the *Public Sentinel.* Lawrence Hill, owner and editor, saw Daniel from his desk at the big front window and waved. Daniel waved back but didn't cross to chat. He would see Lawrence tonight at the planning meeting for the new schoolhouse.

The slope now leveled off, just before reaching the inn. From here he could see the river and the small log school building this side of it. Directly across from the schoolhouse stood a structure that had long been a favorite with Mount Laurel's children—and the subject of endless speculation and gossip for the adults: Willmar's Carousel.

The carousel was, at least in Daniel's estimation, quite a work of art. Painstakingly handcrafted by an early settler—a German fellow named Friedrich Willmar—the apparatus never failed to stop traffic. Even those who had lived within view of it for years could scarcely pass by without slowing to admire the detail of its workmanship: the intricately painted panels and cornices, each bearing a different scene from Willmar's home country of Germany; the flamboyant gondolas; and the fanciful, vividly colored animals—horses and unicorns, gazelles, and even a zebra—all of which appeared to be in flight.

Daniel stopped for a moment. Jamie MacPhee, who managed the carousel and saw to its maintenance, was nowhere in sight, as rides were available only on the weekend.

Willmar's story was a terrible tragedy. It was also a favorite subject of gossip, especially among those older residents bent on shocking the occasional newcomer.

Willmar, an unmarried carpenter from Germany, had arrived in Mount Laurel in the late eighteenth century, before the town was even incorporated. A taciturn, private man who apparently had never revealed his reasons for leaving his native land, Willmar reputedly earned a good living almost from the beginning building houses and furniture and doing odd jobs throughout the county. He also wasted no time in building himself a sizable frame house with a vast upstairs and an intricate, hand-carved stairway.

He remained a bachelor for several years after his arrival but eventually took a wife from one of the hill families, a girl years younger than Willmar himself. The couple kept almost entirely to themselves, limiting their social involvements to church attendance and marketing.

The carousel, according to local historians, had been a labor of love, begun right after the birth of the Willmar's first child, and continued throughout the years as other children were added to the family—six in all, nine if you counted the miscarriages. Supposedly, Willmar completed the final work on his *objet d'art* the very day his sixth child, a son, was born.

Late one winter's night, Friedrich Willmar returned from a two-week job in the northern panhandle to find his house an inferno, with the townspeople gathered in a furious—and futile—attempt to save his wife and children from the blaze.

The poor man lost his entire family that night, all except for the youngest boy, still a toddler in didies. He buried them the next day and, with his surviving child, departed Mount Laurel.

He never returned, but to this day the carousel stood, a weathered but undeniably magnificent piece of artistry. The youth of the town never seemed to tire of it, but to some of their parents it represented an almost macabre reminder of those long-ago children who had not lived to enjoy their father's handiwork.

Some years past, an ugly rumor had begun to circulate that Willmar's wife had in fact set the fire herself. Speculation had it that she might have been a bit mad, that she had been so miserable with her austere, older husband that, rather than go on living with him and having his children, she decided to take the lives of them all.

Daniel paid the tale little heed, having neither seen nor heard any evidence whatsoever to support it. Besides, rumors about one thing or another were fairly common in a small town. But not long after he arrived in Mount Laurel, a number of local families had made a short-lived effort to have the carousel removed. The instigators cast all manner of aspersions on the fixture, declaring it to be a kind of idol, a bearer of ill fortune, even a work of the devil.

Their efforts had been quickly defeated, and the furor had

eventually subsided. But there were still occasional murmurings about the carousel and its history.

Ah, well. He supposed there would always be those who loved a scandalous story.

At the front door of the inn, Daniel stopped, looking toward the river that divided Mount Laurel from the mining town of Owenduffy, which folks around here referred to as a "camp."

Owenduffy meant, literally, "black river." Although the river that separated the two communities wasn't actually black, the mining town itself was, or at least appeared to be. A company-owned town perched against a large seam of bituminous coal— "soft coal," it was called hereabouts—Owenduffy was little more than a dismal warren of gray, unpainted row houses, a cluttered company store, and a few other equally dingy buildings in addition to the coal mine itself.

Populated almost entirely by immigrants—mostly Irish, with some Welsh and Italians—Owenduffy was within shouting distance of Mount Laurel, with only the river between them. Had they not been so startlingly different in appearance, they might have even been called sister cities because of their close proximity.

In reality, however, Daniel knew that far more than the river separated the two towns. As he stood looking out over the valley, it occurred to him, not for the first time, that another kind of river ran between Mount Laurel and the neighboring Owenduffy: a river of social, religious, and economic differences as dark and as bitter as the relentless black dust that fell over the mining town and sifted out over the water, creating yet another source of contention between the residents of the two communities.

There was an ugliness on this land that belied its beauty, and even in the short time since he'd settled here, Daniel had sensed that the blight was spreading, eating away more and more of the charm and goodness that had first attracted him to the quiet, appealing countryside. He could only hope that the ugliness wouldn't eventually contaminate all that was good and lovely here—or even consume it and destroy it altogether.

The Newfoundland interrupted his musings with a well-timed whimper of complaint and a doleful look. Daniel nodded. "I hear you, old boy. Guess you've had enough of my lollygagging for one day. Well, come on, then, let's go stuff ourselves, why don't we?"

The Newfie gave a shake of his head as if to indicate it was about time and then claimed his place in front of the inn, where he would wait for his owner to serve up his first course.

THREE

A HOLLIDAY MEAL

Better than grandeur, better than gold,
Than rank and titles a thousandfold,
Is a healthy body and a mind at ease,
And simple pleasures that always please.
ABRAM J. RYAN

*D*aniel could think of few things he enjoyed more than a meal at Esther Holliday's table.

He made it a point never to be late. Not for anything would he miss out on the jumbo glass of sweet lemon tea Esther always served him before supper.

She met him at the door promptly at six thirty. "Where's Sarge?"

"I left him at home. He's feeling the heat."

"Aren't we all? Well, I hope you brought your appetite."

"My appetite—and a basket of flowers for the hostess," said Daniel, kissing her lightly on the cheek as he handed her the flowers.

Predictably, she blushed. Esther blushed often and easily, but especially when pleased, outraged, or embarrassed.

"Well, come in, come in!" she fussed, patting the neat roll of hair at the back of her neck. "It's a good thing you're on time. I was just pouring your tea."

Daniel followed her to the kitchen, grinning with satisfaction as she went to the sideboard and added an extra slice of lemon to his tumbler before handing it to him.

"Strong and sweet," she said.

"I was looking forward to this all the way out here."

A man did enjoy being taken care of every now and then. Being a bachelor had its distinct disadvantages.

❧

Daniel was the first to push back from the table a little, feeling the need to rest his stomach before dessert.

He smiled as he sat watching the others. Supper at the Hollidays' was a noisy event. Everyone talked at once, and talked loud and fast.

There was no keeping track of how many times Esther asked Stephen, her husband, if he wanted another helping of a particular dish and then proceeded to pass it to him without waiting for his reply. Stephen was waving his fork around, no doubt to his wife's despair, as he decried the foolishness of the latest folks who had moved away to seek their fortune out west.

Stephen Holliday was fiercely loyal to his God, his family, and his hometown, in that order. He tended to take defections as a personal betrayal.

Miss Ruth Ann all of a sudden observed that she had not seen Labonah Vance at the cakewalk and wondered if she and that boy from Keyser were still keeping company and if they might not get married soon.

"Labonah and Charley Henderson have been married going on ten years now, Mama," Esther replied matter-of-factly as she urged some more potatoes on her husband.

Stephen's elderly mother frequently added a somewhat startling and completely irrelevant remark to the mix. Miss Ruth Ann suffered from a pitiless kind of dementia that Daniel had seen before in persons of her advanced years. She was also extremely hard of hearing, and that, combined with the ongoing attacks of confusion, tended to bring some surprising twists to any family discussion.

Daniel noticed that only Clay was uncommonly quiet this evening, saying little, but glaring at his father when he wasn't stabbing his roast beef with a certain ferocity. Obviously, there had been a tiff between the two before supper.

Not an unusual event, that. At twenty-two, Clay Holliday had seemingly adopted the attitude that his father was unreasonable, uncompromising, and just plain mule-headed. Stephen, for his part, was quick these days to declare his son willful, wayward, and wild.

Knowing them both fairly well by now, Daniel would have to say that at least some of their charges against each other were justified. Even so, he was more than a little troubled by the growing tension between father and son. He knew that while Stephen also despaired of the problem, he was just stubborn enough that it was questionable whether he would ever take steps to heal the rift. Meanwhile, Clay seemed to have dug himself deep into a den of self-righteousness, convinced that his father was under some sort of misguided conception that he had the right to wield authority over a son who was no longer a child.

They were at a stalemate that seemed to be forcing them further and further apart.

Ever since Daniel had arrived in Mount Laurel to deliver Ben Holliday's personal effects after his death, Ben's family had taken him in and treated him as a second son. He suspected his friendship with Ben would have ensured approval from the Hollidays in any event, but the fact that he had been with their older son when he died in a Gettysburg field hospital had been the final stitch in the fabric of their acceptance.

For his part, Daniel had come to care deeply for the entire family, and consequently, when he saw trouble in the making for any one of them, his inclination was to try to help. Unfortunately, this thing between Stephen and Clay seemed to be rapidly approaching the point where help might not be possible.

He sensed a storm brewing—a storm with the potential of becoming a full-blown tempest unless something happened soon to take the energy out of it. The ordinary, everyday tensions between a father and a grown son who lived together and worked together had escalated drastically over the past several months, until by now they seemed to have reached a total impasse. But surely those minor fires might have been put out without too much damage had it not been for a much bigger blaze that showed no signs of being extinguished any time soon.

Her name was Elly Murphy, and Daniel had the uneasy feeling that this particular flame was about to flare out of control.

After supper, Stephen headed for the front porch in hopes of catching the occasional breeze that might drift down from the mountains. As for Clay, he excused himself the moment he took his last bite of dessert.

Daniel remained in the kitchen long enough to offer Esther his help with the dishes.

"Don't be silly," she told him in a tone that brooked no argument. "But stay a minute if you will. There's something I need to ask you."

"Ask away." Daniel helped himself to another glass of tea and then leaned up against the pie safe. "That was truly a fine meal, Esther. As always."

She shrugged, wiping her hands on the dish towel. Daniel noticed that her face was flushed, no doubt from the heat in the kitchen.

"Why don't you go outside with Stephen and Clay and let me finish in here?" he suggested. "There might be a bit of a breeze by now."

"As if I'd let you clean up my kitchen," she shot back. "But I did want—"

Abruptly, she stopped, going to the doorway that led onto the hall and peering out as if to make certain no one was close by.

When she returned, she busied herself with putting the baking dishes in the cupboard. "I think I need to see you, Daniel," she said, not looking at him.

"Well, here I am."

"At your *office*."

She seemed nervous. Perhaps even troubled.

Daniel studied her. Esther Holliday was a tall and full-bodied woman who gave the appearance of vitality and uncompromising good health. Now that he thought about it, he couldn't recall that he'd ever heard Esther so much as complain of a head cold or a sore throat. At the moment, however, her face was damp with perspiration, and the flush he'd noticed earlier had intensified.

When she said nothing more but merely stood there, not looking at him as she proceeded to wring the dishcloth into a rope, he moved to prompt her. "Esther? What is it? Are you having problems?"

"No," she said a little too quickly. "No, I'm sure it's nothing."

Daniel waited.

Finally, she turned but still didn't quite meet his eyes. "I think—most likely it's nothing more than my age, but—"

She let her words drift off as she turned back to the dishes.

"Your *age*? Why, Esther, you don't look a day over thirty-five, and that's the truth."

He knew how old Esther Holliday was. She wasn't a woman to dissemble about her years, and besides, he'd attended the birthday party her family had hosted for her in May, at the time of her forty-third birthday.

Even so, he hadn't exaggerated her youthfulness. Esther truly did not show her years. At the moment, she looked as flustered as a schoolgirl. Even so, the significance of her reference to age finally registered with Daniel.

"I see," he said.

She nodded, staring down at her hands gripping the counter. "I don't know why, but I confess I've never thought about—that. Not until recently. I feel foolish, bothering you with woman problems, but I thought perhaps I ought to just make sure it's nothing else."

"Well, of course you should. And you're not bothering me, Esther. It's my job."

As if she hadn't heard, she went on. "It's embarrassing, really, what with you being almost like family and all—"

"Esther—"

"If there were any other doctor nearby—"

"Esther."

She shot him a quick glance.

"You don't need to be embarrassed," Daniel said gently, hoping to put her at ease. "Why don't you come down to the office in the morning? Around ten thirty?"

She hesitated before nodding. "You won't say anything to Stephen?"

"Not if you don't want me to."

"I don't. It's not necessary, and he fusses so."

"All right, then. But I'll expect to see you tomorrow morning."

"I'll be there," she said, her usual brisk demeanor returning. "Here," she said, handing him a paper-wrapped bundle off the counter. "I thought Sarge might like a bone from the roast."

"Ah. He'll thank you for this."

Daniel watched her for another moment and then left the kitchen. Not for the first time, he found himself wishing that he had a nurse or at least an assistant—a woman—to help him attend to his female patients, who invariably delayed as long as they could before bringing what they referred to as their "woman troubles" to him.

The thing was, sometimes they allowed their modesty to interfere with their good sense and delayed too long.

He fervently hoped that would not prove to be the case with Esther Holliday.

~

Outside, Daniel lowered his long frame to the top step. Stephen sat in his usual place, in the big plank rocker with the gingham cushions Esther had made. Clay was nowhere in sight, and Daniel didn't ask his whereabouts. Lately, it seemed that any attempt to strike up a discussion about Clay merely served to fuel Stephen's impatience or, on occasion, his temper.

Besides, after the lively meal, he enjoyed simply sitting and enjoying the quiet. It was a sweet summer evening, heavily scented with mountain laurel and Esther's climbing roses. Down at the stream that bordered the back pasture, the frogs were griping to one another like a bunch of bad-tempered old geezers airing their complaints of the day, while the cicadas tried in vain to drown them out. Oscar, the old hoot owl that Stephen claimed as a farm fixture by now, put in a question every now and then from his perch in the sugar maple tree. Other than the night creatures, it was peaceful as always, a peace Daniel never failed to savor.

The two men exchanged idle talk about the coming autumn and the lumber business—Stephen owned a prosperous lumber mill up the valley in addition to his sprawling farm acreage—and talked in brief of their ideas about the new schoolhouse.

"Speaking of which," Daniel pointed out, "hadn't we best be leaving for the meeting?"

Stephen nodded but made no attempt to move. "This is the kind of evening Ben loved. Sometimes he would sit out here on the swing for hours, watching the night settle in."

Daniel smiled a little, fighting off a twinge of sadness. He figured neither Stephen nor Esther would ever get over missing their older son. The fact was, he still missed him too. Ben Holliday had been as good a man as any he'd met before him or after, and every now and then he still felt a slam of the old guilt-laced pain that he hadn't been able to save his young friend's life.

So many good men had fallen that day, and although he and the other surgeons had managed to save a number of brave soldiers, the memory of those they *hadn't* saved still clawed at him like a hair shirt.

Stephen brought him back to the present when he stood and said, "Well, I'd best tell Esther we're leaving."

He started to open the door and then delayed. "How did you find Mother by the way? Do you think she's failing?"

Daniel thought a minute. "Not since I saw her last, no. At least not physically. But the other—"

"Her mind."

Daniel nodded. "It's as I told you earlier, I'm afraid. There's not likely to be any improvement."

"It's hard to see her…like that, you know. Mother was always so bright. And clever. She had such a wit."

"Miss Ruth Ann is still a delightful lady," Daniel pointed out.

"She is, isn't she?" Stephen agreed, but his smile was obviously forced. He hesitated a second or two and then said, "Daniel, I've wanted to ask you as well…have you noticed anything…different…about Esther?"

Remembering his promise, Daniel hesitated. "Different? How do you mean?"

Stephen Holliday was a big, strapping man, tall and deeply tanned, and as rugged and straight as an oak tree, but at the moment he was clearly concerned, appearing almost bent with anxiety. "Well, I'm not exactly sure. It's just that she seems so dog-goned jittery most of the time. And cranky too. She takes offense at the least little thing. You know Esther. That's not like her. Not a bit. I don't know what to think."

"Perhaps it's just the heat," Daniel replied, uncomfortable with the need to be evasive. "Lots of folks are getting weary of it."

With his hand still gripping the screen door, Stephen's expression cleared somewhat. "I hadn't thought of that. I expect that's exactly what it is, now that you mention it. The heat. We haven't had much of a break for quite some time now."

"That's a fact."

Stephen nodded, looking relieved as he opened the door and went inside.

For his part, Daniel felt less confident than he'd tried to sound. Now that he'd done his best to reassure both Esther and her husband, he was somewhat unsettled to realize that he felt a need to reassure himself.

FOUR

BIG NEWS

Within the future do not look,
But live to-day—to-day.
LYDIA AVERY COONLEY WARD

*D*aniel sent Esther Holliday to his office after her examination, telling her he'd be back shortly.

He had to give himself a few minutes before facing her.

There was no telling how she would take this. He wished Stephen had come with her today, but apparently Stephen didn't even know his wife was here. According to Esther, she had driven into town in her own buggy, combining her visit to Daniel with a visit to the dry goods store.

At the moment Daniel stood in the small but neatly ordered pharmacy where he mixed his medications. The morning was already sweltering, the sun baking through the small, high window on the outside wall.

With a swipe to his forehead with his sleeve, he ran a hand through his hair, which the humidity had turned into a tangled mass of stubborn curl. Esther was wont to nag him about his unfashionably long hair, pointing out that soon he'd be taking on

the appearance of one of the mountain men who lived up the hol-
ler. He smiled a little at the thought. Esther did like to tease him
as she might have one of her own boys, mentioning how the "salt"
seemed to be gaining on the "pepper."

Nor was it beyond her to hint that Serena Norman might
show a little more interest if he would increase his visits to Arlie
Simpson, the town barber.

He glanced at the door, sighed, and then started across the
room. He had delayed long enough.

~

Esther sat in the chair across from Daniel's desk, staring at her
hands and praying for the grace to accept the change that had
come upon her. If indeed that's all it was—the "change," as her
women friends referred to it. When they referred to it at all.

She felt her hair slipping free of its knot and reached to tuck it
back in place. Her hands left a damp spot on the front of her skirt
from where she'd been wringing them, and she tried to brush the
material dry. There seemed to be not an inch of her that wasn't
clammy this morning. The heat was awful.

It isn't the heat...

She might just as well stop trying to fool herself. It was one of
those hot flashes she'd heard her mother and Aunt Josie whispering about, years ago.

And there would be worse things than the hot flashes to come,
from what she remembered of those conversations about the
"change."

*But what if it isn't the "change"? What if something has gone wrong
inside me and will eventually make me ill and out of my head, like
Letty Kincaid was for the few months before she passed away?*

Her stomach knotted. *Please, Lord, let it just be the "change." I'll accept it and even try to be glad for it, if that's all it is.*

Her gaze swept Daniel's office. Clearly, he had worked hard—with Ira Birch's help—to give what had once been Sidney Franklin's domain Daniel's own stamp of individuality.

The exterior of the building had never been much: a white frame structure on a small piece of ground, with a vacant lot on one side and the foundry on the other. From where she sat, she could look outside and see the cemetery.

Daniel admitted that he'd taken more than his share of ribbing from the town jokesters about the proximity of the burial ground to the doctor's office. Inside, though, he and Ira had created a comfortable and, as best as Esther could tell, a reasonably well-appointed medical facility. In addition to the examining room and the pharmacy, there was now a small waiting room with benches and chairs—all built by Ira—and a counter that fronted Audrey's reception desk. And Daniel's office, of course, where she now sat waiting, trying not to be impatient.

~

Daniel stopped just outside the open door, seeing that Esther had her head bowed.

Esther was a praying woman. She would likely be praying even more than usual once she left his office today.

Well, Lord, here goes. Brace Esther for this, and brace me too as I deliver the news to her.

He cleared his throat and walked the rest of the way into the room.

~

Esther looked up as he entered, her eyes like those of a doe trapped in the sights of a hunter's gun. Clearly, she thought she knew what he was about to tell her and was dreading it. She had indicated that she believed herself to be at the end of her womanly cycles and now faced the inescapable approach of middle age.

Daniel sat down behind his desk, picked up a pencil, and began rolling it around between the thumb and index finger of his left hand.

"Well?" Her voice was strained. She sat poised on the edge of her chair, as if she might bolt from the room at any moment. "So…is it what I thought, then? My age and all?"

Daniel studied her. "Ah, actually, no. It's…something else, Esther."

She blinked and then looked away from him. He noted the damp splotch on the front of her skirt just before she wiped her hands down over it.

"Well, what is it, Daniel?" she said, still not looking at him. "What's wrong with me?"

When he didn't answer right away, she turned back to him. "Just tell me, for goodness' sake! I can't abide not knowing. Am I going to die?"

Daniel saw that she was trembling. It dawned on him then that the usually stoic, imperturbable Esther Holliday was badly frightened. He could have kicked himself for not seeing her fear sooner and reassuring her.

"No, Esther. You are most certainly not going to die."

She squeezed her eyes shut for an instant, her entire body appearing to sag with relief.

"I promise you," Daniel added carefully, "I have never lost an expectant mother yet."

Her eyes flew open. So did her mouth. "What?"

Daniel nodded, unable to stop a smile. "You and Stephen are going to have a baby, Esther."

"That's impossible!"

"I can assure you that it's not."

Her face flamed. "I didn't mean...*impossible*. I just meant..."

Still smiling, Daniel put the pencil down and leaned back in the chair a little. "I know what you meant, Esther."

"A baby... Oh, Daniel. Are you *sure?*"

Again he nodded. "I'd say sometime in December."

He didn't believe she had moved since he'd given her the news except to draw a breath. But now she quickly stood, her gaze roaming around the office as if she couldn't quite decide where she was.

Watching her, he also rose from his chair. "Congratulations, Esther."

She looked at him. "I...I can't believe it. A baby, after all this time—" She broke off. "Daniel, I'm forty-three years old!"

He knew he was grinning but couldn't seem to help himself. "A very *youthful* forty-three, as it happens."

She gripped her hands and brought them to her throat. "Oh, mercy. What in the world will Stephen say?"

"Well, now, if I know Stephen, he'll light up like a barn fire. After the shock wears off."

She stood motionless, her hands still clasped at her throat as if in prayer. "I never dreamed..."

"Nevertheless—"

"I feel so foolish!"

Daniel frowned. "Foolish? I can't think why. Didn't you tell me once that you and Stephen always wanted more children, and you were disappointed when none came along after Clay?"

"Yes, but we were young then! But now… Why, Clay's a man grown. And Stephen is forty-nine. We're—middle aged." She stopped. "What will people think?"

Daniel struggled to keep a stern face as he came around the desk. "Esther Holliday, you are the one person I never thought I'd hear ask such a question! It's never bothered you before what people think. Why would you let it matter now when you've been given nothing less than a gift from God?"

Gradually, her expression changed, as if she had only then thought about the baby. "But the baby… Daniel, I've heard stories. You know, about babies born late in life. That sometimes things aren't…as they should be. Will the baby be all right?"

Daniel could imagine what kind of stories she'd heard, and some of them might have been true. But he would talk to her about the risks later, not today. One thing at a time.

"Esther, you and Stephen couldn't be in better health. And it isn't as if this is your first child, after all. You've given birth twice before. And I am going to see to it that you and your baby have the very best of care."

"Oh, I know you will, Daniel!" She was quiet for a moment. "How do you think Stephen's going to react to this?"

Daniel raised an eyebrow. "Do you really need to ask?"

For the first time since she'd walked into the office that morning, she smiled. A genuine, bright, Esther Holliday smile. "No doubt he'll be strutting like a peacock for the next few months," she said, her tone dry.

Daniel looked at her and then laughed at the almost certain truth of her reply.

～

Later that afternoon, Daniel wasn't the least surprised to see Stephen pull his buggy up in front of the office. Indeed, he would have been more surprised had Stephen *not* shown up.

He rose from his knees, where he'd been nailing down a loose board on the porch, and watched as Stephen took the steps like a man half his age.

"Afternoon, Stephen." Daniel wiped the dust off his hand before extending it to his friend, who pumped it so hard Daniel thought he might have heard a bone or two snap. "And congratulations."

The other's expression was that of a man not quite recovered from shock but rejuvenated enough to sport a slightly foolish, crooked grin.

After the bruising handshake, however, he sobered. "Just tell me she'll be all right, Daniel. That's all I need to know."

"Let's get out of the heat," Daniel suggested, starting for the door.

Inside, Stephen declined to take a chair in the waiting room. "I can't sit down. Truth is, I've been as jittery as a long-tailed cat in a room full of rocking chairs ever since Esther told me the news."

"Understandable," Daniel said, thinking, not for the first time, how much he liked this man, how greatly he valued his friendship.

Stephen Holliday was as solid as they came. "Salt of the earth," some would say. Strong. Honest. Smart. A man with a bedrock of integrity and the heart of a lion. Yet a man who wasn't ashamed to show his adoration for his wife of more than two decades.

Daniel had often wondered, somewhat longingly, what it would be like to be married to a woman whose very name could still, after so many years, make your eyes glaze over with love.

He wouldn't mind finding out for himself.

"Esther is going to be just fine, Stephen," he said firmly. "You and I will see to it."

"And the baby?"

Daniel chose his words carefully, unwilling to dissemble with his friend, but also reluctant to put a damper on his obvious elation. "There's always a risk for a mother and baby in childbirth, Stephen. And the risk increases when the woman is past the usual childbearing age. But there are certain things Esther can do to minimize the risk, and I'll make certain she knows every one of them."

He paused before adding, "I hope you can both relax and enjoy this time. Esther is a strong, healthy woman, and there is no reason she shouldn't have a strong, healthy baby."

His friend's ebullient grin returned. "That's what I needed to hear, Daniel! Sorry for barging in like this, but I just had to have a little reassurance."

Daniel nodded. "Well, consider yourself reassured. And may I say that I couldn't be happier for the both of you."

Stephen grabbed his hand in another bone-crushing grip. "Thank you, Daniel! Boy, this is some news, isn't it? And I just want you to know how much it means to have a good doctor and a good friend to take care of Esther and the baby."

"Well, then, you'd best ease up a bit on that handshake, Stephen. When the time comes to deliver your baby, I expect you're going to want me to have both hands in working order."

FIVE

A VISIT TO OWENDUFFY

The dwellings of the virtuous poor,
The homes of poverty,
Are sacred in the sight of God,
Though humble they may be.
ELIZABETH WILLOUGHBY VARIAN

Late Friday night, Daniel was sitting on the sofa in front of a cold fireplace, reading the *Public Sentinel* while Sarge dozed at his feet.

The feature story was an in-depth account of the progress being made on the new schoolhouse. Lest any of the more skeptical citizens of Mount Laurel still needed to be convinced of the need for a new facility, Lawrence Hill, the owner and managing editor of the newspaper, used his weekly editorial to condemn the "outdated, overcrowded, and unsafe" conditions of the present structure.

Daniel smiled at Lawrence's final volley:

Our own Miss Serena Norman, a schoolmistress who would be a credit to even the largest and most cosmopolitan of urban school districts, recently remarked to this editor that "disgraceful" is too mild a word to describe the state of the present building. According to Miss Norman, when the students enter the schoolhouse at the beginning of the new term next month, "they will be entering a structure which is ridiculously inadequate, too small by far, as well as a building of such hasty construction and in such disrepair as to be positively hazardous. I'm certain, however, that the parents and other responsible citizens of our town are eager to do everything they can to remedy this deplorable situation as soon as possible."

Daniel could just see Serena, little bitty thing that she was, looking cool and collected with not a single blond curl out of place as she quietly issued what amounted to nothing less than a challenge—or was it a threat?—to the entire town.

Serena Norman was no less ladylike when she announced a call to arms than when she was pouring lemonade at a church social. Even so, the folks who knew her weren't likely to make the mistake of underestimating her.

He put the paper aside and had just started to doze off when a loud banging on the door brought him bolt upright to his stocking feet. Sarge stirred and growled in unmistakable annoyance, hauling himself up with a look of obvious pique. He seemed to care not even a little when Daniel yelped at the pain that went shooting up his leg when he banged into the storage chest in front of the sofa.

Out of sorts entirely now, he flung open the door to find a thin, dark-haired boy scowling back at him. Cap in hand, the youth was clad in the familiar coveralls and boots of a miner, but then it wasn't unusual for children as young as eight or nine to go into the mines. This boy looked older—fifteen or sixteen at least.

"Are you the doc?" The boy's voice was unexpectedly deep, his tongue thick with an Irish accent.

"I am," Daniel said.

"I need you to come with me, then. It's me sister. She needs doctorin' bad."

Daniel noted the utter lack of appeal in the boy's tone. He wasn't making a request so much as issuing a demand.

"You're from Owenduffy."

"Aye." The boy's eyes glinted with defiance, as if he expected Daniel to close the door in his face.

"You have your own doctor there. Isn't that so?"

The boy twisted his mouth as if he'd tasted something foul. "*That* soak! He's nowhere to be found. Passed out somewhere in his cups again, sure."

Daniel didn't doubt the truth of the lad's remark. It was no secret that Harley Bevins, the company doctor, was a poor excuse for a physician. A hard drinker who had almost destroyed his own health, he was said to be more menace than healer to his patients.

Unfortunately, the coal company officials who virtually owned the town of Owenduffy didn't seem to care.

"What's your name, son?"

"Flynn. Rory Flynn."

"What's wrong with your sister?"

"Bevins said last time he looked at her that she has a bad chest.

Said there was nothing to do for her anymore." The look in the boy's eyes was as sharp as broken glass, but Daniel saw fear mirrored there as well.

"She's took worse ever since," he went on. "She's on fire with the fever, and she fights for most every breath. I couldn't think what to do except to come here." He paused. "She's only nine years."

Something wrenched inside Daniel. It was a hard thing for him to turn someone away, especially a child. But he wasn't supposed to be practicing medicine in Owenduffy, not even in an emergency. Everything over there was run by the coal company, and he doubted they would welcome his interference with their own doctor's practice.

"Will you be coming or not?"

Daniel looked at the boy standing on his porch and saw that the gruffness of his tone had nothing to do with the worry in his eyes.

"You might just as well know I've got no money," Rory Flynn added in the same rough voice.

Still Daniel hesitated. "It's not the money."

He studied the narrow face, the faint shadow of a youthful beard, the look of contempt that didn't quite conceal the youth's desperation.

Finally, he sighed, saying, "Let me get my shoes."

The boy crushed his cap onto his head, making no attempt to mask his impatience.

Meanwhile, Daniel managed to ignore what he knew was a purely irrational urge to apologize for the delay.

～ふ

Although Daniel had never been in Owenduffy in a professional capacity, this wasn't his first visit to the mining town. Not long after his arrival in Mount Laurel, he had driven into the mining town to make the acquaintance of the company doctor. As it happened, Bevins had been gone, so they didn't meet. Another time Daniel passed through simply to familiarize himself not only with Owenduffy but with the surrounding countryside.

The miners' houses were at the entrance to the town, two long rows of ramshackle shanties separated by a rutted dirt road. Unpainted and in various states of disrepair, the houses looked to have been backed up against the side of a hill, without foundations, balanced on somewhat treacherous-looking support posts. Each had an empty space underneath where children could be seen playing amid the rubble and trash. In back, animals, including chickens and goats, roamed free around the outhouse.

From the little Daniel had learned about coal company towns, it seemed the owner of a mine seldom lived anywhere near the town. More commonly he would make his home in the city, often out of state. That wasn't the case here, however. The presence of the mine owner, Allen Slade, loomed over Owenduffy like an ominous shadow.

Slade's sprawling mansion on the hillside west of town had been built to his design years before Daniel arrived in the area. It resembled nothing so much as a British castle and was almost obscenely out of place in its proximity to the hovels it overlooked. Daniel wondered if the inappropriateness of the house and its location wasn't Slade's way of trying to safely distance himself from the workers who padded his pockets.

Although the area wasn't quite as squalid as one of the

shantytowns Daniel had seen in New York City, it still bore the look of a place where folks faced a daily battle simply to survive. Seated on the buggy's bench beside Daniel, Rory Flynn pointed to a house nearly at the end of the row. "This is our place."

After stepping down, Daniel left Sarge on the porch with a stern order to stay before following the Flynn youth indoors. He had never been inside one of the coal town homes before tonight. The Flynn house was little more than a shack, small and dingy, barren of any adornment. The front door opened directly onto a sitting room and combination eating area, furnished with only one worn, overstuffed chair and two wooden ones, as well as a rickety, scarred table. In the center of the room an aged iron stove squatted like an ugly troll. To the right were two rooms that appeared to be bedrooms, their shabby curtains pulled aside. Daniel caught a glimpse of a tiny kitchen toward the back of the house.

Like the exterior, the inside walls were bare of paint. He noted in passing, though, that the cramped quarters were clean and uncluttered, and he saw that someone had placed a glass jar filled with wildflowers in the middle of the table, a brave attempt to bring a touch of beauty to an otherwise grim existence.

The Flynn youth showed him to the bedroom just off the kitchen, where a little girl lay listlessly on a sagging iron bed. She was covered by a thin quilt, and although the night was warm and close, she was shivering.

The child watched Daniel's approach with the burning eyes of fever. Before he reached her, she coughed, a harsh, labored sound that let him know the girl was in trouble.

Her older brother hung back, but he spoke to her in a tone far gentler than Daniel had heard him use thus far. "This is the doctor from over the river, Molly Maureen. Dr. Kavanagh. He's come to make you better."

Daniel cast a look over his shoulder, irritated by the boy's assumption. From the looks of the little girl in the bed, it would be best not to make any overly optimistic promises. But when he bent over the child, he could only smile, for little Molly Maureen Flynn was smiling at *him*.

And what a smile it was.

In spite of her thin, pinched features, she was a lovely little thing, with a heart-shaped face and a fluffy cloud of dark hair. Rory had said she was nine years, but in truth she didn't look to be that old. The small hands clutching the quilt were those of a mere wisp of a child. Her form scarcely gave rise to the bed quilt that covered her.

An angry crimson flush blotched her face, and when Daniel put a hand to her forehead, the heat from her skin seemed to sear his. She coughed again, a hard, incessant, barking sound. With an expression that was almost apologetic, she grasped the quilt ever more tightly.

"Can you give her something for the cough?" asked Rory, behind him.

Not answering, Daniel sat down beside the child on the bed and waited until the coughing spasm subsided. Gently then, he took her hands in his and was appalled at the hot, paper-dry feeling of her skin. He knew at once the little girl was nearly dehydrated.

"Does your chest hurt, Molly?" he said.

She nodded shyly.

"Well, we'll have to do something about that," Daniel told her as he opened his case and retrieved his stethoscope.

The child's eyes grew large, and he hastened to reassure her. "I'm just going to listen to your lungs with this, Molly. I'll bet you didn't know your lungs made noises, did you?"

Again she gave a shake of her head. Daniel waited until she smiled at him again before helping her to sit upright. "Well, they do, and this thing here—it's called a stethoscope—lets me hear those noises. Now it won't hurt a bit, I promise you. But it likely will feel a little cold."

He examined the girl as quickly as he could, for she was weak to the point of trembling. It was just as he'd feared. Bronchitis, and a nasty case of it.

Molly Maureen Flynn was a very sick little girl.

Her brother had come to stand on the opposite side of the bed and now took his sister's hand in his.

"Has she had a bad cold in the past few weeks?" Daniel asked him, fumbling about in his medical case for some chloride of ammonia.

The boy nodded. "Aye, we both did. I got over mine in a couple of days or so, but Molly Maureen, she can't seem to shake it off."

Daniel glanced around. "Where are your parents?"

"Dead," the boy said flatly.

Daniel looked at him. "Both of them?"

"Aye. Mum died on the way across, and our da died in the cave-in last March."

Several men had been injured in that cave-in, and Daniel remembered that three had died.

"So...the two of you live here alone? You take care of your sister by yourself?"

The boy's eyes glinted with a spark of defiance. "We do just fine, Molly and me."

"I'm sure you do," Daniel said evenly. He hesitated, then asked, "You work in the mines?"

When the other nodded, he went on. "And who takes care of Molly during the day?"

"She takes care of herself for the most part, when she's not in school. But the Murphys look after her when I'm not here, especially since she's been sick."

His tone was defensive, even hard-edged, but Daniel didn't miss the slight trembling of his lower lip. The boy had more than he could handle, that was clear, and he knew it. No doubt he felt frustrated that he couldn't do more for his little sister.

"The Murphys? Is that Elly Murphy's family?"

Rory Flynn gave him a suspicious look. "How is it you'd be knowing Elly?"

"I don't know her," Daniel said. "But a friend of mine does. It's good of her and her family to help. Get me a spoon and a cup of water, would you? I've got some medicine here for Molly."

The boy left the room, and while he was gone Daniel used the small table beside the bed to mix the tinctures he wanted, talking to Molly as he worked.

He stayed another half hour, administering the ammonia and applying a mustard poultice to the girl's chest. He managed to coax a bit of barley water down her, but the effort tired her so quickly and she choked so fiercely that he feared she hadn't taken in enough to be of any real benefit.

Before he left, he gave strict instructions to young Rory. The boy would do his best, Daniel knew, but the fact that he left the house each day before dawn and didn't return until dusk left him precious little time to tend to his sister.

"You talk with the Murphys. It sounds as if they'd be willing to help, and Molly needs someone with her while you're away. Your sister mustn't be left alone, do you understand? She's very ill and very weak, and someone needs to see that she eats and gets her medicine."

He could tell Rory was taking his every word to heart, and somehow he knew this youth with the hard mouth and the eyes that were far too old for his years would do his best to follow the instructions he was given.

"Elly will stay with her if her mum will lend her for a spell," the boy said. "She'd probably be glad for some peace from the little ones. There's a houseful at the Murphys."

"Elly sounds like a good girl."

"All the Murphys are good people. Though Dom—Elly's da— can be a hard man entirely, his heart is in the right place."

Daniel nodded slowly. "Well, then, I'll look in on the two of you when I can. And, Rory—"

The other looked at him as if surprised to hear his name used.

"It's probably best if you keep quiet about my coming here tonight. The company might not like it."

The boy's face went dark. "The company don't like anything that's of help to us. They want us kept as their dogs, don't you know?"

Daniel didn't know, though he'd heard enough over the years to suspect Rory was right.

"Remember now, make sure she gets plenty of fluids. That's as important as the medicine I left with you."

"I'll see to it."

And he would, Daniel was certain.

He could tell the boy's next words were uttered with some difficulty. "I'll find a way to pay you when I can."

Daniel regarded him with interest, realizing he could grow to like the boy. "You can pay me, for now at least, by carrying out my instructions and making sure your sister gets proper care."

The boy gave a short nod. "You're Irish."

Daniel nodded. "I am." He was well aware that his own accent was still noticeable, despite his years in the States. It also occurred to him that he would have been only slightly younger than Rory Flynn when he and his mother made the crossing. The thought warmed him toward the boy even more.

For a moment Rory looked uncertain, and then he wiped a quick hand down the side of his trousers and extended it.

Daniel accepted the youth's handshake with pleasure, for he imagined that that calloused young hand was neither casually nor often offered.

⟿

As he drove the buggy out of town, Daniel gave vent to the melancholy that had been crowding in on him ever since he'd ridden into Owenduffy.

"Well, boy," he said to the big Newfoundland perched on the bench beside him, "it's this kind of place—and this kind of night—that ought to make us mindful of just how well-off we are, I expect. Not much of a life over here, especially for young 'uns like the Flynns. Not much of a life at all."

The Newfie shook his shaggy head in tacit agreement and then hefted his sturdy shoulder against Daniel's as if to comfort him.

It was Daniel's way to make prayer a part of his treatments, and almost straightaway he began to lift Molly Maureen Flynn and her protective older brother to the Lord, for surely those two could use more help than they were getting.

He didn't stop praying until he reached home, where he took a long look around his surroundings with a bit more appreciation than usual.

SIX

Sunday Special

Oh, the comfort—the inexpressible comfort, of feeling
safe with a person—having neither to weigh thoughts
nor measure words, but pouring them all right out.
Dinah Maria Mulock Craik

*T*he merciless heat had finally broken, leaving the valley
not exactly cool, but somewhat cloudy and pleasant. So
pleasant that Daniel decided to walk to church Sunday morning,
accompanied by Sarge, of course.

At the Methodist church, he slowed down as much as possible without making himself conspicuous. If Serena had returned
from Buckhannon by now, perhaps he'd meet up with her before
she went inside.

For a moment he was tempted to go inside rather than continuing on to the chapel but then decided that *would* be conspicuous. He could hardly sneak into a church sanctuary other than
his own just to manage a moment with Serena.

All the same, he did slow his pace considerably, coming to a
complete halt when he met Stephen and Esther. She was glowing

like a young girl, while Stephen clutched her arm as if he feared she might topple over if he let go.

Miss Gladys Piper was just pulling up in her buggy—which she drove herself, as always—so Daniel hurried to help her out and escort her to the church door.

"I can't think why you simply don't join us," she said somewhat sternly before going inside. "Reverend Jeffords does tend to run on at times, I'll admit. Nevertheless, he usually delivers a fine sermon."

"Oh, I'm sure he does, Miss Gladys, but I'm kind of settled in at the chapel now. Perhaps I'll pay a visit one of these days, though."

On his way down the steps to reclaim Sarge, he greeted Lida Broomhall and J.D., whose shirt collar looked to be starched so stiff it threatened to choke off his windpipe.

"You're goin' in the wrong direction, Doc!" boomed J.D.

"I've heard that before," Daniel rejoined with a wave, not stopping to talk, since he was already running late for his own worship service.

"No Serena this morning, Sarge," he told the Newfie as they trotted on down the street. "Maybe tomorrow."

Sarge chuffed softly as if to acknowledge his own disappointment, and Daniel put a hand to his companion's silky head, rubbing his ears a little before parking him in the lobby beside the church door, where he would faithfully wait until the end of the service.

Not for the first time, he congratulated himself for having the good sense to choose a dog with such a sensitive spirit.

Sandy MacIver, in Daniel's opinion, was an inspiring man, in or out of the pulpit. He was also, in addition to being his pastor, Daniel's closest friend in Mount Laurel.

As Daniel sat listening to the concluding remarks of the morning message, he felt genuinely blessed and uplifted by the worship service. While Sandy's sermon wasn't the sole source of the blessing, it was certainly a vital part of it.

Sanderson MacIver was a sinewy Scot with a neat mustache and a watchful gaze, a man whose easygoing manner might have caused him to appear somewhat ineffectual to those who didn't know him. Because Daniel did know him, he was keenly aware that there wasn't a fellow in town more capable of exerting his influence or changing minds and hearts than the wiry redhead who occupied the pulpit of the Mount Laurel Chapel every Sunday.

Sandy—who refused to countenance the title "Reverend" when applied to himself or anyone else—was a man whose intelligence was surpassed only by his compassion and kindness. A man as quick to weep with his flock as he was to celebrate with them. A man who extended as much grace to nonbelievers as he did to the most faithful churchgoers. And a man clearly on intimate terms with the God he served so enthusiastically and wholeheartedly.

He was also, Daniel had come to realize, a man who kept the door firmly closed on his own personal struggles. Even to his friends, although he had shared at least a part of his story with Daniel.

There was sorrow behind that door, Daniel knew. An old sorrow, a long-standing, never-quite-healed sadness that accounted for the air of reticence and the occasional moodiness that seemed to shadow his friend.

Long before Daniel first arrived in Mount Laurel, Charlotte MacIver had died giving birth to the child for which she and Sandy had hoped and prayed for nearly ten years. The infant, a boy, had also died.

Daniel had witnessed much tragedy in his years as a physician, but he could only imagine Sandy's grief. To lose both wife and a long-awaited son at the same time had to be almost more than a man could bear.

Sandy had never remarried nor shown any inclination to do so, although Daniel was fairly sure that he was viewed as a highly eligible prospect by a number of single women around town—not to mention their mothers, who would like nothing better than to see their daughters wed to a fine, upstanding man of the cloth like Sanderson MacIver.

On that infrequent occasion when he voiced this conjecture to his friend and pastor, however, it was quickly pointed out that a bachelor *physician* might prove just as desirable a target for some matronly matchmaker as an unmarried clergyman, and that perhaps Sandy ought to bring his good chum, Daniel, to the attention of some of the more determined ladies and their unmarried daughters.

This usually put an end to Daniel's fun, at least until next time.

In the midst of his musing, Daniel suddenly realized that those around him were rising for the closing hymn and benediction. As he scrambled to his feet, he glanced up at the pulpit and saw from the look of wry amusement on Sandy's face that he'd been found out for his wandering thoughts.

He grinned back and then jumped right into the final chorus of "Just As I Am," with a little more verve than was his habit.

His pastor merely lifted a knowing eyebrow and went on singing.

～

Some months ago, Helen Platt—of Helen's Mountain Inn—had dubbed them "The Bachelor Brigade."

Daniel Kavanagh, Sandy MacIver, and Lawrence Hill—doctor, pastor, and newspaper publisher—now sat at their usual table by the window, enjoying the "Sunday Special" of glazed ham, corn bread, and sweet potatoes. Three unmarried men, each a professional, each still young enough that their single status was not necessarily a permanent condition.

A fact that Helen seldom missed a chance to point out.

The only other bachelor in Mount Laurel—at least the only other one old enough to shave and young enough to bother to do so—was Bernard Cottle, proprietor of the local shoe shop. The threesome had invited Bernie to join them on more than one occasion, but the somewhat shy, bookish Bernie seemed to prefer the company—and understandably, the cooking—of his mother.

It wasn't that Bernie was standoffish or overly particular. But Josephine Cottle made the best black walnut cake and the most sinfully delicious custard pie in the county. Having sampled both of these delicacies at various town socials and church functions, Daniel figured it only stood to reason that Mrs. Cottle would also set a savory Sunday dinner table.

That being the case, he had long accepted Bernie's ongoing refusals as the wisdom of a man who had better choices.

Although Daniel spent more time with Sandy and felt closer

to him, he also liked and genuinely respected Lawrence. The handsome, silver-haired publisher of the town newspaper was Mount Laurel's most sophisticated resident.

Having tired of the hassle of city life some years before the war, Lawrence had uprooted and moved to Mount Laurel, seeking, in his own words, "the luxury of a peaceful place and a slower pace." He had bought the then struggling newspaper from its elderly owner and set about turning it into a fairly prosperous weekly that served not only Mount Laurel but most of Randolph County as well. As a pastime, he wrote political articles for one of the New York City magazines, but the *Public Sentinel* received the best part of his time and energy.

Daniel, at thirty-four, was the youngest of the three, and, in his own judgment, the least cosmopolitan. He felt quite certain that Lawrence had never had any rough edges, and if Sandy ever had, he'd clearly lost them by now.

As for himself, he couldn't quite shake the image of a raw-boned Irish immigrant boy still trying to grow into his own skin. No small undertaking, he reckoned, since he stood a good six feet four and had the long arms and "generous" feet of a plowboy.

"So, Daniel. I hear you've expanded your practice."

Daniel frowned at Lawrence's remark. "Expanded?"

The other took a sip of coffee. "Word has it you made a visit to Owenduffy the other night."

Daniel stared at him. "How in the world did you hear about *that*?"

Lawrence shrugged. "No secrets in a small town. Besides, newspapermen are unconscionable snoops, you know."

"Well, even for Mount Laurel, my comings and goings aren't

exactly news," Daniel groused. "Or at least I shouldn't think they would be. But, yes, I did see a patient over there Friday night. A little girl."

"Where was the company doctor?" Sandy put in.

"Most likely where he usually is," Lawrence replied sourly. "Either on a binge or sleeping one off."

From what Daniel had heard, Bevins didn't just indulge himself with the occasional binge. He simply stayed drunk most of the time. But Daniel kept that bit of gossip to himself.

"So how did you come to step in for him?" Sandy asked.

Daniel told them then about Molly Maureen Flynn and her brother, Rory.

"Bad situation," said Lawrence when Daniel had finished his account. "But it may have been a mistake for you to go over there. The company doesn't take kindly to interference from outsiders."

Daniel looked from Lawrence to Sandy, who lifted his eyebrows in tacit agreement.

"The child was seriously ill," Daniel said slowly. "Apparently, Dr. Bevins was nowhere to be found. What would *you* have done?"

"Probably the same thing," Sandy admitted, while Lawrence merely shrugged.

"But that doesn't mean the company will see it that way," added Sandy. "They won't hesitate to take you to task. Or try."

"Well, they can take me to task today if they like. I plan to check on the child again later this afternoon."

Lawrence shook his head. "Better leave it alone, Daniel. Those company bosses can be a tough bunch."

Surprised at his friends' comments about what Daniel considered a purely natural response to a call for help, he laughed a little.

"What do you think they'll do to me? Impale me on my own scalpel? I didn't abduct the girl. I simply examined her and gave her some medicine."

After a pause, Sandy said, "Just be careful, that's all. I don't think you realize how territorial the coal company is. You may think we're making too much of this, but—"

"I *know* you're making too much of it," Daniel told him. "And quite frankly, I couldn't care less what the coal company thinks. If they're that concerned about who takes care of their people, then maybe they ought to consider hiring on a new doctor. One who can be found when he's needed."

Daniel squirmed a little at what sounded, even to his own ear, like a touch of self-righteousness. But from what he knew—admittedly gleaned for the most part from rumor and fence post gossip—the situation with the company doctor was an ongoing problem. The man was supposed to be looking after the miners and their families. A full-time job, or at least it ought to be. Bevins, however, was reputed to be entirely indifferent to his responsibilities and made something of a mockery of the profession with his bad behavior and his indifference toward his own patients.

Worse still, Daniel wondered if the man might not be downright dangerous—a threat to those he did treat, given the tales about his often being thick tongued and bleary eyed in the middle of the day. The idea of a man like that treating the critically ill—a child like Molly Maureen Flynn, for example—chilled his blood.

The thought of the little girl he had promised to look in on made him push back from the table and get to his feet. "Well, this has been pleasant as always, fellows, but I have to be on my way."

"We don't mean to pick on you, Daniel," said Lawrence with a rather sheepish smile. "Just looking out for your well-being, you know."

Daniel shot him a wry look as he retrieved his wallet. "And I appreciate your concern, Lawrence. I would never take lightly the wisdom of your advanced years. Or my pastor's sage advice."

Lawrence curled his lip, and Sandy grinned as Daniel gave them a wave and headed off to pay his bill.

SEVEN

SERENA

And O! She was the Sunday
In every week.
AUSTIN CLARKE

*I*f Daniel had left Mount Laurel when he'd planned to, he
might have missed Serena.

As luck would have it, though, he forgot his medical bag on
the kitchen table and had to go back inside to retrieve it. Sarge
leaped from the buggy to follow, only to be sidetracked by a dev-
ilish tomcat out on an afternoon foraging expedition. By the time
Daniel reclaimed the big Newfie—much to the relief of the cat,
no doubt—it was almost half an hour later than he'd planned to
start for Owenduffy.

He glanced back at the house before they neared the edge of
town. He had chosen the site not only for the exceptional view
of the surrounding mountains and the river, but also for the way
it overlooked the valley and the town itself, just below the ridge.
From his vantage point, Mount Laurel took on the appearance of
a hand-hewn miniature village, each piece carved with the same

excellence and minutiae of detail the tragic Friedrich Willmar had applied to the artistry of his carousel.

Most nights he fell asleep staring at the moon-silvered slopes of the hills while listening to the river run its languid course down the valley. And almost every morning, except in bitter weather, he would walk to the edge of his property, a mug of coffee in hand, and feast his eyes on the town and the mountains he had come to love with an almost proprietary kind of affection, as though a part of his very soul were somehow bonded to his surroundings.

He liked living where he did, pressed against the hillside at the tip of Mount Laurel. Some of his patients seemed to think he ought to keep residence at his office, probably so they wouldn't have to go too far in search of him if he happened to be needed. But Daniel had never much liked the idea of living where he worked. He seemed to need at least the illusion that his profession and his personal life were separate.

The truth was that it was difficult if not impossible to separate his personal life from his work. It sometimes seemed that almost everything he did was somehow wrapped up in the practice of medicine.

No doubt that made him a very dull fellow. At least his friends seemed to think so. They liked to nag that he should join them more often for "recreation." Daniel was just as fond of telling them that he did not consider sticking a hook through a helpless worm simply to entice an equally helpless fish a particularly civilized form of recreation. Nor did bringing down a tree squirrel with a hunting rifle relax him. Not a bit.

If he found some perverse form of relaxation in inflicting pain on one of God's creatures, he would tell them, he might just as well lance a boil or set a broken bone. At least he got paid for that kind of "amusement."

⁓

The afternoon sun seemed to brighten considerably as he caught a glimpse of Serena Norman's fussy little buggy parked in front of the schoolhouse. It brightened still more when he spied Serena herself striding down the boardwalk in front of the building.

He pulled up behind her buggy, ran a hand through his hair, and jumped down to meet her. She smiled, and he figured he was grinning like a lovesick schoolboy. But then, Serena ought to be used to that by now. She had the same effect on most of the male population in town.

"Isn't she something now?" he observed to Sarge, who leaped from the buggy and would have galloped full bore toward Serena had Daniel not restrained him with a hand on his head. The Newfie looked at him, but only for a second or two before returning his full attention to Serena.

By the time she reached them, Daniel's mouth was almost too dry to speak, and his voice actually cracked when he tried. "I was wondering when you'd be back."

Still smiling, she touched one small hand to straighten the blue bonnet she was wearing, the one Daniel always fancied because it so perfectly matched her eyes. "Well, here I am."

"Indeed," he managed. "Here you are."

"I thought I told you I'd be back by the weekend."

She reached to pat Sarge's head, and he whimpered with doggie delight. The great oaf had no pride at all, it seemed.

"Yes, I suppose you did tell me that, now that you mention it. It just seemed…longer." Clearly, his own pride was also sadly lacking.

Her mouth twitched a little when she turned back to Daniel, as if she found him mildly amusing. Which often seemed to be the case.

"So, how was your aunt?"

"She's doing much better."

The conversation went on that way for another minute or two, with Daniel growing more and more uncomfortable, his wits seemingly too fogged to say anything even mildly intelligent. He might just as well have made comments about the lack of rain and the dust in the air.

Instead, he gestured toward the school building. "You weren't working on the classroom today, were you?"

She lifted an eyebrow. "Hardly on Sunday, Daniel. I thought I'd just take stock to see how much is left to do before we open. Quite a lot, it seems."

"I told you I'll be glad to help."

"And I plan to hold you to your offer. So, where are you off to so late on a Sunday afternoon?"

"Owenduffy." At her puzzled look, he went on to explain. "I treated a little girl over there for a bad case of bronchitis the other night. I thought I'd just check and see how she's doing."

She frowned. It seemed to Daniel that Serena was the only woman he'd ever known who could disarm a man with either a smile or a frown.

"You're not supposed to treat those people, Daniel. They have their own doctor."

"I know. But the girl was seriously ill, and her brother couldn't find the company doctor, so I took care of her."

She wrinkled her nose. "That doctor over there must be a perfectly awful man. Everyone says he's nothing but a drunk."

"Well, he does seem to be absent more often than not. Anyway, I was glad I went. The girl needed attention."

Serena regarded him with an expression that bordered on disapproval. "That really shouldn't be your concern, should it? Surely you have enough to do looking after our own people."

Our own people. Daniel thought that seemed an odd way to put it, but then he suspected that Serena was probably no different from most long-time residents of Mount Laurel when it came to Owenduffy. There was always that dividing line—in reality more like a dividing wall—between the two towns. The river that ran between was just a symbol of the "them versus us" mentality that separated Mount Laurel's locals from the immigrant miners and their families.

"It wasn't all that much out of my way," he said with a shrug.

Her look was skeptical, but then the smile returned. "You're such a softie, Daniel. Well, I'd best be getting home. I told Mother I'd be back in time for supper."

Daniel hesitated before asking, "Could I...stop by later?"

Her reply was quick in coming. "Not this evening, Daniel. I'm really tired from the trip, and I still have to unpack my things and get settled before morning. I want to start getting the classroom in order first thing tomorrow. It's only two weeks now before the beginning of the term, and I have a lot to do."

Disappointed, he merely nodded his understanding. "Maybe later in the week then."

"Of course. Perhaps you can come to supper one evening," she offered, raising herself up on tiptoe to brush a hint of a kiss on his cheek.

Ordinarily, this gesture of affection, which was as much of a kiss as Serena ever allowed him, would have caught him completely off guard—and pleased him no end. But while her light-hearted words and the kiss itself seemed entirely sincere, he knew from experience that the invitation to supper might well be forgotten in the busyness of her week. He found himself unreasonably annoyed by that simple awareness.

He helped her into her buggy, watching her start off before resuming his own drive. The rest of the way to Owenduffy, he puzzled over his feelings for Serena.

He wasn't ready to concede that he was in love with her. Could a man actually be in love with a woman he'd never even kissed?

Not likely, he decided.

Infatuated, then? Was it merely the kind of schoolboy crush that would wear itself out given enough time—and enough evasiveness on her part?

He knew most of their friends and acquaintances took it for granted that he and Serena were a couple. They attended many of the town's social events together, and Daniel called at the Norman house with as much frequency as she would allow—usually no more than once a week and almost always on Sundays. But no matter what anyone else might assume, Daniel knew they were leagues away from any sort of a commitment.

In truth, he wasn't exactly sure if he wanted a commitment, or even what, exactly, his real feelings were. He did know that she managed to make him feel awkward and even somewhat foolish on a fairly regular basis. He couldn't help but wonder, though, if his ineptness was due solely to the effect Serena had on him or had just as much to do with his own awkwardness and lack of experience where women were concerned.

He heaved a somewhat dramatic sigh, and the Newfoundland looked over at him with disdain.

He could hardly fault the hound for his contempt. Was there anything more pathetic, after all, than a man losing his mind… not to mention his dignity…over a woman?

~∂

As he bumped across the corded covered bridge linking Mount Laurel to Owenduffy, Daniel's mood darkened still more.

He had no inclination now to bask in the grace and tranquil glory of the late summer countryside or take comfort in the knowledge that Serena was back in town. Instead, he steeled himself to face the soot-dusted, gloom-clouded community held captive by a company of men who saw not the sin of enslaving their own kind, but only the profit to be gained from that servitude.

It was always a bit of a jolt to cross the bridge from the placid beauty and quiet of Mount Laurel and its environs to enter a place that seemed the very antithesis of all he'd left behind.

He had an unsettling sense that the town of Owenduffy existed in the bowels of a shadowed cave, much as did the mine from which its inhabitants drew their sustenance. The few houses that had windowpanes seemed to glare at them as they passed. In one yard, a scrawny black dog growled and ran toward them as if to give chase, but Sarge rose and bared his teeth and the sorry creature scurried off, tail between his legs.

"Well, aren't you the fierce one?" Daniel said to the Newfie, who ignored the taunt, studying him as if to question the wits of a master who would take them into such a place as this.

"Can't say I blame you, chum," Daniel muttered. "Even I'm beginning to wonder what I'm doing here."

The sun that had been at Daniel's back only a moment ago seemed to have retreated, as if its brightness would be found alien and unwelcome in this place. And though the afternoon sun had been steady and warm when he left Mount Laurel, he now shivered and drew his shoulders inward against the sudden chill.

EIGHT

MEETING MURPHY

A fighting-man he was...
Hewn out of the rock.
JOSEPH CAMPBELL

*T*he door was ajar, so after rapping on the frame Daniel
waited only a moment to enter.

His second visit to the Flynn cabin, this time in the dim afternoon light that managed to seep through the windows, revealed
an even harsher view of the poverty of those who lived here. The
few furnishings seemed mostly in a state of disrepair, and the
lack of anything even remotely decorative or aesthetically pleasing marked the forlorn little house as a place where comfort and
contentment would not be easily attained.

He went directly to the bedroom, where he found young
Molly Maureen in bed. Today, however, she was sitting up, with
the help of a quilt propped behind her, while a young woman
with a flaming tumble of copper hair fed her with a spoon.

Both jumped when Daniel walked in. Molly Maureen gave
him a bright smile, but her companion eyed him with a plainly
suspicious stare.

"Sorry," Daniel said. "I knocked, but you must not have heard me."

With what appeared to be a deliberate lack of haste, the young woman set the bowl of food down on the table beside the bed and rose from the chair.

This would likely be Elly Murphy. No wonder Clay Holliday was so badly smitten. She was a beauty. Tall and lithe, with strong features and a long, graceful neck, she might have been one of the ancient Celtic warrior queens instead of the daughter of a small-town coal miner. She also looked considerably more mature than the seventeen years Daniel knew her to be.

Indeed, Stephen would have his work cut out for him, trying to convince his lovesick son to walk away from this girl.

She looked entirely unimpressed when Daniel introduced himself. "And you must be Elly," he said. "Elly Murphy?"

Molly Maureen giggled. "She's Addie, not Elly! Addie Rose is Elly's big sister."

The older girl cracked a small smile but said nothing, instead dismissing Daniel's attempted apology with a wave of her hand.

After another awkward moment he turned to Molly Maureen, relieved to find his small patient looking much perkier than she had two days ago. She was still noticeably weak and too pale by far, but there had been visible improvement.

"Well, now, Miss Molly, I do believe you might be feeling better than you were the last time I saw you."

The little girl beamed. "Addie Rose says I'm doin' ever so much better. She takes good care of me, she does."

"Well, you make sure to show her you appreciate it," said Daniel with a quick smile in the older girl's direction—a smile that wasn't returned.

"All right," he said, sitting down on the side of the bed and taking his stethoscope from the medical case. "Let's have a listen."

After satisfying himself that the child really was significantly improved, Daniel straightened and turned to the young woman. "I think you must be a good nurse, Miss Murphy. Molly seems to be doing remarkably well, considering."

She fixed him with a sharp blue-eyed stare but remained silent. Puzzled by her demeanor, Daniel made another attempt to engage her. "Do you live nearby, Miss Murphy?"

One perfect eyebrow lifted. "Anywhere in Owenduffy would be nearby, I expect."

Daniel looked up. Was the girl being deliberately rude?

This time he was the one who made no reply.

Instead, he turned back to his patient. "I can see that you're on the mend, young lady, so I'll just leave you another bottle of medicine and be on my way. But I want you to promise me that you'll stay quiet and warm for a few more days until you're feeling completely well again. Do I have your word?"

Molly nodded, still smiling at him.

"Where's your brother, by the way?" asked Daniel

"At Mr. Gormant's"

Daniel turned to Addie Murphy. "Gormant—the mine boss?"

She nodded and said shortly, "He works for Mr. Gormant on Sunday afternoons. Does odd jobs and the like."

Daniel wondered if the boy ever got any rest. And working for Hugh Gormant—what would that be like?

The Welsh mine boss had the reputation of being about as coarse and mean a human being as the Creator ever saw fit to breathe life into.

Daniel stood, pressed by a sudden urgency to get out of this small and dismal cabin—indeed, out of the town itself.

On the heels of that thought came a stab of guilt. If the place could have such a bleak effect on his spirit in only a few minutes, what must it be like for the sick child on the sagging bed and her brother, who faced it on a daily basis?

Or for a girl like Addie Murphy, whose beauty seemed so glaringly out of place against the backdrop of hopelessness and gloom that pervaded Owenduffy?

Did they ever dream of escape, he wondered? It was hard to imagine how they could not.

He jumped at the sound of heavy footsteps thumping across the floor. A big man with a face like a thunderhead and shoulders wide enough to heft a barrel on each side came tramping into the bedroom just then. Sharp, hawklike features, a fierce, black mustache, and a shock of dark hair falling over one eye gave the fellow a hard, even dangerous appearance.

Daniel had to check himself to keep from taking a step backward.

"You're to come home now, girl," the man commanded in a deep rumble of a voice with an accent that plainly marked him as Irish. "Your mother is needing your help."

"Aye, Da," said Addie Murphy. "I was just giving Molly her supper."

Gone now was the somewhat sullen air she had presented to Daniel. Her expression conveyed, if not outright acquiescence, at least a measure of respect. Or was it caution?

As the big Irishman turned his fierce gaze on him, Daniel moved to offer his hand. "Daniel Kavanagh," he said.

The man stood unmoving, glaring at Daniel. "You'd be the doctor from across the river," he finally said, the words laced with something akin to disgust.

Daniel dropped his hand back to his side. "I am, yes."

He heard his own accent thicken. It was as if he'd stepped outside of one world into another, one that was different and yet familiar. The rhythm of the west of Ireland had not been completely lost. Even though it had been years since he'd left the small village of Killala and later the back alleys and docks of New York, his tongue could still turn as Irish as a well-worn coat.

"I didn't get your name," he said cheerfully.

The Irishman stood eyeing him as if he were a toad on a rock. "I'm called Murphy," he said, offering no more.

"Well, Mr. Murphy, Molly Maureen tells me that your daughter has been taking very good care of her, and I must say that's obvious. She's doing very well."

Clearly ignoring Daniel's attempt to compliment his daughter, Murphy continued to study him with a less-than-pleasant expression. "Thought you did your doctorin' across the river."

Daniel wasn't about to let this fellow intimidate him. He knew his type well enough, after all. He'd spent his share of time in the midst of hard men with dark tempers.

"Molly's brother came for me. It seemed an emergency."

"Bevins was in his cups again, I expect," said the miner. The hard mouth beneath the heavy mustache turned down even more.

When Daniel made no reply, Murphy gave a nod and glanced at the child in the bed. "She's been bad for a time."

"Well, she's doing much better now. And as I said, I believe your daughters can take part of the credit for that."

The other man's dark-eyed gaze scraped over Daniel like a sharp knife. "They do their share of tending to the sick. We look after our own. No one else to do it." His eyes stayed locked on Daniel. "If you're needing paid for your visits, you'll have something of a wait. The boy's wage barely keeps the two in beans."

Daniel shook his head. "That's already been settled between Rory and myself."

Ignoring Daniel, Murphy went on. "I'll have the girl—" he turned his head toward his daughter—"fetch some fresh eggs and a basket of her mother's sweet bread. That will have to do for now."

Daniel put up a hand. "That's not necessary. I'm not looking for payment."

Again, the man disregarded him. "Molly Maureen, Addie must go and help her mother now. You stay abed until Rory gets home, mind."

The little girl, who seemed accustomed to Murphy's orders and appeared entirely unfazed by him, merely gave the big miner a smile and a nod. "Aye, Mr. Dom."

"Come on, then," said the miner, turning his back on Daniel and starting for the door, his daughter following on his heels.

Daniel said his goodbyes to Molly and then followed the Murphys.

Outside, he stopped at the buggy, where Sarge had stretched out for his late afternoon nap. The big Newfie raised his head, lumbered to his feet, and fixed Murphy with a watchful eye.

"I'll just go and get the things, Da," said Addie Murphy, starting for the road.

Daniel stopped her. "No, please. That's not necessary."

Both she and her father looked at him.

"If you insist, please give it to Molly and her brother."

Murphy studied him before nodding to his daughter to go on.

Daniel watched her make her way to a house that sat a little more than halfway down a slight hill, well away from the road. It was the same one he'd noticed before, one of the few buildings in Owenduffy that sported a coat of paint. Of course, the coal dust had darkened the siding, but even so, the place stood out from the neighboring houses.

In front, two small boys played with a spotted dog and a stick, while a little girl who looked to be younger than Molly Flynn came at a run when she spied Addie.

Daniel turned back to Murphy and found the miner watching him with the same unsettling, narrow-eyed stare. When the man finally spoke again, however, his tone, albeit grudging, might have been slightly less harsh.

"They won't like it, your coming over here to see the girl."

Daniel looked at him.

"The company," Murphy said.

Daniel nodded. "So I've heard."

"You came anyway."

Daniel wasn't sure if Murphy meant the remark as a question or an assessment of his mental state. He merely shrugged, and, propelled by some perverse streak of stubbornness, again extended his hand to the irascible miner. There was no reason whatsoever to expect that this gesture toward courtesy would be accepted any more readily than his first attempt. Nevertheless, he made the offer.

"Well, then, it was good to meet you, Mr. Murphy," he said, purposely letting his own Irish thicken his words.

Murphy, not quite as tall as Daniel but as solid as a stockade, glanced at Daniel's outstretched hand and then his face. After a long, somewhat awkward moment, he finally applied a bone-bruising handshake. "I'll see the Flynn youngsters get the bread and eggs," he said gruffly, yanking his hand away as if it were *his* bones that had been splintered and, without another word, turned and traipsed toward home.

Daniel stood watching, a shadow of uneasiness passing over him as he thought about Stephen and Clay Holliday. Although Stephen could be a hard man and was openly disapproving of his son's involvement with Elly Murphy, Daniel had a feeling that Stephen's censure might be the least of Clay's problems.

Indeed, he would not want to be in the boy's shoes should the man Murphy happen to share Stephen's disapproval of the young couple's attraction to each other.

NINE

AN UNEXPECTED OFFER

I bind my soul this day
To the brother far away,
To the brother near at hand,
In this town, and in this land.
LAUCHLAN MACLEAN WATT

October

Summer rolled into fall like a long, mellow sigh after a
good meal.

It was such a gentle transition that Daniel almost failed to
notice it, until he realized the fragrance of honeysuckle and sun-
baked wildflowers had been replaced by the pungent odor of
wood smoke and apple butter steaming in open-air cauldrons.
Frost had taken the late-blooming roses, and the hills were already
ablaze with scarlet and gold fire, while the roadsides now flour-
ished with goldenrod and milkweed.

There simply was no pageant like a mountain autumn, no event
that could rival the Alleghenies in early October. If this season

wasn't one of the most spectacular displays of the Almighty's creativity and power, Daniel couldn't think what was.

With a long breath, he turned away from the window in the pharmacy. On this particular Monday morning he didn't have the luxury of spare time to soak up his colorful surroundings. The coming days promised to be at least as busy or even busier than those of the previous week.

Within the past two weeks, scarlet fever, one of the diseases he hated most, had appeared among some of the hill folks as well as half a dozen families in town. He'd had his hands full, making home calls in addition to seeing patients in the office. He knew from experience that a full-blown epidemic could strike any time now.

Indeed, before another day passed, he intended to get word to Esther to avoid coming to town. For that matter, she had best avoid people altogether until this latest outbreak passed. He had a number of other patients in the family way too, and he intended to issue the same caution to them. No sense taking chances.

His own mother had nearly died from the vicious illness when he was a boy. And not long after his arrival in Mount Laurel, he had lost at least half a dozen patients during an outbreak. Little Mercy Seaton had been stricken deaf and mute during that same time, while her mother, Lenora, had nearly succumbed to a vicious kidney infection left in the wake of the fever.

Now the menacing disease had returned, and the thought of another rampage struck dread in his heart. He had learned of very few cases in Owenduffy as yet, but even a few guaranteed there would be more.

As he rolled up his shirtsleeves to wash his hands, the thought of Harley Bevins reminded him of little Molly Maureen Flynn and her brother, Rory. From time to time, he wondered how they were getting along. On his last visit, his young patient had been up and about, looking pleasingly fit with some color in her cheeks and even a glint of mischief in her eyes.

And what about Addie Rose Murphy?

Daniel's head came up with a jerk. Again he stood staring out the window above the pharmacy sink as he dried his hands. This wasn't the first time the memory of the Murphy girl had edged its way into his thoughts. For some reason, it unsettled him that he all too clearly remembered what she looked like and even the sound of her voice. Although the thought of Serena could temporarily crowd out the image of the somewhat younger Addie Rose, a memory of the fire-haired beauty lingered, like a soft light that never quite dimmed or went away.

He jumped when the bell over the waiting room door jangled. At the same time, Sarge, who had been snoozing under the table, jolted to his feet with a growl, threatening to topple the table with his bulk.

No doubt the big lug was simply irritated that his nap had been cut short. It wasn't as if he could be startled by the bell—or much of anything else.

Daniel tossed the towel onto the counter and crossed the room. Like Sarge, he was curious as to who might be making an appearance so early on a Monday morning, even before Audrey arrived to police the patients during office hours.

In truth, his office hours were a joke. No one paid the sign on the entrance door any heed whatsoever. Apparently, folks simply took it for granted that he had no personal life outside the office. If they needed to see Doc, they simply showed up in the waiting room, regardless of the hour.

As much as Daniel grumbled about the lack of consideration, he knew he could blame no one but himself. The reality was that he didn't have much of a life outside the office, and he did indeed spend more time here than at home. He was easily found, and his patients knew it.

❧

The last person he would have expected to see in his waiting room at this time of day—or at any time of day—was Hugh Gormant. Daniel had met the mine boss only twice, and both brief meetings had merely served to reinforce the man's reputation for being loudmouthed, contentious, and hardheaded. Simply put, Gormant came across as a bully. It wasn't all that difficult to figure out why his workers were rumored to dislike him with a vengeance.

Gormant stood in the middle of the room, his arms folded across his chest, legs apart in a stance that could only be described as belligerent. It was a harsh assessment, Daniel knew, but the fact was that the man looked like a thug, pure and simple. Gormant wasn't tall, but there didn't appear to be a soft ounce of flesh anywhere on that thickly muscled body. With his unkempt black hair, close-set eyes, and dark stubble of beard, he reminded Daniel of a number of disreputable gang members that had stalked the slums of New York City.

Sarge gave another growl, and Daniel ordered him back to the examining room.

"Mr. Gormant," Daniel said with a short nod.

Gormant's sour look never wavered. "The company's needing a doc. You want the job?"

"I beg your pardon?"

"Bevins is gone. Fired. He couldn't stay sober long enough to do any doctorin'. I've been authorized to hire someone in his place. No one else around here except you. You want the job?"

No beating around the bush here.

"No, actually. I don't."

"What?"

"I can't take on any more patients. I don't have time."

The man smirked. "You had time to come sneakin' over the bridge a couple of months back to do some doctorin' without being asked. I figure the good Christian people on this side of the river must not take sick all that much."

His tone of voice made the word "Christian" sound like a label of contempt.

"A big city doc like yourself can't handle some miners in addition to your own kind?"

Daniel bit down on the first acid reply that came to mind. "I'm afraid not. You'll need to find someone else."

Gormant's mouth pulled down even more as he stood glaring at Daniel. Clearly, he wasn't accustomed to being refused. After another second or two, he dropped his hands to his sides and clenched them. "We got the scarlet fever going around. We need a doctor *now.*"

Daniel's mind raced. He didn't want this. More to the point, he honestly didn't see how he could possibly handle any more patients. He hadn't overstated his time problem. Maybe if the scarlet fever hadn't started up when it did he might have worked something out...

The disease could decimate a town like Owenduffy in weeks. No reliable sanitation system. Too many immigrants who knew little if anything about even the most basic health care. Too many houses and workers crowded together.

Daniel thought of the wispy little Molly Maureen Flynn and her earnest-faced, hard-working brother. And Addie Rose Murphy. And all the children. There were so many children in Owenduffy.

He drew a long breath. "I might be able to give you one day a week," he said on impulse, brushing aside his misgivings. "I don't see how I could do anything more and still take care of my patients here."

The mine boss looked as if he were about to spit. "One day a week won't be enough, and you know it."

"I *do* know it, but that's the best I can do."

Gormant regarded him with disgust but said nothing.

"Look, I would do more if I could, but there's just no way I can."

Finally, the other gave a shrug and curled his lip even more. "I expect we'll take what we can get then. But just so you know, you'd have a steadier income with the company than you do with this bunch of farmers over here. You might want to keep that in mind."

With that, he turned and stalked out, leaving Daniel to stand knotting his fists in frustration.

He was still in the waiting room when Audrey walked in a moment later.

"What did *he* want?" she demanded, loosening the ribbons of her bonnet as she passed briskly by Daniel on her way to the counter.

Daniel looked at her. "He came to offer me a job."

Audrey whipped around, her mouth tightening. "He *what?*"

"It seems the company fired Harley Bevins."

"Took them long enough," she said, her tone dry.

"Maybe so, but now they're in need of a doctor. He thought I might be interested."

Audrey's sharp little chin lifted a good inch. "I hope you put him in his place."

Daniel shrugged. "I told him I'd help them out as much as I can."

She stared at him. "You didn't."

"Well, I'm not planning to move over there, Audrey. I made it clear that I can't spare more than one day a week."

"That's one day a week you're going to be needed right here in *our* town. See here, Daniel—"

Daniel had long ago accepted that he'd never be "Dr. Kavanagh" or even "Doctor" to Audrey. Even if both of them were around for another twenty years, in her eyes he'd still be a boy, never a full-fledged physician. He also knew that her terse "See here, Daniel" always preceded an unsolicited—and usually undesirable—piece of advice. He braced himself.

"What are you thinking, taking time away from all your regular patients right here in town to go over there with…those people? And with this awful scarlet fever bearing down on us now."

Patience, he told himself. *She means well. Audrey always means well.*

"They have scarlet fever in Owenduffy too, Audrey. That's why I need to help as much as I can. Don't worry. I know my limit, and I made it clear to Gormant. One day a week, and no more."

She lifted her chin a tad higher with a sniff that only Audrey could effect. "If truth were told, the fever probably came from that place over there to begin with. Folks aren't going to take to the idea of your going back and forth, Daniel, knowing what you might be carrying in to our own people. They aren't going to like it one bit."

He drew a long breath. "I can't base how I practice medicine on what people like or don't like, Audrey. Any more than Dr. Franklin did."

If he'd hoped that the mention of his predecessor, whom Audrey had plainly revered as a veritable saint for more than two decades, might give her pause, he'd misjudged her. There would be no chance to escape the rest of her reprimand now.

"Dr. Franklin," she said, righteous indignation lacing her very breath, "was uncompromisingly dedicated to his own patients. He would *never* have risked their well-being for that bunch of… *foreigners* across the river."

Daniel rubbed the back of his neck to keep from cracking his knuckles, which he knew Audrey intensely disliked. He also knew that when she began to use words such as "uncompromis-ingly," she would brook no argument from him. He might just as well get this over with. Pulling rank wasn't something he liked to do with his starchy secretary, but he was the doctor and he did pay her wage.

And a fairly generous one at that.

"Audrey, I appreciate your feelings about this. Truly I do. But I'm sure you understand that I have to do what I believe is right when it comes to practicing medicine."

Winter seemed to blow through the room as she fixed her leaden, unblinking stare on him. "Of course, you have to do what you think is best," she said, making it chillingly clear that Daniel obviously didn't know what was best.

"Thank you, Audrey," he said, a little more meekly than he'd intended. "Well, we should get things set up. I expect we'll have a busy morning."

Her only reply was to turn her back on him. Feeling a bit like a schoolboy who'd had his knuckles rapped, Daniel headed for the examining room, making a determined effort not to slink.

It was going to be a long day.

～

As it happened, the day turned out to be even longer than he'd feared. Late in the afternoon, a young girl from the hills, clearly little more than a child, came stumbling into the waiting room.

She appeared to be uncertain, even a bit frightened, by her surroundings, but her mission was clear. Both her mother and a neighbor woman—the child's aunt—needed "doctorin'." Her description of their symptoms left little doubt that both had been stricken with scarlet fever.

Even though his Mondays were usually so busy Daniel seldom left the office, he didn't have the heart to deny the girl's plea that they needed him "right now." He followed her home and then on to her aunt's house.

Two hours later, he made his way to his own home, exhausted and once again discouraged by the all-too-obvious evidence he'd encountered of extreme poverty and lack of even the most basic knowledge in self health care.

Too disheartened to do anything more than feed Sarge and kick off his shoes, he finally collapsed on the couch and slept through the night without waking to fix any supper for himself.

TEN

MIXED NEWS

Drop Thy still dews of quietness,
Till all our strivings cease…
And let our ordered lives confess
The beauty of Thy peace.
JOHN GREENLEAF WHITTIER

*T*wo weeks later, Audrey informed Daniel that she would be retiring at the end of the year.

Her announcement came without warning and with very little explanation, other than the fact that she wasn't as young as she used to be.

Reeling from this unexpected—and highly unwelcome—news, Daniel tried to change her mind. "But, Audrey, I need you. Surely you can see that. You know how I depend on you, and with things as they are now, there's no way I can manage without you."

"You'll get by, Daniel. You'll just have to. I've been coming to this office five days a week at eight o'clock every morning for more than twenty years, and frankly I'm tired of it. I want—I *need*—some time for myself."

Daniel studied her. "Are you feeling all right, Audrey? You're not ill, are you?"

Her mouth thinned as it always did when she thought he was being foolish. "I am perfectly fine. I expect it's never occurred to you that I would like a life away from sick people every now and then."

"I can understand that." Actually, he wasn't sure he could. But then could someone who spent most of his life around illness really be expected to grasp why someone else might not want to? Still, it clearly wasn't the time to say as much. "It's just that this is a bad time—"

"It will never be a good time," she shot back, "what with you intending to trot back and forth between here and that mining camp, taking on everybody you meet with an ache or pain. My mind is made up. This is how it's going to be. After the end of the year, I'm finished. You'd best start looking for someone else right away."

Daniel hesitated before replying. "Have I done something to offend you, Audrey? Is that it?"

"No, that is *not* it. And if you're thinking that this has anything to do with your treating those foreigners across the river, I'll tell you right now it doesn't. It's true that I don't approve—"

"Audrey—"

"But that has nothing to do with my retiring." She gave a long sigh as if she were dealing with a dull-witted child. "It's just exactly what I'm trying to tell you. I'm simply tired of spending all my time around patients. I need to get away from this office and sick people and live a normal life."

Daniel didn't believe for a moment that this unexpected announcement had nothing to do with his decision to give a few hours to the sick in Owenduffy. But he had seen that look in Audrey's eyes before and knew there would be no changing her decision.

Letting out a long breath, he groped for patience. "All right, then. I don't like it, and I really don't know how I'll manage, but it seems there's nothing I can do to change your mind."

She gave a sharp little nod and went around her desk, settling herself in her chair and scanning the daily log. "You're taking Lonny Crawford's cast off this morning. Brownie Teeter is coming in again because of his asthma. And Ruth Lieninger is bringing the baby in for you to see. Poor little thing has that bad rash again."

She went on, ticking off the patients he could expect to see today, although those who actually bothered to make appointments were few. Most simply showed up, assuming he would be available.

"You're going to be late making your home visits," she pointed out.

"I'll get them done."

"Dr. Franklin never held much with this business of scheduling patients for office visits. He leaned more toward making home calls."

How many times had he heard this before? It had been a routine observation ever since he'd taken over the deceased Sidney Franklin's practice.

"Dr. Franklin didn't see a third of the patients I do in a day's time either."

As soon as the words were out, he regretted saying them. Even though he'd spoken only the truth.

Audrey sniffed but made no reply. It was her typical way of indicating disapproval.

As it happened, Audrey seemed to sniff a lot these days.

～

After his last call of the day, Daniel picked up his mail and headed home, eager to read the letter from Evan Whittaker he'd found waiting in the post at the general store.

When he arrived home, Ira Birch was sitting on the front porch, waiting for him. His mouth began to water the moment he saw the large stew pot at Ira's side.

Supper.

As soon as Sarge spied Ira, he jumped down from the buggy and went at a gallop to greet their visitor. Daniel waved, and then he pulled the buggy around the side of the house to free his horse, Ginger, from her harness. "I'll tend to you in a little bit, girl."

On the porch, he went straight to the stewpot, lifted the lid, and smiled with pleasure at the luscious aroma of Sally Birch's hearty beef stew. "Ah!"

"Hello to you too, Doc," Ira said, his tone teasing. "Well, thank you kindly. It's nice to see you again, I'm sure. Oh, I reckon I'm doing good. How about yourself?"

Daniel laughed as Ira uncoiled his tall form to shake hands. "Sorry, Ira. There's just something about your wife's cooking that makes me forget my manners."

"Uh-huh. I believe I've noticed that before."

"You be sure and thank her for me. I can't think of anything nicer to come home to than Sally's beef stew."

"If you'd get yourself a wife, you wouldn't have to be moochin' off my supper," Ira said dryly.

"If I ever find a woman who can cook like your Sally, I'll marry her the same day I meet her."

"Uh-*huh*. Well, if that's one of your conditions, I suspect you might be livin' alone for a long time to come."

"You're probably right."

Sarge followed them inside, his expression hopeful.

"Don't get any ideas, chum," Daniel warned him. "This is *my* supper."

In the kitchen, Daniel started a pot of coffee before joining Ira at the table. Only then did Sarge give up his longing looks at the stewpot and plop down at the back door.

"You can go ahead and eat," said Ira.

Daniel shook his head. "No, I need to relax a bit first."

"Busy day?"

"They're all busy of late. And I was up in the middle of the night. Elphea Simpson's baby arrived."

"Do babies ever show up in the daytime? Seems as though every time I hear you mention a new arrival, it's one that took place in the middle of the night."

"You know, I've noticed that too."

"You ever wish you'd been a travelin' salesman so you could sleep nights?"

"I'll admit that the thought has occurred to me."

"You go over to Owenduffy today?"

"Not today." Daniel rubbed his shoulder. "Come to think of it, I didn't even get lunch. There wasn't time."

"Then you need to eat. I have to get back home anyway," Ira said, standing. "Sally warned me not to be late if I want some supper of my own tonight. Besides, she'll need my help with the children."

Daniel pushed himself up from his chair, suppressing a groan as his back clenched with pain. "Give Sally my thanks as always—and a hug."

"I'll do that."

After walking Ira out, Daniel stood watching him ramble down the hill, headed home.

Ira Birch had become one of the first friends Daniel had made after settling in Mount Laurel. The freed black man had been recommended by a patient who knew of Daniel's need for some carpentry work, both on the office building and his own house. To say Ira was a good carpenter was like saying Bach wrote some pretty fair music. Ira Birch was a master carpenter, and that was the truth. Not only did he excel at his primary trade of carpentry, he could fix just about anything that needed fixing.

With the help of some abolitionists and Quakers, Ira had run away and brought his family north before President Lincoln issued the proclamation freeing the slaves. Both Ira and Sally had been slaves on the same large, prosperous farm in Tennessee until their escape. According to Ira, they had been among the "better-treated" slaves. He had worked his way into his owner's favor with his carpentry skills, while Sally served as a personal maid to the owner's youngest daughter. Apparently, during their early years at different plantations, they had suffered their share of brutal mistreatment but had fared better with their most recent owner. Even so, Ira's resolve to come north had not wavered.

Daniel never failed to feel an edge of awkwardness when his friend spoke of that earlier life. He couldn't imagine the quiet, gentle-natured Ira or the warmhearted, easygoing Sally living in bondage. For that matter, had he not seen for himself a type of bondage foisted upon his own people in Ireland, he would not have been able to conceive of the evil inherent to the practice.

As a boy, however, he had learned all too well about oppression. He knew what it was like to be the victim of a power that cared nothing about bending others to its will. The British Crown had been doing its best to enslave the entire country of Ireland for centuries and had almost achieved their purpose by using the cataclysmic potato famine to rob the Irish of their land, their humanity, and, in countless cases, their very lives.

Millions had died of starvation and famine fever or—like Daniel and his mother—had immigrated to America and Canada in a desperate measure to survive. So not only did he sympathize with another man's bondage, but he also understood the need to escape that bondage by any means possible.

He took Sarge with him to see to Ginger's water and food, and then Daniel allowed him to follow him inside. The aroma of Sally's stew was already wafting through the rooms, tempting Daniel in the worst way, but he decided to read Evan's letter first. The Newfie plopped down in front of the fireplace as Daniel stretched his legs out in front of the sofa and began to read.

> *Dear Daniel,*
>
> *I trust this will find you well. From your last letter, I feel sure it will find you busy, given your many patients and your ever-expanding practice.*
>
> *Your mother is sitting here beside me at the desk as I write, fussing at me to tell you this and tell you that and to also make quite certain you know how much she—and I—miss you. Although Teddy isn't*

all that far away at the Academy, obviously he can't
leave the Point and make a trip down river when-
ever he feels like a visit. So Nora and I must con-
tent ourselves with caring for our other children here
at Whittaker House, all the while missing our own
boys in the worst way.

Daniel stopped reading, smiling a little even as a faint twinge of sadness nagged at him. He still remembered the night his brother—his half brother, actually, although he seldom thought of him in that regard—had been born. Teddy had arrived a few weeks earlier than expected, but from the beginning seemed to thrive. Daniel, then in his teens, had waited with Evan—his step-father—throughout that long night, both of them wrung through with anxiety and exhaustion, cringing at every cry of his mother's pain, worrying through the late hours until a baby's cry finally replaced his mother's.

So many years ago…

Teddy was now nineteen going on twenty. A cadet at the United States Military Academy at West Point. A man.

Shaking off the memories, he returned to Evan's letter.

We added a set of twins to our flock just last
week. Two little boys of color about three years old,
from the looks of them, abandoned near the mission
house on Chatham Street. One of them is ill with a
bad chest cold. Dr. Rogers comes regularly to see to
him and assures us he will recover in time and with
proper care.

We've no idea of their names, as no note or any

*form of identification was found with them. So
we've named them Peter and Paul for now, still hoping a parent will eventually turn up, though as you
know, once a child is left in the street, that's usually
the end of any family involvement.*

*How cruel this world can be for so many, espe-
cially these little ones!*

It occurred to Daniel that, were it not for people like Evan
and Daniel's mother, the world would be even crueler than it
already was. Evan was responsible for aiding Daniel and his
mother's escape from Ireland, at the same time acting as their
self-appointed guardian during the harrowing ocean crossing to
New York. There could scarcely have been a less likely scenario
than a young British employee of a landowner in County Mayo
befriending an impoverished widow and her son. But to make the
situation even more incredible, Evan had been shot aboard ship,
resulting in the loss of an arm, only to resume his role as their pro-
tector once he began to recover from his injury.

A few months later, he married Daniel's mother.

Daniel had come to trust and respect Evan Whittaker as
he had few other men. To this day, at the age of thirty-four, he
believed beyond any doubt that Evan had been sent to him and
his family as a gift from God.

It seemed that Evan had also been sent as a gift to the orphaned
and abandoned children of New York City. Over the years, Whittaker House had become a sanctuary for the unwanted children of
the city. Evan's vision expanded, and there were now two homes
for the homeless, filled with children who otherwise might not
have survived the brutal streets of New York.

A prayer of thanks for this man who had played such a vital part in his own life and in the lives of so many others rose in Daniel's heart as he went on reading.

> *As always, we are crowded to the limit both here and at the Orchard Street house, but we have an increasing number of volunteers from the churches and benevolent societies who make it possible for us to continue. Remember, I told you once that God had promised to take care of us if we would take care of His children. He has been faithful. Always faithful.*

By the time Daniel finished reading Evan's letter, his eyes were heavy. So weary was he by now that even the thought of Sally Birch's savory stew couldn't lure him from the sofa to the kitchen. Putting the letter aside for the time being, he finally gave in to his need for sleep.

ELEVEN

LONG DAYS

We are not here to play, to dream, to drift;
We have hard work to do, and loads to lift;
Shun not the struggle, face it, 'tis God's gift.
MALTBIE BABCOCK

Fall gathered in on Mount Laurel with crisp, painted days and quilted fields of wildflowers. The days grew shorter for most folks in town, but for a doctor trying to keep ahead of scarlet fever and a surprising number of babies making their entrance, those same days seemed to grow only longer.

All the days—and most of the nights—had been long this past week. Daniel ate on the run, slept not nearly enough, and felt as if his favorite season of the year was flying by without his finding the time to even notice. It also occurred to him that he hadn't seen Serena in nearly two weeks. There simply had not been time for anything but work. He'd like to think she understood, but Serena had never been all that patient with the hours he kept.

Today he was spending the afternoon in Owenduffy. So far he had seen two children with bad ear infections, an elderly miner with wasting lung disease, and Tom O'Riordan, another miner, with a broken arm. At the moment he was returning his instruments to his medical case after delivering Gemma Fortunato's new daughter. Because the mother spoke no English at all, Daniel had all he could do to communicate his follow-up instructions to her.

He was quickly learning that delivering a baby in Owenduffy often differed from the same process in Mount Laurel. With some of these mothers, he was little more than an assistant. Many of them were delivering not their first child, but the fourth or fifth, and seemed to view him as an unnecessary distraction. He would concede that by this time some of them knew more about the birthing process than he did. At times he actually felt as if he were in the way. But the husbands, and, on occasion, an aunt or a sister, continued to send for him, so he continued to respond.

Today's newborn was the second child of the Fortunato family, and although the mother found it difficult to communicate, she at least made Daniel feel welcome. In fact, he had enjoyed getting to know the family. The father was a cheerful fellow, shaking Daniel's hand repeatedly after the baby's birth, while the mother, Gemma, couldn't seem to stop smiling and making what seemed to be appreciative gestures.

And the new baby girl was plump, pretty, and obviously in good health.

He felt good when he left the house. He also left with a fragrant loaf of bread under his arm from the surplus that Gemma Fortunato had baked only early that morning before taking time out to give birth.

Fearing that his next call might not be nearly so heartening as this one, he determined to savor the pleasurable experience along with the bread.

～

Addie Rose Murphy sat at the side of ten-year-old Nainsi Clery's bed, holding the little girl's hand and getting up only long enough to wet a sponge to cool the child's forehead.

She studied the girl, the red spots that blotched her pale skin, the heat that seemed to boil from her. Where did this awful disease come from? Why had three of the Clery children escaped the dread sickness so far while wee Nainsi came down with it?

"My throat hurts, Addie Rose," Nainsi whispered.

"I know it does, dear. It's best not to talk."

She was so ill.

Addie Rose hated scarlet fever with a vengeance. Children seemed its favorite victim. They grew so miserable and fared so poorly under its attack that some were struck deaf or even died.

The thought spurred her to get up again and pour a small cup of the mixture she had blended that morning. Helping Nainsi to sit up a bit, she coaxed the child to rinse her mouth.

"What's that you're giving her?"

Addie Rose was so startled by the sharp male voice that she nearly dropped the cup.

It was the doctor from Mount Laurel. She had heard he'd been in and out of town over the past two weeks, but this was the first time she'd run into him since meeting him at the Flynns' house.

She deliberately took her time easing Nainsi back to her pillow and setting the cup down on the table before turning to face him. "'Tis only a rinse for her throat."

He came to stand at the other side of the bed. "A rinse of what?"

It struck Addie Rose that, even though the doctor looked hollow-eyed and weary at the moment, he was clearly younger than she had taken him to be the first time she'd seen him.

She resented his tone and let him know it. "'Tis only a few drops of eucalyptus oil and a bit of myrrh with some water," she said, her tone equally sharp. "It seems to help her mouth and throat."

He looked from her to Nainsi, then back to Addie Rose. "How did you know to use eucalyptus?"

Addie Rose shrugged. "I just knew, is all."

He eyed her with a doubtful expression. Addie Rose met his look straight on.

"You make the rounds, Miss Murphy. Your name comes up surprisingly often among the patients I see. Seems as though you're always one step ahead of me."

Addie Rose stared at him, but his expression gave nothing away. Was he making fun of her or reprimanding her?

She made no reply but moved away from the bed so he could tend to Nainsi. Instead of leaving the room, though, she returned to what she'd begun earlier. Her mother had taught her to keep a sickroom neat and clean, and her own instincts told her it might be important to wash away as much of the disease as possible. So when Una Clery—Nainsi's mother—had sent for her to come help, Addie Rose had set about cleaning everything within sight in the room, using a mixture of vinegar and lye soap.

She had started the cleaning while Una was tending to the little ones but then stopped when Nainsi grew fretful. Now as she washed down the iron rails at the foot of the bed, she watched the doctor's every move while he examined Nainsi.

He was still standing when, as if he had eyes in the back of his head, he said, without turning, "What are you using in the water?"

"Soap. And some vinegar."

"Lye soap, is it?"

"Aye, and what else would it be?"

"Well, there are other kinds of soap." His tone sounded dry but less cutting now.

"Not in Owenduffy," Addie Rose replied with a shrug.

She knew she probably sounded cross, but he wasn't exactly a sweet-talker himself.

He kept his attention fixed on Nainsi, speaking quietly to the ill child as he continued to examine her.

Addie Rose tried to keep her eyes averted, but in spite of her slight pique her gaze traveled back to him. The doctor was what her sister Elly would call a well-setup man. He closely resembled a drawing she had once seen in a book—a book she had tried to keep from her mother's sharp eye, it being an adventure novel loaned to her by Sally Gerrigan, who seemed to always have a book or two on hand. In truth, it had been a romantic adventure novel, which Ma would have disapproved of even more.

The Murphys were among the few folks in Owenduffy who could actually read. For the most part, Addie Rose was grateful that her parents were book-taught and had passed on to their children the ability to read, but it sometimes made things difficult if her reading choices didn't meet with their approval. Da had threatened more than once to make her eat a book he didn't think she ought to be reading. Not that he would, of course. He was softer on his womenfolk than the miners under his sharp eye would ever have believed.

Her thoughts went back to the doctor. The illustration he

brought to mind was that of a Spanish buccaneer. He was said to
be as Irish as...well, as Irish as the Murphys. Indeed, at times she
could hear a distinct touch of the Irish curl in his speech. Yet he
had a look about him that spoke of dangerous men in capes who
swept in and out of dark doorways and spoke in threatening whis-
pers. He was startlingly tall, with a face so lean it looked sculpted
from stone and hair the color of jet, so thick with waves that by
rights it should have gone to a girl, not a man. She had noticed the
first time she'd seen him, that night at the Flynns' cabin, and again
today, that his deep-set eyes seemed to change color, deepening
from a smoke blue to dark gray, depending on the light. Though
he was clean-shaven, the heavy shadow of a beard, a prominent
mustache, and his sun-darkened skin gave him the look of a ren-
egade...and he had a way of lifting his chin that hinted of a certain stubbornness she found strangely annoying.

He wasn't exactly handsome—at least not like the adventurer
in the novel she'd read. For one thing, his nose was a bit too high-
bridged and sharp, but in spite of his almost rakish appearance,
he had a kind of stillness and a steadiness about him that was hard
to ignore.

Abruptly, he turned to look at her, and Addie Rose felt like a
guilty child caught in some mischief. She found it difficult to look
directly at him, but the force of his stare drew her in.

He motioned for her to follow him across the room. "Have
you had this disease?" he said when they reached the door.

"Years ago, aye."

"Good. So, then, how long can you stay with her?" He went
on without waiting for her to answer. "The girl's mother clearly
has her hands full with the younger children. Besides, she seems
the nervous type. I'll talk to her, but I'm not sure she'll remember

what has to be done. The child needs to be sponged all over her body with cool water repeatedly. I want to get her temperature down as quickly as possible. And she needs to be watched for any breathing problems. No food—understand? Nothing but fluids. Lime water or rice water, all right, but no solid food." He stopped long enough to again ask, "How long can you stay with her?"

"As long as need be, I suppose, but I'll have to send word home."

"All right. I'll leave you some belladonna. I'll show you how much to give her. And I'll also leave something to put in your cleaning water along with the soap and vinegar." He paused. "Keep the other family members out of here. I'll talk to Mrs. Clery about that before I leave."

Addie Rose continued to nod, her mind racing to take in everything he told her. For Nainsi's sake, she needed to remember it all.

"Listen, now——" He had a stern, blunt way about him as he spoke, and yet his eyes hinted of kindness. "This is crucial. You can spread the fever simply by taking care of someone who has it, so you need to scrub yourself before making contact with anyone else. And your clothes——" he hesitated as if uncertain whether to go on, but finally he did. "If you can't afford to burn them, then they need to be washed in a strong disinfectant. You absolutely *must* take care not to infect anyone else."

Addie Rose almost felt as if he were accusing her, and she resented it. "I know what to do," she said sharply.

One eyebrow lifted. "And how is it that you know what to do, Miss Murphy?"

"My mother is a wise woman. She used to tend the sick in her village."

"In Ireland, was it?"

"Aye, in Ireland. She taught me what she knows."

His gaze continued to go over her face. Then he smiled a little, and what a difference that made in the man! With the hard
set to his mouth suddenly eased, and his eyes, so stern only a
moment before, now bright with a glint that bordered on humor,
he seemed warmer, even friendly.

"And it seems she taught you well. All right, then. I'll jot a few
things down for you and Nainsi's mother and leave some other
things you'll need. And I'll do my best to come again by day after
tomorrow, but I can't make any promises. It's a difficult time. I
can't seem to stay ahead…"

His words drifted off unfinished as he crossed the room again
and started drawing things out of his medical case.

Addie Rose watched him, wondering how long ago he had
come from Ireland, if he'd grown up here in the States or was
a more recent transplant. Even though he spoke with an educated tongue, an underlying current marked him as distinctly
Irish. And there was his name, of course: Kavanagh. Even so, he
might not have come across.

No. He had. She was sure of it.

He closed his medical case and then turned back to the bed
and bent low, listening to Nainsi's breathing for a moment before
chucking the girl under the chin, straightening, and starting for
the door.

And then he was gone, leaving Addie Rose to stare after him,
confused by the flurry of emotions he left behind.

TWELVE

WHEN THE WORK IS EVERYTHING

Who is so poor that I should not take notice?
Who is so low that I should help deny?
Who should call in need for healing mercy
And I pretend I did not hear the cry?

ANONYMOUS

*T*he road between Owenduffy and Mount Laurel was tedious, even in the best of weather. It was pocked and pitted, with deep ditches on either side. During a dry spell, the horse and buggy turned up enough dust that Daniel sometimes wore a bandanna over his mouth to keep from choking. But during a rainy season, things could get downright treacherous. Every ridge became a slick gully, every rut became a puddle, and the ditches quickly filled with mud and stones that could tip a buggy completely over, injuring a horse and driver if they should go off the road.

It had rained every day that week, so by late Thursday afternoon the road was a danger to both man and beast. The way over from Mount Laurel had been bad, with ruts and enough bumps to make Daniel feel as though jumping beans had taken up residence in his stomach.

The way back was a nightmare. A hard, wind-driven rain had been coming down for hours, and by the time he left Owenduffy, the road was little more than a mud-slicked creek. The river, swollen almost to its banks, was running hard and fast. The bridge swayed slightly in the strong wind, spooking the usually calm-natured Ginger, who took up a faster trot than usual in her eagerness to leave behind the rushing water.

Daniel wasn't immune from a twinge of uneasiness as they clattered across the wooden planks. While the horse probably couldn't hear him in the din from the river and the wind, he talked to her all the way across, keeping his voice low and calm, though in truth he was just as anxious to get to the other side as she was.

They were just over the bridge when Ginger stumbled in a particularly deep rut. The buggy teetered and then lurched, throwing Daniel hard across the bench as they slid into a ditch, the right front wheel crashing into an enormous rock before jamming against the hillside.

Ginger shrieked but almost immediately found purchase, remaining steady while Daniel jumped down from the buggy to assess their situation. Sarge leaped directly into the ditch, his feet instantly sinking into the thick mud. He shot Daniel an accusatory glance while slugging out of the ditch onto the road, the mud making a sucking noise as he freed himself.

One look told Daniel they were stuck fast. Both right wheels of the buggy were sunk into the mud, the back skewed at an angle. He stood, rapidly getting soaked, looking from the wheels to the horse, trying to think what to do. There was no way he could pry free of that much mud by himself. Still, he had to try. He didn't welcome the idea of leaving the buggy and riding horseback in this downpour. He had a hunch that a buggy left by the side of the road for any length of time in Owenduffy might end up being "unstuck" by someone other than the rightful owner.

He was still standing, getting soaked, calculating his options, when he spotted what looked to be a coal wagon coming up behind him. Relief swept through him, but when the wagon pulled up close enough that he could recognize the driver, he wondered if his relief might be premature.

The driver appeared nearly as drenched as Daniel, water running off his cap and down his face, his coat dripping like a waterfall.

Dominic Murphy.

The miner looked from the buggy to Daniel. He finally gave a short nod. "Looks as if you have a bit of a problem."

Daniel choked back a sarcastic reply. "We hit a rut. Do you think you could help me get back on the road?"

Murphy jumped down from the wagon and, tossing water off his cap before replacing it, walked around the buggy to inspect the embedded rear wheel. "I'd say the axle's broke."

Daniel groaned.

Murphy took one more look before straightening. "I'm making a delivery over to the bank manager's house at Mount Laurel. Hitch your horse to the back of my wagon if you want, and I'll get you home."

Daniel hesitated, but not too long. There seemed nothing for it but to take the miner up on his offer, grudging though it appeared to be. "I hate to trouble you. There's my dog as well."

Murphy cast a sour look at Sarge. "There's room for the both of you. As I said, I'm on my way."

As he went to unhitch Ginger from the buggy, Daniel found himself wondering if Murphy would have offered the ride if he'd not been "on the way."

"Will my buggy be safe, do you think?" he said climbing onto the bench and waiting for Sarge to leap up behind him.

"You've little choice in the matter in any event, I expect."

ᕘ

Clearly, Dominic Murphy was a man of few words. They would have passed the first minutes of the drive in total silence had Daniel not repeated his thanks for the miner's help more than once, just as a way of trying to make conversation.

Finally, Murphy waved a hand of dismissal. "It's no trouble." His tone was impatient, his expression annoyed.

Daniel let out a long breath and decided to try a different tack. "So—you also make deliveries."

"Man who usually delivers to Mount Laurel broke his arm. This team is a handful, so I took the delivery for him."

"Tom O'Riordan?"

Murphy glanced over at him, pulling his cap down a little more snugly against the rain. "How would you know that?"

"Just a guess. I set his arm earlier today."

The miner said nothing for a time. Then, "You've been over to Owenduffy a lot lately, I hear tell."

The man had a way of making every statement sound like an accusation.

Daniel nodded. "I suppose I have."

"Would that be mostly because of the fever, then?"

Daniel wondered how long ago Murphy had left Ireland. His accent was still thick. Again he nodded. "Your daughter—Addie Rose—is a good nurse. She was at the Clerys' house today when I was there. She helped a lot."

The miner shot him another look. "Who's down there? Is it the fever?"

"Nainsi. And yes, she has the fever."

Murphy pulled a face. "And her not strong to begin with."

"Your daughter was going to stay with her, at least for a while. She seems to have a way in the sickroom."

"I'd as soon she stay away from those sickrooms," Murphy said sourly. "But she's like her mother that way. Jana—that's her mother—was the same back home. Folks always sending for her when there was a need. Still do, but the girl goes more often in her place now."

Daniel felt strangely pleased that the big miner actually seemed willing to finally carry on a conversation with him. "How many children do you have, Mr. Murphy?"

"You needn't 'Mister' me. The name's Dominic. There's five— three girls and two boys." He paused. "Addie Rose and her next sister are the oldest."

The "next sister" would be Elly, Daniel concluded. The source of contention between Stephen and Clay Holliday. "How long have you been in the States Mr.—Dominic?"

Murphy's answer was slow in coming, as if he had to calculate the time. "Ten years or so now." He clicked his teeth, and the team struck up a quicker pace in spite of the mud-pitted road. "County Clare is where we're from. Near the Shannon. And yourself? I figure the West."

Daniel looked at him.

"Well, your name, man," Murphy supplied in a dry tone. "And there's still a trace on your tongue."

"You figured right. I grew up in Killala. We came over when I was sixteen—nearly eighteen years ago."

Again Murphy glanced at him. "That would have been when the Hunger was at its worst."

"It was."

Silence settled between them for another moment or two before Murphy broke it. "I hear you're a city fella."

"We settled in New York when we first came over. But I don't fancy myself much of a...city fella...no." Daniel waited. "So how did you end up here?"

"Well, wouldn't that be my good fortune now?" Murphy said with a twist of his mouth. "An uncle came over before us, found me a job in one of the Pennsylvania mines. We moved here after a couple of years because the conditions were said to be better." He gave a short, humorless laugh. "I'm still lookin' for those golden streets of Amerikay, though."

Daniel nodded, not knowing quite what to say. Reality was that things had been better for him and his mother when they arrived. He'd had a family and two patrons—his Uncle Mike and Lewis Farmington, a New York shipbuilder—who had helped him get through medical college. He might not have found the streets of America to be made of gold, but they'd turned out to be a sight smoother for him than the starving roads of County Mayo.

Somehow, though, he didn't think Dominic Murphy would care much one way or the other, so he kept his feelings to himself.

Indeed, Murphy lapsed into another silence at that point, and they spent the rest of the drive to Mount Laurel without speaking.

~

By the time Daniel got Ginger, the Newfoundland, and himself dried off and warmed up some soup for supper, he was so tired he could scarcely eat. Later, in front of the fire, he attempted to read the papers, but he was too exhausted to focus, so he gave up.

How many hours of sleep had he managed so far this week? He prayed there would be no emergencies tonight, for he wasn't sure he had it in him to take care of anyone other than himself.

In front of the fireplace, Sarge was wherever dogs went when they dreamed, and he looked so content that Daniel decided to join him. Yet when he put his feet up and tried to nap, sleep wouldn't come. His thoughts seemed to be stuck in Owenduffy.

After the year he'd spent at Bellevue in New York, and especially after his battlefield experiences during the war, he had almost convinced himself that the thing to do would be to set up a practice where most of his patients would be clean, reasonably well educated, and afflicted with less hideous injuries and fewer malodorous diseases than he'd encountered up until then. He had grown bone weary of the putrid, ugly side of medicine, not to mention the accompanying exhaustion and discouragement that came from never seeing real progress or improvement, much less actual cures.

A visit to return his friend Ben's effects to the Holliday family had sent that resolve flying. Not only had Stephen and Esther taken him into their home and their hearts in a matter of hours, treating him like another son, but he'd fallen in love with Mount Laurel and its surroundings.

Of course, he hadn't known much about Owenduffy when he decided to settle in the area. Even if he had, there was no way he could have known that he'd end up taking on what amounted to a second practice in the neighboring mining community. But it seemed that he had done just that, and when he took the time to give his situation any measure of thought and realized what he'd brought on himself, he couldn't help but question his own common sense. Even so, here he was, and it was no one's doing but his own. Well, maybe the Hollidays' encouragement had entered into his decision more than he'd realized at the time, but certainly they weren't altogether responsible.

In any event, his days had turned into a numbing cycle of not enough rest, not enough regular meals, and not enough free time to spare for any real personal life. To make matters worse, the woman who only weeks before had occupied far too many of his waking thoughts and more than a few of his recurring dreams might just as well be living in another state for all the time and attention he had been able to give her.

But did she even mind? Did his absence really make any difference to her?

Naturally, he'd like to think so. But he was never sure of anything with Serena. Sometimes he thought she shared his feelings but was too reserved to express them.

Other times he thought he just might be the worst kind of fool.

Until lately, he'd given his pride the boot and taken whatever crumbs of attention she offered. He didn't much like himself at those times, but the truth was he had never been very good with women. He had been far too busy in medical college and later with his work at Bellevue, followed by the war, to get involved in a serious relationship. At least that's what he'd told himself. If he were altogether honest, however, he had isolated himself from women for so long he was as awkward as a callow schoolboy when it came to knowing how to treat them. What did it say about a man when midway into his thirties he was more comfortable with his dog than with a pretty girl, even one he fancied?

Especially with one he fancied.

He was supposed to be reasonably intelligent. He had made it through medical college after all. But his life had become so absorbed in his work that he now found it difficult to come out of the fog of his days, much less function as the kind of man a woman might find a proper suitor.

Yet he wanted what most other men seemed to want: a home and a life with a family. In fact, he had always envisioned himself with a fairly large family. Well, he was about to turn thirty-five, and so far the only woman he had ever even thought of marrying hadn't exactly encouraged his attentions. And instead of doing whatever he could to remedy the situation, he was digging himself deeper and deeper into a way of life that would only make matters worse.

But what was he supposed to do? The miners and their families needed a doctor too—deserved a doctor—just as much as the folks in Mount Laurel did. With the high number of injuries common to a coal miner—and with the scarlet fever raging even more viciously in Owenduffy than in Mount Laurel—he couldn't ignore the needs of either community, could he? And it wasn't as if there were a supply of other physicians lining up to take his place.

The thing was, he was a good doctor. That much he knew about himself. He'd had the benefit of some excellent medical training and experience. As a boy in his teens, he had made rounds with Nicholas Grafton, one of the finest doctors he'd ever known. He had studied under him, assisted him, and learned all he could from him.

That was the point at which many doctors ended their education. Instead, he'd gone on to medical college and then trained in the wards at Bellevue, where he had encountered just about every kind of imaginable illness—mental as well as physical. For several months he'd also done a concentrated apprenticeship in surgery with the brilliant Dr. Jakob Gunther. Later, he had applied a great deal of what he'd learned with Gunther in the field hospitals of the war.

Medicine was what he had wanted for as long as he could remember, though he recognized that his passion for it was a kind of contradiction. Why he would allow himself to become consumed by a life that reeked of such ugliness, such hideous pain and suffering to the human soul as well as to the body, would, he suspected, forever be a mystery even to him.

More than once, his mother had shaken her head in puzzlement at the idea of his becoming a physician. "You have a poet's spirit, Daniel," she would say. "You've always loved beauty and music and gentleness. What would make you want to work with such brutal and ugly things? How will you survive the pain? I'm so afraid you'll end up with your own spirit wounded or even broken."

And sometimes, during the really bad times, he wasn't so sure but what she hadn't been right.

As a boy in Ireland, he had watched his father die. And then his sister. And his older brother. He had survived the sight of neighbors and friends being evicted from their homes in the dead of winter and then dying of exposure and starvation along the side of the road. He'd survived the unspeakable horrors of an ocean voyage in the bowels of a ship not fit for animals, much less human beings. In New York, he had encountered suffering and deprivation on a scale beyond imagining in the slums of the Five Points and the alleys of the Bowery.

Why indeed had he opted for a career that would only surround him with more of the same? Had he somehow known that dealing with patients' pain would help him bury his own pain?

What had saved him from that broken spirit his mother had feared? In some inexplicable way, medicine had actually seemed to strengthen his spirit. Every murmur of pain he could silence, every broken limb he could make right again, every dread disease he could hold at bay, and every death he could prevent, or at least stave off, seemed to set off a kind of singing inside him, a quiet anthem of praise for what had been accomplished. No matter how small the victory.

He had discovered that in medicine, for every loss there was a gain, for every failure there was an eventual success. And somehow it was enough. Enough to keep him from losing heart. No matter how weary he became, and in spite of the discouragement and frustration and even the anger that sometimes accompanied his profession, there resided in the deepest part of him a faith that it was all worthwhile, a conviction that God was in charge after all and there was an order to life—and to death—and that he was merely an instrument used to help maintain that order.

Over the years he had also found a haven, an escape, when the failures mounted and the successes seemed to come few and far between, if at all. Music had become his retreat, the place where he could go and find his own healing, where he could be cleansed and calmed and renewed when the work, and the world, became too much to bear.

He glanced over at the Kavanagh harp propped against the bookcase, the fiddle next to it, the tin whistle on the shelf.

Not tonight. He was too tired. The only retreat he needed tonight was sleep. He should stir himself and make for the bedroom, but the fire was so warm, the sofa so comfortable.

He released a long breath, and Sarge raised his great head just long enough to cast an indignant look in his direction.

"Oh, sorry," Daniel said, his voice thick. "Did I wake you, you big slug?"

The big Newfoundland gave a long-suffering sigh, and then he lowered his head and returned to his snoozing, leaving Daniel soon to follow.

THIRTEEN

THE PROBLEM OF SERENA

She smiled and that transfigured me
And left me but a lout.
W.B. YEATS

*I*n the city, Daniel hadn't kept hours on Saturday, other than to make calls at the hospital. But it hadn't taken him long to discover that the residents of Mount Laurel and Owenduffy didn't acknowledge Saturday as being different from any other workday. The good people of both towns and the surrounding areas kept their doctor just as busy on a Saturday morning as on a weekday.

Today was no exception. In fact, he'd been even busier than usual. By the time he unhitched the buggy and unlocked the office door, at least half a dozen patients had been standing outside, waiting to see him. After letting them in, Daniel did his best to see them as promptly as possible, calling one at a time into the examining room.

It turned out to be a long morning. Little Billy Kehoe showed up with a bad case of poison oak. Cecilia Potter arrived with a black eye, signaling that her husband, Leonard, had been drunk again the night before. Of course Cecilia wouldn't admit to the abuse that seemed to be escalating, even though Daniel asked her a number of pointed questions. This time she blamed her injury on a fall. Over the past few months she'd "bumped into a piece of furniture" as well as tripping over "a loose board on the porch."

Later in the morning he'd seen Eliza Duncan, an elderly widow with an almost debilitating case of rheumatism, and Pete Boyner from the livery, who was in misery with a high temperature due to a particularly vile ear infection. His patient at the moment was little Peggy Pardue, who had broken her finger by slamming the back door on it in pursuit of her puppy.

Peggy was a golden child who had managed to charm Daniel from the first time she'd appeared in his office with a case of tonsillitis. Six years old, she was usually a whirling cloud of blond curls, deep dimples, and boundless energy. At the moment, however, she was a quivering bundle of not-quite-suppressed tears while her mother stood by, holding her good hand. Daniel tipped her chin up and smiled into her eyes. "That finger isn't going to hurt for very long. I promise," he told her. "It will feel much better by tomorrow."

Another sniffle. "Are you sure?"

"Absolutely," Daniel said, his tone solemn. "Today, however, it might be best if you play quietly with your dolls."

"Can I go to Sunday school tomorrow?"

"Oh, I should think so." Daniel glanced at Susan Pardue. "Your mother will have the final say on that, though, in the morning. All right?"

Peggy nodded, as she held up her hand and investigated the

splint on her finger. "I have to go to school Monday too. I'm in first grade, you know."

"I do know. And I'm quite sure you'll be able to go to school on Monday."

"Miss Serena will be especting me."

"And I see no need to disappoint her."

The mention of Serena's name pricked his conscience. He simply had to find time—make time—to see her. They hadn't been separated for this long for months. Probably not since summer a year ago when she'd gone with her parents on vacation to the Adirondacks.

Seeing Peggy and her mother out, he noted with relief that the waiting room had finally emptied. But just as he started back to his office, the bell over the door clanged. He turned to see a highly unexpected visitor enter the waiting room.

"Serena!"

From the corner of the room where he'd been napping, Sarge hauled himself to his feet and trotted over to reach her before Daniel could. It was no secret that Serena was one of the big Newfie's favorite people.

Serena stopped just over the threshold, arched one delicate eyebrow, and gave Sarge a head rub while favoring Daniel with a mere hint of a smile. "So you *are* still in town."

Daniel stopped short. "What? Oh…yes! In fact, I was planning to come by your house today and…well, I'm really glad you're here." He started to cross the room but then stopped again. "You're not ill?"

She waved off the question. "You know I'm never ill. No, I was concerned about you."

Daniel gave an awkward shrug, trying not to feel pleased by

her words. "I'm really sorry," he said, meaning it. "I've just been
swamped, what with the scarlet fever and all—"

She dismissed his stammering with a flick of her wrist and
came the rest of the way into the room. "I know. It's all anyone can
talk about. We've had so many absences at school—but of course,
you'd know all about that. Anyway, I assumed you hadn't had any
free time, or else I would have heard from you. Still, I was beginning to wonder if you'd forgotten all about me."

It wasn't like Serena to be coy, but the petulant look and the
tone of her voice could hardly be described as anything else.

Daniel closed the distance between them. She was wearing a
perky bonnet that made her eyes look as blue as the larkspur that
grew wild on the hills behind his house. A ruffle of blond curls
peeked out around the foolish little hat, and she looked so adorable he had all he could do not to crush her to him.

Instead, he settled for taking her hands in his. "You know very
well I could never forget about you."

She actually lifted her cheek for a kiss.

Maybe I should absent myself more often...

It took only a moment to dismiss that thought as he touched
his lips to the cool satin of her cheek.

"I hope you've come to have lunch with me."

"Actually, I came to invite you to dinner. Mother said to tell
you she's making one of your favorites: her peach preserves cake."

He nearly groaned in anticipation. "Nothing could keep me
away." The only thing that could eclipse the thought of Louisa
Norman's peach preserves cake was this unexpected and person-
ally delivered invitation from Serena.

"We could still have lunch," he said.

"I suppose you skipped breakfast."

He had to think. "Guilty."

She frowned.

Daniel had never known another woman who could look so pretty when she frowned—or when she smiled. Of course, it would be physically impossible for Serena not to look pretty.

"I can't, Daniel. Papa's out of town until later, and I promised Mother I'd do some marketing and other errands for her. Besides, we'll have the evening together."

"Promise?"

"*You're* the one who hasn't had time for *me,*" she pointed out. "But before I go, I want to know if you're really all right. I heard that you wrecked your buggy. Were you hurt at all?"

"How did you hear about that? And, no, I wasn't hurt. The only thing hurt was the axle on the buggy, and Ira's working on that today."

She studied him. "Why are you doing this, Daniel?"

"Why am I doing what?" he asked, puzzled.

"Going back and forth to Owenduffy." She said the town's name as though it scalded her tongue. "Especially as busy as you are with your practice here."

"They're without a doctor over there, Serena. And the scarlet fever has hit them even harder than Mount Laurel. I wouldn't feel right not doing what I can. I don't plan to keep it up forever."

"You shouldn't be doing it at all. You're running yourself ragged. You look awful."

"Well, you surely don't," he said, trying for lightness. "You're absolutely sparkling."

He tugged at her hands to pull her a little closer.

"Daniel—a patient might come in."

"And see his doctor holding hands with the prettiest girl in town. Now there's a scandal."

"Daniel." She continued to regard him with a disapproving look. "Those people in Owenduffy need to have their own doctor."

The way she said "those people" bothered him some, but in the next instant she was all dimples and smiles, so perhaps he'd imagined the distaste in her tone.

"Now you're impatient with me," she said with a pout.

"No, I—"

"Yes, you are. I can tell. All right, I won't nag. At least not until later. Why don't you close up now and go home to get some rest while you can?"

"I just may do that. What time should I come this evening?"

"Mother said about six. She asked if you'd bring your minstrel's harp too. She loves it when you play."

"I'll bring it, but I suspect your mother is the only one in the family who really enjoys listening to me play."

"That's not so."

He grinned at her. "Last time I played, your mother listened and you and your dad dozed."

"I did not!"

"You did. But that's all right. I want your mother to like me."

"She does like you. A lot." Again now she lifted her face to his, standing on tiptoe to reach him. "I really do need to go."

What was going on here? One kiss on the cheek was usually all she allowed, and then he most often had to maneuver a bit before it was granted.

He decided to act quickly before she changed her mind. This

time he lingered a little longer than usual. When she didn't pull away, he put his arm around her waist to pull her even closer.

But she slid smoothly out of his reach. "Don't be late for dinner."

"If I camp out on your front porch the rest of the day, will you take pity and let me in early?"

She laughed at his foolishness. "Just come hungry," she said, giving the Newfie another pat on the head. "You can bring Sarge, but he'll have to stay outside. You know how Mother is about animals in the house."

"One whiff of that peach cake, and he might ram the front door. I think I'd best leave him at home."

The big Newfoundland raised his head, his interest obviously piqued by the sound of his name.

After Serena left, Daniel went to wash up. When he came back to the waiting room, Sarge was again snoring. "It's just you and me for lunch, fur-bucket. Rouse yourself."

At first the Newfie stirred only a little, but the promise of food never failed to get his attention. With an oversized yawn, he got to his feet and went to wait at the door.

~

Later that afternoon Daniel lay sprawled on the couch, intent on taking Serena's suggestion to get some rest. To his increasing frustration, however, he remained wide-awake.

In truth, sleep hadn't come easily to him for years. He'd grown so accustomed to little rest during his time at medical college and throughout the war that he seemed to have set up a kind of pattern. Being called out at all hours of the night also didn't help. Uninterrupted hours for sleeping were always rare in a doctor's life, especially for a doctor serving two different communities.

He had finally resigned himself to staying awake and was about to get up when someone pounded on his front door. The pounding continued as he pushed himself up from the sofa and lumbered to the door without his shoes. "Coming!"

He opened the door on Dominic Murphy. The miner was in his work clothes, his hands and face streaked black with coal dust. "I figured you hadn't had time to get your axle fixed," Murphy said without preamble, "so I came for you with the wagon. 'Tis our neighbor's youngest in need of you. She's but a wee thing and in a bad way with a fit of some sort. No one knows what to do for her. Will you come?"

There was no time for hesitation in the case of a convulsion. Daniel motioned Murphy inside. "I'll have to get my case." He glanced down. "And my shoes."

The miner stepped inside but didn't follow him to the other room, instead waiting just inside the door.

Daniel dreaded convulsions almost as much as a ruptured appendix, especially in babies and toddlers. Unpredictable and terrible to witness, they usually frightened the entire family, not only the child. Truth be told, they often gave him a scare too.

"How long since the child was taken ill?" he asked Murphy as they climbed onto the wagon bench a few minutes later.

"I'm not sure. I was no more in the door after work than Moira—that's the child's mother—came running to see if I'd fetch you. She's in a state. Her man is dead, so there's just herself and the wee one."

Not until they had pulled away from the house did Daniel

remember about Serena and his dinner date. With a silent groan, he squeezed his eyes shut for a second and pulled a deep breath. Talk about miserable timing.

"Mr. Murphy—"

"Didn't I tell you there's no need to 'Mister' me? Just Murphy will do. Or Dominic." After a brief pause, he added, "Mostly I'm called Murphy."

"All right, Murphy. I need to make a quick stop on the way. Do you mind?"

The other glanced at him. "Seems a poor time to be stopping."

"I have to. I had another appointment—an important one. I can't just not show up."

Murphy let out what seemed an exaggerated long breath, but nodded. "Show me where, then."

Daniel felt as if he might be ill himself. Here Serena had finally showed some interest in being with him, and he was about to stand her up.

⌒

As it happened, Serena's mother showed more understanding of his plight than her daughter did.

When Serena opened the door and saw him standing there, she blinked in surprise, then gave him a stern frown. "Daniel! It's scarcely five! What are you doing here so early?"

"Serena—" He clenched the nape of his neck with one hand, knowing even as he groped for the right words that she was going to be unhappy with him. To say the least.

"The thing is—" He stopped and then started over. "I'm afraid I can't stay."

"But what are you doing? What's wrong? What's happened?"

"It's…a patient. A baby. A toddler, actually. In convulsions." He was stumbling all over himself, but he couldn't seem to make a great deal of sense. "I'm on my way there now, and no doubt I'll be late getting back, so I wanted to tell you now, before it gets any later—"

"But surely it won't take all that long. Whose child is it?"

"Well…the family is in Owenduffy, so no doubt I'll be awhile."

"Owenduffy?" She stood staring at him. "You're going to Owenduffy instead of coming for dinner? Mother's worked practically all afternoon on the meal, and so have I."

"I'm so sorry, Serena. But I have to go. Convulsions are dangerous. I'm sure I don't have to tell you that. And I need to get there as soon as possible."

"What's going on out here?" Louisa Norman came to stand at the door beside her daughter. "Why, Daniel! How nice. You've come early. Goodness, Serena, don't leave him standing at the door."

"Daniel isn't staying, Mother. He has something more important to do."

Serena's words were as sharp as shattered glass.

"Mrs. Norman," Daniel started in, "I'm so sorry. I hate this." He hurried to explain, or tried to, his gaze darting back and forth from Serena to her mother. "I have an emergency in Owenduffy. A toddler who's convulsing. I feel awful about this, I really do. But I have to go."

"Well, of course you do," said Mrs. Norman. "You shouldn't even have taken the time to stop here. You just go on now. We'll do this another time."

Finally, Daniel caught a deep breath. "Thank you for under-standing." He hesitated another moment, hoping for something from Serena. What came wasn't what he might have hoped for.

"Mother's right," she said evenly, her eyes totally without warmth. "You needn't have stopped. We'll do this another time."

"Serena—"

She practically shut the door in his face. Daniel felt as if he'd been slapped, but he delayed no longer.

Murphy gave him a long look as he plopped down on the wagon bench, saying nothing.

"Seems you might have been better off if I hadn't come for you," the miner said.

Daniel looked at him, delaying his reply. Finally, he turned to stare at the road ahead. "No, you were right to come," he said woodenly. "This is what I do."

Murphy continued to watch him before nodding and turning back to the road. "Aye, it is that."

～

The Corcoran toddler was two years old, a fact that made Dan-iel grit his teeth. Convulsions were all too common—and could be deadly—in an infant or a toddler.

"If you need anything, I'll be in the kitchen," said Murphy as they entered the house. "I'll stay to give you a ride home. The child's in back, first room to your right."

Daniel nodded and then made for the stairway. He was relieved to find Addie Rose at the child's bedside, trying to soothe the tot, while at the same time restraining her as best she could so the little one didn't hurt herself. He had already seen that the Murphy girl had a decidedly calming effect on children. More to the point, she had proven herself to be quite capable in the sickroom.

There was no time for introductions, but Daniel knew at once that the woman who stood weeping and wringing her hands on the opposite side of the bed was the mother.

Addie Rose gave him no more than a quick glance, but for a change she appeared almost glad to see him.

He found the little red-haired toddler much as he'd expected from Murphy's description: with a high temperature, eyes rolled back, the small body contorted and caught up in the throes of violent muscle contractions.

Clearly, he had to work fast. He had Addie Rose coax the mother to the kitchen. When she came back, he snapped instructions. "I need warm water—not hot, mind, just warm—for an enema. And while I give the enema, I want you to fill a washtub or sink with tepid water." He paused. "We have to do this quickly."

As he had feared, the enema helped, but not enough, so he placed the child in the washtub Addie Rose had filled, dipped her and sponged her, over and over again, for more than an hour until the convulsions finally ceased. Then he wrapped her in a warm blanket and proceeded to walk the floor with her, keeping her bundled snugly against him for almost half an hour. She looked up at him once, her blue eyes confused and a little frightened, but alert. After a few minutes more, she dozed off in his arms, and Daniel handed her over to her mother so she could put her to bed.

He looked in on her once more before leaving the house and saw that she was in good hands, with her mother sitting close on one side of the bed and Addie Rose on the other. He would come back Monday to check on her and get some information on her diet. So often convulsions could be traced back to a poor diet or severe allergic reactions.

He glanced at his pocket watch. Nearly eight o'clock. So he had been right to stop at Serena's before leaving Mount Laurel. Now if he could only figure out a way to get back in her good graces.

Something told him that might take some time—perhaps a great deal of time.

And, he feared, considerably more charm than he knew himself to possess.

FOURTEEN

An Idea from a Friend

Friends... They cherish one another's hopes.
They are kind to one another's dreams.
Henry David Thoreau

The past few days had been enough to test the endurance of an elephant.

By Friday morning, Daniel knew he had to do something. But what?

To make things even more hectic, Audrey had worked only one day this week, pleading a headache. She was prone to "pounders," as she called them, routinely dismissing Daniel's suggestion that she might do well to avoid her garden and the field behind her house, at least until after the first frost.

Daniel was fairly certain that her headaches were related to the time she spent pulling weeds and taking a scythe to the high, coarse weeds at the back of her lot. Audrey, however, wasn't one to heed unsolicited advice. At least, not that of her employer.

It was midweek, however, before she'd delivered the real blow that not only caught him totally off-guard, but left him almost dazed, wondering how in the world he would ever manage now.

She hadn't even made an effort to visit him in person to deliver the news that she wouldn't be returning to her position. Instead, she had sent a brief, curt note, delivered by her neighbor, Ruth Reilly, informing him that due to her "increasing physical problems," she found it necessary to resign sooner than she'd originally planned.

It was all Daniel could do to not go to her house and plead with her to reconsider, but the cold finality of her words—and his awareness that she had never really been satisfied with her job since his predecessor resigned—stopped him from what he knew would almost certainly be a complete and possibly embarrassing waste of time.

With no idea how to even begin looking for a replacement for Audrey, he had managed to block the dilemma from his mind—at least temporarily. He would have to deal with it as soon as possible, of course, but for now his patient load and the situation with Serena were demanding all the time and energy he could muster.

By late morning, he was relieved to find his waiting room empty at last. He wasted no time in removing his lab coat and washing up, hopeful of managing the first real lunch hour he had taken all week. Perhaps once his afternoon calls were completed, he'd be able to drop by Serena's on the way home and do whatever it was going to take to repair the rift that had developed between them.

He didn't want to wait any longer. He'd hoped to talk with her before now, but there had simply been no time to manage even a quick meeting before today. He had the weekend ahead of him, of course, but there was no guarantee he'd have any real free time even then. Especially given the illness that was sweeping both Mount Laurel and Owenduffy. No, he was determined to see Serena today and attempt to make amends for what she no doubt considered his deplorable behavior last Saturday when he'd begged off dinner because of the emergency in Owenduffy.

He caught himself wondering if she would have been as put out with him if his reason for canceling had involved a patient in Mount Laurel. The thought made him uncomfortable, and he quickly forced it from his mind. Still, there was no way to dismiss the awareness that most anything to do with the mining community seemed to trigger a negative reaction in Serena.

⟿

Lawrence Hill was sitting alone when Daniel walked into Helen's. The newspaper publisher half stood and motioned that Daniel should join him.

"Well, this is a surprise," Hill said, eyeing Daniel as he sat down. "I was beginning to think you'd left town." Upon closer inspection, he added, "You don't look so good, my friend. In fact, you look downright exhausted."

Daniel waved off the remark. "It's a busy time."

They made small talk for a few minutes before Lawrence shot him another inquisitive look. "So...I expect the scarlet fever is the reason you've been so busy?"

Daniel nodded. "That, plus the usual caseload. I can't seem to keep up."

Lawrence continued to study him as he took a sip of coffee. "You're still seeing patients on both sides of the river, then?"

"Well, yes. The miners need medical care as much as anyone else." Immediately, Daniel regretted the defensive tone even he could hear in his reply.

"Of course they do," Lawrence said mildly, leaning back in his chair. "Have you ever considered getting some help?"

In truth, Daniel had thought about it quite a lot lately, especially given the additional problem of Audrey's resignation. But he wasn't in a position to seriously consider taking another doctor into the practice. During normal times, the patient flow wasn't enough to support two physicians.

But will normal times ever come again?

It was highly doubtful any reputable doctor would be interested in a part-time position, and that was all he could offer for now.

He shrugged and then went on to explain that the situation was complicated.

"I can understand that," Lawrence said.

Daniel continued to push his potatoes around on his plate. "Besides, even if that were a possibility, I don't know of any other physicians in the area. And I surely don't have time to go conducting a search for someone."

Lawrence remained quiet for a time. Then, "What about someone you could train yourself? An apprentice?"

"That used to be fairly common practice, but not so much anymore. These days most fellows interested in medicine are going for more formal training in the colleges and hospitals. Apprenticeships are frowned on now. More rules, more restrictions. That's a good thing, of course, but it won't help me find a part-time assistant." He went on then to confide the problem of losing Audrey as well.

Finally, frustration rendered him completely uninterested in the rest of his food. He put down his fork and pushed his plate away.

Lawrence began to tap his fingers on the table. A sure sign he was thinking. "All right. What about a nurse? Or someone who could serve as an assistant while being trained as a nurse?"

"Well, that's a great idea," Daniel replied with no real enthusiasm. "But I don't know of anyone who'd be qualified, or even interested, for that matter—"

Or did he? Without warning, the face of Addie Rose Murphy rose in his mind. For once his thoughts didn't linger on the girl's loveliness but moved to process what he'd observed about her—her capabilities, her quiet competence, and what he had already perceived to be a genuine concern for the well-being of others.

More than anyone else he could think of, Dominic Murphy's daughter had the makings of a capable assistant. Indeed, from what he'd seen so far, she most likely possessed real potential for becoming an excellent nurse. All she needed was training. And wasn't he capable of administering that training?

In addition, while she was learning what she'd need to know about the medical aspects of the position, couldn't she also serve at least as a part-time receptionist? That would make her an even more valuable addition to his practice than Audrey had ever been, given the latter's total lack of willingness to take on any nursing responsibilities.

Suddenly energized by where his thoughts had taken him, he knew what he needed to do and decided he needed to act now.

His chair scraped the floor in his haste to stand. "I hate to rush off," he said, digging down into his pocket for his wallet. "But I just remembered something I need to take care of. Will you be here tomorrow?"

"No doubt I will," the other man said, frowning a little. "Because it's just about the only place in town where you can get a decent meal. What's your hurry anyway? Didn't leave a patient on the examining table, did you?"

"I hope not," Daniel said with a laugh. "Just so you know, you've given me an idea. A good one, I believe. At least one I want to think about."

"Well, I hope you'll find time to let me in on my own brilliance. Maybe you can take time out again tomorrow for lunch."

"I'll try," Daniel promised, already on his way around the table, his mind racing ahead to such unfamiliar subjects as how to make a part-time job offer attractive to someone like Addie Rose Murphy and what sort of salary would be proper—a salary he could afford, that is—for such a position.

~

Once Daniel was finally free to leave the office for the day, he found himself in a quandary over the best way to contact Addie Rose. He supposed it made sense to simply drive to Owenduffy and go to her house. But this late in the day, the girl's brothers and sisters—and her father—would most likely be at home, perhaps even gathered for supper, although he had no idea what time miners usually had their evening meal. It might be difficult to have a conversation with her in the midst of such a large family.

There was also the possibility that Dominic Murphy might not take kindly to the idea of employment for his daughter, especially within the confines of an unmarried doctor's office, much less her traveling about the town unchaperoned. Something about the miner's usual tough demeanor had given Daniel a sense that Murphy would be even more hard-edged in his capacity as a father—especially where his daughters were concerned.

Then, too, it was more than possible that Addie Rose might be elsewhere, perhaps helping to tend to someone ill with scarlet fever. In reality, he simply had no idea what might be the best way to approach the young woman and offer her a job.

He decided to get on his way to Owenduffy, hoping the ride over would clear his mind from the clutter of the day and present a workable way to approach Addie Rose Murphy with a job offer she'd be eager to accept.

More to the point, an offer her father would *allow* her to accept.

So, once more, at least for the time being, he relegated calling on Serena to the back of his mind, telling himself he needed to address one problem at a time.

FIFTEEN

A REJECTION—AND SOME ADVICE

May God be praised for woman
That gives up all her mind.
A man may find in no man
A friendship of her kind.

W.B. YEATS

*D*ominic Murphy flung the door open, his face set in the dark scowl Daniel had come to recognize by now.

After a second or two, his expression eased just a bit to a raised eyebrow and a lift of his chin in obvious surprise. "Your wagon broke down again, Doc?" he said, removing a pipe from his mouth.

Daniel chose to ignore the note of sarcasm in the other's tone. "Not this time. Thanks be," he added. He knew he was stalling for time, uncertain as to how to proceed.

"I was wondering if I could talk with you," he finally managed. "Or am I interrupting your dinner?"

"Supper's over," Murphy said, still studying him. He hesitated only another second or two. "Well, come in, then. Too bitter to stand out there."

Daniel expelled a long breath and stepped inside.

The front room was a bit of a surprise. By now, Daniel had been inside a number of the miners' homes, and with few exceptions their furnishings were meager and inadequate, with decorating so sparse as to be almost nonexistent. The Murphy place was humble enough, but the furniture, while for the most part homemade, looked sturdy and quietly attractive. The sole window was curtained, the room painted and cheerful. Clearly, this was the family's attempt at a type of parlor.

The middle room was similar, though it appeared to be more lived in and more often used. This was obviously the dining room. A long wooden table with a glass vase of dried wildflowers graced the center. It was warmer than the front room thanks to a large, cast-iron, coal-burning stove going strong. A rocking chair flanked each side of the stove.

By the far wall of the room, two small boys and a little girl knelt playing marbles on the floor. An attractive woman doing needlework of some sort sat in the smaller of the two chairs by the stove. She looked up at her husband and Daniel with a shy smile.

"My wife, Jana," Murphy said without preamble. "This is the doc from Mount Laurel I was telling you about."

Daniel acknowledged the introduction, at the same time wondering exactly what Jana Murphy might have heard about him. But then, given her husband's dour attitude toward him, he figured he might be better off not knowing.

He was disappointed to see no sign of Addie Rose, but he

hesitated to raise the subject of his visit. In the next moment, Murphy's wife excused herself and told the children she'd be helping them get ready for bed. Once they left the room, Murphy indicated that Daniel should take the seat she'd vacated beside the stove as he sat down in the other chair.

As Daniel had already learned, the big miner wasn't one to beat around the bush. Murphy had no sooner seated himself in the larger of the two rockers than he turned and faced Daniel directly. "So what's on your mind, Doc?"

"I'm in need of help."

Murphy lifted an eyebrow. "That would seem to be a fairly common problem with you, I've noticed."

Daniel leaned forward a little. "No. What I mean is that I need help with my practice. My patients."

Murphy frowned a little. "From what I hear tell, you're doing a fine job."

"I could do a better job if there were two of me."

"Afraid I can't help you there, Doc."

Daniel watched him. "Actually, I think you can. If you will."

Now the miner looked genuinely puzzled.

"Here's the thing," Daniel said, still uneasy about what to expect. "I need someone to help out in the office. With paperwork. Making appointments. Possibly going along on house calls now and then. A number of things, actually. I'm getting buried in work, what with trying to take care of patients on both sides of the river. Especially since we were hit with scarlet fever, I can't seem to ever keep up with all that needs to be done."

Murphy tilted his head a bit. "Well, I can see where that might be a problem. But I don't understand what I could do to help."

Daniel swallowed hard. "I thought…I was wondering…if perhaps your daughter, your oldest daughter, might be interested in a job."

Slowly, Murphy drew himself up a little straighter in the chair. "Addie Rose? You want Addie Rose to come and work for you?"

Relieved that the miner seemed more surprised than put off, Daniel nodded and then plunged ahead. "I thought I should talk with you first. I didn't know how you'd feel about it, so I thought it best to ask you before approaching her with the idea."

Murphy kept his gaze fixed on the stove. "I suppose the girl is of an age to make up her own mind…"

Daniel finally drew a deep breath. "I was hoping you'd approve—"

Murphy shot him a hard glance. "I didn't say I approve."

Daniel blinked. "Oh."

Murphy said nothing for a moment. Finally, cracking his knuckles, he asked, "So, there's no one else in the office besides yourself, then?"

"Well…no. That's why I'm looking for someone."

Murphy ran a hand over his beard. "Surely, you could find someone if you looked a bit. Wouldn't another doc be of more help?"

Daniel shook his head. "Not necessarily. I believe I could keep up with the treatment of patients if I had someone to help me with everything else. Besides, there's not another doctor in the area that I know of, and I don't have any free time to go looking for someone. I need help now."

The miner kept his piercing gaze riveted on Daniel. "I see your problem, Doc. But I'm afraid Addie Rose isn't the answer to it."

Daniel kept his silence for a moment. "Do you mind telling

me why? Your daughter is good with the sick. She seems to have a natural gift for helping where it's needed." He paused. "I'd pay her well."

He saw Murphy's hands go white-knuckled on the arms of the chair.

"She's but a girl. She has no real experience in the sickroom."

Surprised by the miner's remark, Daniel frowned. "Really? I've had any number of patients mention how she's helped them. And from what I've heard, it's becoming fairly common for some folks to ask for her when they need help for themselves or a family member."

"Addie Rose is always willing to help out a neighbor, but it's not as if she's had any real training," Murphy said with a shrug.

Daniel hesitated. "Well, I've always thought that experience is the best training. And from what I've heard, your daughter has had a great deal of that."

Murphy gave him no opportunity to say more, but went on. "I like you, Doc. You seem a decent enough sort. But that doesn't change the fact that I don't know you all that well. Surely not well enough to be easy with my daughter spending time cooped up alone with you and traveling about the countryside with you. I expect if you'll just think about that, you'll understand where I'm coming from."

Daniel had thought about it, and because he had he wasn't all that surprised to hear the man voice this concern. In truth, he'd given the matter enough thought that he believed he had an answer ready.

"Tell me something. I've been practicing in the area for more than three years now. Not as long here in Owenduffy as in Mount Laurel, I know, but still—have you ever heard so much as a word about any…impropriety on my part? With, say, a patient, or with any other woman? Anything at all?"

Murphy's eyes narrowed, and he opened his mouth as if to say something, but then he seemed to change his mind.

Daniel went on. "Look, Murphy, I probably understand your concern better than you might think. If I had an attractive daughter, I'd likely want to lock her up and keep her out of sight until I saw her safely married to a man of my choice. As it happens, you've nothing to worry about where I'm concerned. I'm already a bit of a fool over a certain young lady in Mount Laurel—so much that I honestly don't believe I've even looked at another girl for a year or more now. I promise you, my interest in your daughter is strictly professional and would remain so."

He stopped to catch a breath before adding, "Addie Rose would be perfectly safe with me. You can trust me on that."

He searched Murphy's face carefully, but if he had hoped to make an inroad on the other's resistance, the expression on the big miner's face quickly discouraged that notion.

Apparently, there was nothing else he could say that would convince the man he was trustworthy so, reluctantly, he stood, saying, "Well, I've taken up enough of your time. But I wish you'd at least think about this, and maybe even talk it over with Addie Rose." Before he turned to go, he couldn't resist adding, "I suppose it must be a hard thing to accept that one of our children is grown up and old enough to make her own decisions. But I can't help but believe, based on what I've seen for myself and heard from others, that that's the case with your daughter. Just let me know if you change your mind."

Murphy said a civil enough goodbye, and Daniel left then, frustrated that he had been unable to win the trust of this man he had come to respect and somehow even admire. On the ride home, he realized with some surprise that he had been hoping Murphy might esteem him enough to trust him with the protection and reputation of his daughter.

He was even more surprised, as he grasped that this wasn't the case, that this itself was as much a disappointment as his failure to secure an assistant.

～

Dominic tiptoed into the bedroom, stopping short when he saw his wife propped up in bed, reading.

"I thought you'd be sound asleep by now."

She smiled at him. "I wasn't about to go to sleep until I found out what the young doctor wanted."

He sighed as he sat down on the side of the bed to take off his shoes. "What he wanted," he said gruffly, "was to hire our daughter on as his 'assistant.'"

"Which daughter?"

He looked at her. "Addie Rose, of course. Word apparently gets around about her being of good help in the sickroom."

Jana nodded. "She is that." She put her book down. Then, "You said 'hire her.' You mean he wants to give her a job?"

"Indeed."

"And what did you tell him?"

"Why, I told him no, of course."

Her reply was slow in coming. "Why 'of course'?"

He turned to look at her. "And what else would I say? I'll not have her going off to spend her days with a man we scarcely know, just the two of them."

Again, she delayed answering him. "You did mention not long ago that you liked the young doctor, that he seemed a good enough sort."

He stood to unclasp his suspenders. "I like that rascal of a storekeeper Tom Corcoran well enough too, but I'd not trust him in a closed room with one of our girls."

"Oh, Dom! Sure and you'd not compare the likes of Tom Corcoran with the doctor."

"I don't know the doc well enough to compare him with any-one. And the fact that I don't know him is reason enough to keep him away from Addie Rose, is all I'm saying." He lifted an eye-brow. "It seems you took to him well enough."

She pursed her lips. "All I have to go on is what you've told me about him. And the two minutes I spent with him tonight. But he does seem to be a nice young man."

He groaned. "You're not thinking I should agree to let Addie Rose work for him?"

"What, exactly, would he be wanting her to do?"

He explained then what young Kavanagh had described to him, what he'd be expecting of anyone he happened to hire.

When he finished, she folded her arms and took on that look she had when deep in thought.

"So?" he prompted.

She studied him for a moment. "Dom, Addie Rose is twenty-two years old. She's not a child any longer. She's a woman."

"And don't I know that well enough?"

She patted the side of the bed, and he sat down.

"I'm just thinking that it might be time to let her be her age," she said slowly.

"Meaning what?"

"I know your intentions are good—" she stopped.

"Well, I should hope you know that."

"But you can't keep our girls children forever. Here's the thing, Dom. Addie Rose is gifted with the healing. People ask for her. They trust her in the sickroom. She has something special. 'Tis as if she senses the needs of others and knows what to say, what to do." She reached to touch his hand. "Our girl has something others need…those who are ill, that is. I'm not sure we'd be doing right to keep her away from what the good Lord may have called her to do."

She squeezed his hand, but Dom didn't respond. It was a rare thing when his Jana spoke her heart so. But then hadn't he always known she was a different kind of woman from others? She knew things, Jana did. The Old Ones might have said she was fey. For certain she understood their children better than he ever would.

"I mean only to protect her," he muttered.

Her pressure on his hand increased. "I know that, husband. I know. But we can't keep them out of the world forever. They have their own lives to live. Addie Rose is old enough to be living hers. And so, for that matter, is Elly."

He withdrew his hand. "Now, that one hasn't a grain of sense. Don't be telling me how grown up she is."

Jana shook her head. "Elly has more sense than you credit her for. But she's in love, Dom. All of us can be more than a little foolish when we're in love." She stopped, smiling. "Even a man like yourself. I seem to recall you once had a bit of *leibideacht* in that hard head of yours."

He tried to pull an annoyed look, but given her smile, he figured it had had no effect at all. "If that was ever the case, it was no doing of my own," he said gruffly. "You were the cause of my losing my wits back then. In truth, you can still turn me to a green *gorsoon*."

"So you've said before."

"Well, then, what is it you're getting at?"

Again she reached for his hand. "I believe you should tell Addie Rose about this offer from the doctor and let her make up her own mind as to whether she wants it."

He drew a long breath. "You'd trust her alone with a man we scarcely know, then?"

"As I recall, my da trusted me with you when he knew you little better than we know the doctor. And you had a far more questionable reputation."

He drew himself up. "Your da threatened to take a horse whip to me if I so much as looked at you the wrong way."

Again she smiled. "Aye, he did, didn't he? Mum told me. She thought it was funny."

"To save me, I can't recall so much as a glint of humor in that black look she turned on me every time I darkened the door."

Her smile broadened. "Neither of them had it in mind to make things easy for you, that's true."

"Indeed." His scowl held fast. "So what is it you're saying, then? What would you have me do?"

"Well, if you ask me," she said quietly, "I think you should do nothing. Let Addie Rose make up her own mind. If she accepts, then of course we'll keep a close eye on her behavior and how the job seems to suit her."

"That's giving the girl more freedom than I'm comfortable with."

"Dom…" Her look was reproving, even severe. "'Tis time."

"Oh, all right," he growled. "But whatever comes of this is on your head, not mine."

"Of course, dear."

He narrowed his eyes again. "That's it, then?"

She nodded. Then she reached to kiss him on the cheek. "That's it," she agreed.

He pulled her a bit closer. "That's it for now, you mean."

"Aye," she said. "For now."

SIXTEEN

An Early Morning Surprise

Her hair was a waving bronze and her eyes
Deep wells that might cover a brooding soul...
JOHN BOYLE O'REILLY

When someone knocked on the door of his office just past daylight Monday morning, Daniel immediately assumed there was trouble at the mine. The whistle hadn't blown yet, but it wouldn't be the first time he'd been summoned before news of an emergency was made known to the town.

He could not have been more surprised to find Addie Rose Murphy standing before him when he opened the door. Bundled in a dark woolen coat, her hands in her pockets, the girl appeared thoroughly chilled. Her cheeks were nearly as red as her hair, much of which tumbled free from a colorful headscarf.

"Miss Murphy!" It took a moment for him to realize he was staring. When he finally came to himself, he opened the door a little more and stood aside. "Come in! Please, come in!"

She hesitated only a moment before stepping inside.

"Surely you didn't walk here? You must be chilled to the bone."

"No, I came in the wagon with Da on his way to the mine." She stopped just inside the door and stood watching him, as if she were waiting for something. Finally, she spoke. "Da said you wanted to see me."

Caught off guard, Daniel could manage only a blank stare.

"Something about a job," she said, eyeing him curiously.

"A job—" Daniel's mind stalled for a moment. Dominic had made it blazingly clear that he wouldn't so much as even tell her about the job opening. What was going on?

"Your father talked with you about my needing help here in the office?"

Her smile was uncertain. "He did. You might have noticed that he didn't much like the idea, but Mum convinced him to let me decide for myself."

Ah! So, thankfully, Jana Murphy hadn't seen eye to eye with her stubborn husband!

"And you're interested?"

"I am. Very interested. But you do know that I've had no real experience, not in nursing or office work of any kind?"

"Yes, I know. But I'm sure you can learn the office routine in short order, and from all I've heard, you've had a great deal of hands-on experience in the sickroom. While I need someone to handle most of the clerical work and keep the office running, I'm even more interested in a nursing assistant. Whatever you might lack in that area, I feel sure I could help you learn."

To his dismay, her expression suddenly changed from its previous interest to one of suspicion. "Why would you do that?"

"Why? Well…because from what I've heard it seems you just might have the potential to make an excellent nurse." He stopped before adding, "And because I need help and need it now."

She blinked, and the look of mistrust gave way to the same interest he'd seen a moment before. "You'd train me then? To be a proper nurse?"

"If that's what you want—and if you're willing to work hard. Yes, I'd teach you as much as I can. Certainly, as much as I believe you'd need."

He wouldn't have wanted her to know just how much he was silently urging her to agree. As it happened, her reply wasn't long in coming.

"I do want the job. And I'm a hard worker. What do I have to do to apply?"

"What—well, don't you want to know about the pay?"

She looked at him and pressed her lips together. In that moment, Daniel realized that she hadn't even thought about the matter of salary yet.

"To be honest," he hurried to say, "I haven't thought through all the details myself yet. But I'm sure we can work out something satisfactory to both of us."

"When would I start, then?" She stopped. "If you hire me, that is?"

Daniel hesitated only a moment, studying her. "How about now?"

He hadn't expected her to take him seriously. But before he could add anything more, she began taking off her scarf and muffler.

"What should I do first?"

He wasted no time in helping her with her coat.

～

In spite of the good things Daniel had heard about Addie Rose Murphy, she managed to surprise him. By late afternoon, he could scarcely believe how much she had accomplished—and with so little help and instruction from him.

Moreover, his patients had clearly taken a liking to her. Vito Eneo, an irascible farm laborer who spoke barely coherent English, at first seemed to resent her very presence, but he clearly softened when she spoke a few words of broken Italian while handing him a container of ointment for the raw sores on his forearm.

When Daniel asked her later about her knowledge of Italian, she simply shrugged. "The little I know I learned from the Benedetta twins. I took care of their mother when her leg was broken."

And then there was the almost instant rapport she'd established with the elderly Martha Arbogast, a usually sullen-natured widow who seemed to find fault with most treatments and suggestions Daniel had on occasion offered for her rheumatism.

"I'm impressed," Daniel said when Addie Rose came back inside after helping Martha to her buggy. "That's a different side to the Widow Arbogast than I've seen since she first started coming to me. What magic did you work with her?"

Addie Rose smiled. "I asked her about her two-year-old grandson, Nathan. He's absolutely adorable, and she dotes on him."

Daniel stared at her. "I didn't know she had a two-year-old grandson."

"Well, she does. I took care of him one afternoon while she helped her daughter bake pies for Lon Weaver's funeral." She paused. "Don't you get to know your patients at all, then?"

The question caught Daniel off guard. It also made him think.

Did he actually treat the patient or merely the disease? Especially lately, had he been so busy, so intent on keeping up with his patient load that he had become too preoccupied with the treatment to be sufficiently interested in the patient?

An uneasy feeling snaked through him, the feeling that he already knew the answer to his own question. He certainly hadn't intended to become that kind of physician, but was it possible that in the press and rush of his life lately he had unwittingly let that happen? Shaken, he forced a smile. "I thought I did. Apparently, I need to know them better. It seems I'll be able to count on you to help me with that."

A puzzled frown pinched her features, an expression that seemed to indicate she found him strange indeed. Feeling more than a little uncomfortable under her stare, Daniel started for his office.

He stopped to turn and ask, "Will your father be picking you up?"

"Aye. He should be here most anytime now."

"Well…you did a fine job today. And I promise, tomorrow we'll settle on your salary." He paused. "You will be back tomorrow, won't you?"

"If you want."

"I do," he said quickly. "Of course I do."

And he did. In spite of the fact that something about her made him strangely uncomfortable, he very much wanted her to come back.

SEVENTEEN

A NEW PATIENT

*The fear that is sometimes hidden in the heart
is not so easily erased from the face.*
ANONYMOUS

*D*aniel could not have handpicked a more efficient and helpful assistant than Addie Rose Murphy. Over the next two weeks, she proved not only to be a highly competent organizer and office manager, but also to possess an innate nursing instinct. Indeed, in a matter of just a few days he had come to not only admire her and appreciate her, but to rely on her. He could scarcely believe that in such a brief time she had his office running more smoothly than he would have believed possible.

Seated at his desk late Friday afternoon, on impulse he decided to tell her how pleased he was with her work—and to show his appreciation, albeit in a small way. The timing was good, as she stood across from him, about to receive her week's salary.

"I just wanted to tell you that I think you're doing a fine job," he said, handing her the brown envelope that held her pay. "You'll

157

find a modest increase in there this week. You deserve more, but for now this is the best I can do."

She actually blushed as she reached for the envelope. "I... thank you," she said, stammering a little. "It's...I like the work. I like it a lot."

"Good! Then I'll hope I don't have to worry about losing you. You've actually made my job a good deal easier."

"Oh, no. I mean, I plan to stay."

She stuck her pay envelope into the pocket of the lab apron he'd provided for her. Daniel couldn't help but notice—not for the first time—the unusual grace and unexpected elegance of her hands. Long, slender fingers with perfectly shaped nails, yet with a visible strength and grace to each movement.

In contrast to Serena's small, almost childish hands, often knotted in tense fists...

He started, wondering where that had come from. It wasn't the first time this had happened. More than once he had caught himself jarred by a sudden, out-of-place thought or observation about Addie Rose in contrast to Serena that caught him completely off guard and left him uncomfortable, to say the least.

He was almost relieved when the bell over the office door sounded. He pushed up from his chair so quickly it screeched across the floor, but Addie Rose was already on her way out of the office, leaving him to follow her.

He stopped just inside the waiting room, watching as Addie Rose met the latecomer halfway.

The woman who remained standing close to the door was a stranger to Daniel, but obviously not to Addie Rose.

"Glenna?" she said. "I haven't seen you in an age."

The other seemed to attempt a smile, but it quickly fell apart, unfinished. Without speaking, she put a hand to her throat. Daniel stood, not yet moving as he took in the woman's appearance. Her wheat-colored hair was long and heavy, unkempt, her coat well worn and at least a size too small. Dark shadows deepened her eyes, and her face was blotched in two or three places with bruises.

She had the look, Daniel thought, of one dogged by an old and relentless fear. He had seen that look before. It was the look of a wild-eyed animal, poised to run.

Without meeting Addie Rose's eyes, or his, she visibly trembled as she asked, "Am I too late to see the doctor?"

Addie Rose started to reply. "Well, it is after hours—"

On impulse, Daniel spoke up before she could finish. "It's all right," he interrupted, motioning the newcomer the rest of the way in and then turning to Addie Rose. "Can you stay a few minutes more?"

She glanced from him to the woman just inside the door. "I can. Da said I shouldn't look for him before five thirty today."

Daniel nodded, and when the woman finally looked at him, he gave her what he hoped was a reassuring smile before turning back to the examining room, waiting for them to follow.

~

Daniel knew almost as soon as he began the examination that the woman—whom Addie Rose had introduced as Glenna Mac-Mahon—had been mistreated. She was quick to explain that she'd fallen the night before, but what he was seeing wouldn't have been caused by any fall. Ugly bruises marred her upper right arm and webbed onto her neck. A cut over her right eye was still crusted with blood. The eye would be black before morning. She flinched every time he touched her shoulder, and when he attempted to check her ribs, she gasped with every touch.

He glanced at the cheap, thin wedding band on her finger. This woman wasn't his first case of ill treatment. After a few years in practice, he recognized abuse when he saw it.

The reality was that Glenna MacMahon was wracked with pain and soreness. Two broken ribs, a number of bruises, and a badly sprained shoulder weren't the only causes of her misery, but they definitely contributed to it.

With her face turned away, she said, "Is my arm broken, then?"

Daniel shook his head as he finished binding her ribs. "Not broken, but badly sprained. Most of the pain in your arm is coming from your shoulder. And as I told you, you have two broken ribs. I'm afraid you're going to be extremely sore for several days."

He glanced at Addie Rose, who stood waiting. After binding the patient's ribs, Daniel said gently, "Addie Rose will help you with your things. Then we'll talk in my office."

"Oh, but I have to get back. I don't have time—"

"You need to make time," Daniel said firmly. "It won't take long."

Dismayed, Daniel realized that what he was seeing in her eyes at that moment was nothing short of panic. Her voice trembled as she again protested. "No, really, I can't! I have to get home. I shouldn't have stayed away this long."

She was already off the examining table and reaching for her things. When Daniel put a hand to her arm in an attempt to persuade her to stay, she shrugged him off almost violently, flinching with the pain the movement obviously caused her.

"Please," she choked out. "I have to go!"

Across the table, Addie Rose gave a quick shake of her head to warn Daniel off, so he stepped back. "All right," he told her with reluctance, "but I want to see you again in two or three days."

He followed them to the waiting room, watching while Addie Rose helped the woman with her coat. "Don't forget," he told her, "I want to check on you again. Soon."

She made no reply as she hurried out the door.

Later, as they tidied the examining room, Daniel said, "She won't be back, will she?"

Addie Rose's expression was troubled. "Most likely not."

"Since you obviously know her, fill me in."

"I'm afraid I don't really know her all that well. We went to school together for a time, but she dropped out and got married before graduation."

"You were in school together?" Surprised, Daniel added, "She looks a good deal older than you."

"She's not, though. We're about the same age." Addie Rose stopped but then went on. "I think Glenna has had a hard life."

"She's been abused," Daniel said flatly.

She hesitated, but only for a moment. "I've heard as much."

"What do you know of her husband?"

Her back was to him as she washed her hands. She didn't reply until she turned around and faced him.

"I believe he's several years older than Glenna."

"A miner?"

She nodded.

"Are there children?"

"No. At least, I don't think so. I've never seen her with any."

That in itself was somewhat odd. Most of the miners Daniel had come to know had fairly large families.

Thinking, Daniel stuck his hands in the pockets of his lab coat. "I'm not comfortable with letting her go like that. She's in a lot of pain, and it's not going to get better right away." He stopped. "Will it make things worse for her, do you think, when he learns that she came here? And he will find out, since I bound her ribs and put iodine on those cuts."

"You had to do what was needed."

Daniel drew a deep breath. "And yet I may have caused her more trouble than she had before she came." He stopped, knotting his hands into fists in his pockets. "I hate these kinds of cases!"

She shot him a look. "There have been others?"

"Too many."

"Well, at least you care. I can't think that other doctor would have been concerned one way or the other. Not from the tales I've heard about him."

"Oh, I care," Daniel said. "But what's frustrating is that there's nothing I can do about it, nothing except to treat her wounds. There should be a way to keep it from happening in the first place. Or at the very least, those responsible for the abuse should be punished."

"I doubt that's likely to ever happen," she said, her tone bitter. "No one talks about it, but it's common knowledge that the law turns a blind eye to a man who beats on his wife."

She was right, of course. He had dealt with wife-beating too often not to be aware of the ease with which most men seemed to evade even the feeblest form of punishment for abuse of their mate. And in a rough-edged community such as a mining town, ill treatment of women—and even children—seemed to occur all too often.

Not that such abuse was limited to the poorer classes. He had encountered firsthand in his practice a number of women married to well-to-do-professionals who had carried on the despicable vice of wife-beating. He had even treated one tormented victim in New York who adamantly refused to admit that a particularly vicious form of abuse had been perpetrated upon her by her husband—a well-known clergyman.

After a moment, Daniel realized that Addie Rose was staring at him in confusion. Apparently, she'd asked him a question and he hadn't answered. He sighed, realizing he had most likely drifted off into one of his more annoying habits—annoying, at least according to Serena, a habit that she had more than once described as his "bothersome woolgathering."

He was quick to apologize. "I'm sorry?"

"I said you're obviously upset about this—about Glenna and the abuse problem."

Daniel nodded. "It's just so….wrong. Something needs to be done about it, but what you said about the law turning a blind eye? That's what I've run into anytime I've reported a similar case, even though I could document it. It doesn't help that most women won't accuse their husbands. They stay silent, pretend that they've fallen or hurt themselves in some way."

"That's because they know what will happen if their husbands find out they've reported them," Addie Rose said quietly.

Daniel looked at her. For someone so young, she seemed extremely wise.

He was growing to respect her more and more, this daughter of the mines, for a number of reasons—and not only for the wonders she had worked in his office in such a short time. In fact, if he were to be altogether honest with himself, he was becoming uncomfortably aware that his feelings toward Addie Rose Murphy might possibly be edging toward more than respect.

And that was no good. No good at all. For one thing, she was too young for him to be thinking of her with that kind of interest. And for another, he suspected that hard-edged father of hers might take a very dim view—to say the least—of even the hint of an inappropriate "interest" in his daughter. He liked Dominic Murphy, even respected the man, but he had no illusions about what the irascible miner might be capable of should someone even appear to step over the line with him.

Besides, what about Serena?

Just then Addie Rose appeared at his office door to announce that her father had arrived and she'd be leaving for the day.

With a strange kind of relief, Daniel stood to say goodbye, but he refrained from walking with her to the door as he usually did.

EIGHTEEN

MORNING MUSINGS— AND A SURPRISE

Lord, give me faith!—to leave it all to Thee...
JOHN OXENHAM

Stephen Holliday greeted the late September morning by taking his usual walk just after sunrise. He wanted to make the most of these days. Too soon the trees would be losing the season's fire to dry and decay on the ground, adding the scent of approaching winter to the air. As he always had, he would hold on to the sights and sounds that were a part of his morning walks as long as possible, sorely reluctant to let them go into his storehouse of memories.

He always chose this time of day for traipsing about, checking on the animals and the property, scouting for any needed repairs, and simply enjoying in his own way his quiet morning meeting with what he thought of as the family farm. If it bothered him that the "family" part of the farm had dwindled, he usually managed to bury his mixed feelings of discontent and sadness in the reminder that a small family was still a family. He was realist enough to know that the tragedy of losing his older son in the war would never stop gnawing at his heart, but he still had his younger boy, Clay, and, of course, his wife, Esther. His love and steadfast drive to protect them and provide them with a good life had been enough to keep him from sinking into relentless despair.

Almost from the day the shattering news of Ben's death had arrived, and through every day after, he had resolved to keep his own grief from increasing Esther's and Clay's. The two boys had been close, as much friends as brothers, so he knew Ben's passing had left a terrible void in Clay's life. And Esther—although he had sensed her making an effort to be strong for his sake, he knew all too well what the pain of losing a son could do to a parent.

He found it harder some days than others to keep from giving in to the heartache that nagged at him like a predator, but he continually fought it as best he knew how. For the most part, he thought he had succeeded more than he'd failed. And these days, thanks to the good Lord, it couldn't be more obvious that Esther absolutely glowed with happiness.

He smiled to himself. Even after all these weeks since his wife had unveiled the startling news that they were going to be parents again, he couldn't control his raw delight and eagerness at the thought of a new baby around the house. If he had asked for a God-given gift, one to put the joy back in Esther's heart—and, yes, in his own heart as well—he couldn't have imagined such a sweet, special answer to a prayer as this one.

His mood grew more solemn as he was reminded—not for the first time—that Clay's attitude toward the baby was the only dark cloud on the horizon. It wasn't that the boy seemed averse to the idea of a new baby brother or sister. It was more that he appeared to be indifferent. He'd shown almost no interest when they first announced the news, and as time passed, his apparent lack of interest couldn't have been more obvious. Any attempt to engage him in a conversation about the baby brought a detached, if not downright rude, response.

Esther thought the boy would come around after the baby actually arrived, but Stephen wasn't so sure. If he wasn't mistaken, the only real interest their son had these days was focused on Elly Murphy. Clay worked the farm as he always had, did the tasks he had always done, and still maintained his part-time job at Sam Riegel's leather shop, but so far as Stephen could tell, he did it all with little enthusiasm. The only time he showed any real eagerness was when he left the house in the evening, presumably to spend time with that girl.

Esther had tried to be a kind of buffer between him and Clay. She seemed to have a good deal more patience for their son's romantic obsession than he did. He could tell she tried not to be too obvious when she chided him for his disapproval of Clay's interest in the girl, teasing him that he had been even more distracted when they were courting, but Stephen couldn't help but be concerned. Even though he knew his impatience with the situation created a rift between him and his son, he couldn't very well pretend to approve of the relationship when he didn't, could he?

On his way back to the house now, he heard Clay calling for him. Something in his son's voice made him pick up his pace, and when the boy shouted again, Stephen took off at a run.

～

As usual, Sarge beat Daniel to the door when the knocking sounded. The last person Daniel would have expected to see was Clay Holliday. One look at that tanned, sharply chiseled face— so much like Stephen's—made it all too clear that something was very wrong.

"Clay?"

Over the boy's shoulder, he saw the russet-and-white quarter horse Clay always rode. The stallion had clearly been ridden fast and hard.

He opened the door a little wider. "Come in, come in."

Clay shook his head. "There's no time! Dad said could you come right away? It's Mother. She thinks the baby is coming."

Daniel quickly calculated the time. Esther's delivery date was a good month away, possibly a bit more. "I'll have to get my bag and the buggy. You go on back home. I'll be there just as quickly as I can. Make sure your mother stays warm. And get some water boiling."

Clay nodded and ran back to his horse.

Sarge was at his heels as Daniel scrambled to grab his bag and a jacket before hurrying to the barn. Although he knew an early delivery wasn't unlikely in cases like this, he still didn't like the idea. He reminded himself that Esther was in remarkably good health, always had been, and was a strong and vital woman. She had dedicated herself to this baby, and she was determined to do anything and everything possible to see that it was born strong and well. God willing, this should be a relatively easy delivery—if that was even what was about to happen. It could be a false alarm. There wouldn't be anything unusual about that.

Even so, he was still praying as he rushed toward the barn.

NINETEEN

THE BEGINNING
OF A LONG DAY

No morning begins with a map of the day.
ANONYMOUS

*D*aniel stopped only long enough to go by the office and collect Addie Rose. He had a feeling he might need her with him this morning. Fortunately, he'd given her a spare key early in her employment because Dominic often dropped her off as much as half an hour ahead of his own arrival.

He was also grateful for her foresight in having drawn up a sign not long after she started working for him to alert any patients that the office was temporarily closed during an emergency. This morning, it took her only long enough to grab her coat and the extra medical bag he'd given her soon after her hiring, and they were on their way.

Sarge was relegated to the back of the buggy in spite of his obvious intention to park his considerable bulk between them on the bench. The big oaf had wasted no time in appointing himself as Addie Rose's personal guardian. The way things were going,

Daniel figured it might not be long before he was shuttled into second place in his own dog's affections.

Not long before they arrived at the Holliday farm, Addie Rose asked about the family. "You said Mrs. Holliday was in her early forties?"

Daniel nodded. "Which some might say puts her at risk for childbirth. But Esther is a young, healthy forty-three, and other than the fact that it's more than a month premature, if the baby is really coming, she should do just fine." He paused. "All the same, I'll be a little uneasy until I see just how she's doing."

"You're good friends with the Hollidays, aren't you?"

He glanced over at her. "They're like family. In fact, they took me in like family almost as soon as I arrived in Mount Laurel." He turned back to the road but went on to explain. "I took care of their son when he was wounded at Gettysburg. He didn't make it, so after his death I made the trip to bring his family his personal effects—and I ended up liking the area so much I decided to settle here."

She was quiet for a moment. "Their other son—Clay—has been seeing my sister."

He turned back to her again. "So I've heard."

When she said nothing more, Daniel also remained quiet. Then, just before they pulled onto the lane that led up to the farmhouse, she added, "Elly and Clay want to get married." Another pause. "Da doesn't think they should."

Daniel nodded. "What do you think?"

"Me?" She drew a deep breath. "I suppose I understand Da's concern. Elly's only seventeen, and she can be a little…flighty. And they come from really different places in life. But even so, it seems to me they should have the right to decide their own future."

Daniel tended to agree with her but didn't reply. Slowly, he pulled the buggy around to the back of the house and came to a stop. When he glanced up, he saw Stephen standing at the edge of the porch, frowning into the gray morning light.

Daniel could see the tension and anxiety carved into his friend's features. And in that moment, he felt a renewed wave of his own unease, stronger than before, rise up and begin to roll over him.

Stephen met them at the back gate. It took Daniel only an instant to sense that his friend was at the edge of panic. In spite of the brisk cold of the morning, his face was moist with perspiration, his jaw set in a rigid line, and his eyes glazed with something akin to raw fear.

"It's too soon, isn't it, Daniel?" he blurted out even before they reached the gate. "What does this mean?"

Daniel reached to grasp his hand. "First things first, Stephen. I can't tell you a thing until I examine her. But keep in mind that babies don't always cooperate with our expectations. They have a tendency to arrive when it's convenient for them."

Once inside, Daniel introduced Addie Rose while shrugging out of his coat. Although Stephen was clearly too agitated to pay close attention to the introduction, Daniel noticed that he did give Addie Rose a quick, sharp look.

"Murphy, you say?" Stephen said.

She met his gaze. "Yes, that's right."

Daniel cut in before any questions could be asked. "Before you take us to Esther, Stephen, tell me what time her pains began. And has she been nauseous at all?"

Stephen raked a hand through his hair. "Clay called me inside a little before eight. I was out walking." His words came like a spasm, broken and uncertain. "By the time I got to her, she said she'd been having cramps and a lot of back pain for several minutes. I don't know about nausea. She didn't say anything about that. She was restless through the night, but she'd gone back to sleep before I left the house this morning…"

He stopped, catching his breath and clenching his fists at each side. "So—do you think the baby is coming early, Daniel?"

"I'll let you know what's going on just as soon as I know. Now take us to her, and then you go—where's Clay? You go and stay with him."

"He's outside. He's taking care of the milking. I'm staying inside, Daniel."

Of course he was. "That's fine. But you can't be in the room while I'm examining her."

"But—"

"No, Stephen. You're not all that steady now, and you'll just unnerve Esther."

Stephen's hands went up. "All right, all right. But I'm not leaving the house."

Daniel squeezed his arm. "That's fine. Make some fresh coffee, then, why don't you? I promise I'll fill you in just as soon as I examine Esther." A thought struck him, and he stopped in midstride. "Where's Miss Ruth Ann?"

"She's been visiting with my cousin Lorrie and her family. She'll be there the rest of the week."

Daniel nodded, somewhat relieved. Stephen's elderly mother was a dear, but any change in routine tended to set her off, and she could be difficult at those times. They didn't need any additional problems today.

"All right, then. Off with you while we tend to Esther."

When Stephen still hesitated, he gave him a gentle push. "Coffee," he ordered.

"Now."

~

He had to fight down his own concern when they walked into the bedroom. Esther was propped up against the headboard, a blanket thrown over her drawn-up legs. Pale, her face heavily doused with perspiration, she was still in her night clothes and—most telling of all—her hair was damp and falling free of the neat knot at her neck she usually wore. Daniel had never seen Esther looking less than perfect, and for a moment he found himself completely taken aback. In fact, this stark difference in appearance said more than even the grimace of pain on her face.

He managed what he hoped was a fairly casual greeting as he crossed the room. "Well, now, what's going on here that brought me out before my breakfast?"

"Oh, Daniel. I'm so sorry! This is probably totally unnecessary! But Stephen…well, you know how he is—"

"I'm teasing, Esther. And yes, I do know how that husband of yours is. And we wouldn't want him any other way, would we?"

She shook her head, but at the same time she said, "Where is he? And Clay…where—" She stopped short, clutching her abdomen and gasping for breath.

"Don't worry about your men. They're taking care of business while I take care of you, which I'm going to do right now." After quickly introducing Addie Rose, he set about examining her, gently but thoroughly.

Daniel had already seen enough to be almost convinced that this was no false alarm. By the time he completed the examination, he knew it for certain.

And so did Esther. She had delivered twice before, after all.

"I'm in labor, aren't I?"

"You are."

"It's too early," she said, her voice ragged. "I was never early with the boys, Daniel. Does this mean there's something wrong with the baby?"

He hurried to reassure her, at the same time wishing he could reassure himself. He tried to be careful not to say too much. "Absolutely not, Esther. It just means that this baby has decided to come in its own time. We simply have to adjust our schedule to accommodate his—or hers, as the case may be."

He darted a glance at Addie Rose on the opposite side of the bed, and found her watching him closely. "We could do with an extra sheet and another blanket," he told her. "And a couple more pillows, I think. And some boiling water."

She nodded, and while Esther pointed out the linen closet on the other side of the room, Daniel opened his case and placed any instruments he might need on the table beside the bed.

Without being told, Addie Rose also brought some washcloths and soap when she returned with the hot water.

At this point, all that seemed left to do was to try to make Esther more comfortable and let Stephen know what was going on. Then they would settle in to wait.

And pray.

TWENTY

AN EVENTFUL DAY

This is the day which the LORD hath made.
PSALM 118:24

*T*he morning had pointed to a long day ahead, and it more than fulfilled its promise.

By four o'clock, Stephen had made no less than a dozen trips in and out of the bedroom, where Esther labored in obvious distress. Yet as apparent and wrenching as her pain was, Daniel would have had a difficult time discerning which of the two was suffering the most. Somehow, despite her agony, Esther managed to maintain a bright face and relentless optimism, while Stephen, on the other hand, seemed gripped by continuous and nearly debilitating spasms of nerves.

Daniel thought the best he could hope for was that the baby would make an appearance before he had to treat the expectant father for a complete collapse.

He was pleased by the way Esther had responded to Addie Rose, almost from the time of their arrival. This wasn't the first time he'd noticed that the girl had a steadiness, a poise about her that seemed to provide a calming effect on patients, even those in severe pain. With Esther, though, it was more. The two seemed to connect emotionally. It was almost as though Addie Rose could anticipate the times Esther would be close to panic and somehow manage to calm her.

When Daniel thought about it, he could recall times when she'd had a similar effect on other patients, steadying them during a particularly stressful treatment or unexpected crisis. More than once she had caught him by surprise with her keen perception.

Most of the instructors in medical school had trained the students to keep their feelings under wraps, insisting that to show any emotion other than confidence in the presence of a patient was unprofessional. Daniel would have thought he had mastered his own feelings accordingly had Addie Rose not proven so adept at spotting even the slightest hesitation or any hint of distress in him.

As it was, he found himself strangely relieved by the girl's discernment. It was as if she recognized what he would have considered a weakness in himself—a trait that surely Serena would also have identified as a weakness—and found it not such a bad thing after all.

Perhaps because that thought darted unexpectedly into his thoughts, Esther's question during one of her lulls between contractions caught him completely off guard.

"You didn't answer me."

He looked at her. "I'm sorry. Too much coffee, I expect."

"I asked you how things are between you and Serena these days—"

She broke off, clearly in the grip of another contraction.

Without answering her, Daniel checked his pocket watch.

"Your contractions are coming much closer together now. And the pains are sharper, aren't they?"

She nodded, putting a fist to her mouth. "Where's Addie Rose?"

"She went to give Sarge something to eat."

"Let him inside, Daniel. It's too cold to keep him outdoors."

"You just concentrate on doing your job for now. Sarge is in the barn. Most likely Addie Rose will find him sound asleep."

"He's such a good dog." She drew a ragged breath at the end of the contraction. "You didn't answer me," she said again.

He glanced at her. "What?"

"Serena...I asked how things are with the two of you."

He hesitated. "Actually, I haven't seen her for several days."

"Oh?"

"It's been a busy time," he said, knowing he sounded lame.

"Is everything all right?"

Again, he stalled before answering. "Serena has been a little put out with me, I believe."

Esther frowned. A motherly sort of frown. "What did you do, Daniel?"

"Nothing. Literally nothing. I expect that's why she's put out with me. I had to forego an evening with her. I didn't want to, but it just didn't work out, and since then—"

He stopped short when her frown turned to a grimace and a sharp cry. He bent over to grasp her hand. At the same time Addie Rose walked back into the room and, seeing Esther's distress, turned back to close the door before hurrying over to the bed and clasping her other hand.

"It hurts—" Esther gasped, half rising from her pillows.

"I know, dear. I know," Daniel said softly, trying to soothe her.

"We're getting closer now. You just hang on to Addie Rose and me. You're doing so well!"

"You keep a watch on Stephen, Daniel."

"You just concentrate on the baby. Stephen will be fine. Everything will be fine, you'll see. Before the sun sets on this day, you'll have a new little one to fuss over."

She managed a smile before crying out again.

Daniel looked at Addie Rose. "Make sure everything's ready."

"I already have," she said quietly, smiling at Esther. "And Esther is doing really well, don't you think?"

He nodded and glanced at her across the bed. "I'm glad you're here. And I can tell Esther is too."

"All right, you two," Esther said, her voice unsteady but still dry with its usual humor. "I'm still here. Stop talking about me as if I've left the room."

Daniel reached to clasp her hand in both of his. At the same time, he drew a steadying breath as he prayed for Esther and the miracle about to take place.

❧

Within minutes, Daniel realized they were in trouble.

Esther was working hard—so hard her heartbeat was racing, her pulse was pounding, and her temperature was climbing. Addie Rose began applying cool cloths to Esther's forehead even more often in hopes of leveling out her temperature. With relief, Daniel confirmed to himself that the baby wasn't presenting breech, as he'd previously feared. Even so, things were not progressing as quickly as he'd like.

He continued to use the relaxation techniques he had found

most helpful with his other maternity patients rather than the frequent and extreme pushing procedures employed by most other physicians. Although still somewhat controversial among older doctors, he had found his preferred method to be both less exhausting to the mother and easier on the baby.

Addie Rose, who apparently had had some experience with a few births among neighbors, had been present at only three other deliveries with Daniel. Even so, she seemed to easily adapt to his methods, and by now Daniel believed she could most likely see a mother safely through the birthing process without him, at least given a traditional delivery. He noticed that her attention never wavered as she watched his every move and Esther's reaction.

He thought hard about the next step. He knew he had to make a decision now, before Esther became completely exhausted.

"Esther, we're going to walk around the room."

There was no missing the expression of disbelief on Esther's face or Addie Rose's searching look. But after another moment, neither protested when he told Addie Rose to get on one side while he took the other and then helped his patient to her feet.

They walked for several minutes and continued walking even during contractions, when Daniel would hold onto Esther as if they were dancing while Addie Rose watched. They kept this up until he decided to let her rest on the side of the bed for a few minutes.

"One more time," he said as he helped her up again and began to cross the room in the same rhythmic pattern, swaying during contractions, then once more picking up their pace. Finally, he helped her back to bed and did another quick examination. Her contractions were quicker now and maintaining a more even pattern.

"All right, dear," he said. "Now you can push. Addie Rose, help to brace her."

It took another twenty minutes, and by the time the baby made her debut, Daniel was sharing Esther's exhaustion...coupled with his own exhilaration.

After taking care of the umbilical cord, he gently sponged the baby and then handed her over to her mother. "Esther," he announced with a smile, "you have a little girl." He paused and then turned to Addie Rose. "Would you go give the good word to the new father?"

Apparently, the new father's nerves had finally driven him somewhere outside. Clay had left earlier for his job at the leather shop in town, so Addie Rose returned alone.

"I called for your husband several times," she said, squeezing Esther's hand. "He probably just went for a quick walk to get a breath of air. If need be, I'll go and look for him."

Over the next few minutes, Esther occupied herself with examining every inch of her newborn baby girl while plying both Daniel and Addie Rose with questions. She also displayed an exuberance and delight Daniel wouldn't have thought possible, given how tired she must be.

A moment later, though, she sobered. "Daniel, she's all right, isn't she? I mean, she's so tiny."

He squeezed her shoulder. "She seems perfectly fine, Esther. Yes, she is small. But just because she was in a hurry to make her grand entrance doesn't mean she's not healthy. I'll check on her often, of course, but I would have done that anyway even if she'd been full-term. For now, it seems to me that you've nothing to worry about."

As he uttered the words, however, Daniel breathed a silent

prayer that he was right. "Just enjoy her. Have you chosen a name yet?"

"We decided only a few days ago on the name Anna, after Stephen's grandmother, if we had a girl," Esther said. "And of course we'll enjoy her! You know we will."

At that moment, the new and visibly tense father burst into the room. "Did you call me? Is everything—"

His glance went to Esther and the baby in her arms. Daniel thought for a moment he might have to resuscitate his friend, but Stephen finally moved, nearly tripping over his own feet as he rushed to the bed.

At that point, Daniel attempted a few congratulatory words, but he was fairly certain no one heard him, least of all the new father.

TWENTY-ONE

A DISTURBING VISIT

*A whisper of unease
often brings about the entrance of worry.*
ANONYMOUS

aniel had just finished with the last patient in the book for the day and was already in his coat to leave for home when he decided to stop and check in on Gladys Piper.

The elderly spinster had been on his mind quite a lot recently, especially after he'd checked the patient log and realized she hadn't been in nearly as often as usual. In fact, she had missed her last appointment altogether, which wasn't like her. He wasn't actually concerned. Miss Gladys was an independent sort and typically in fine health. All the same, it wouldn't hurt to pay her a call.

He wished Addie Rose were going along, but because of her long day yesterday he'd insisted she take today off. She and Miss Gladys had met only once, but he'd been surprised at how the starchy spinster had seemed to warm to his young assistant. Indeed, he didn't think he had ever seen Miss Gladys drop her frosty reserve so quickly and easily as when Addie Rose struck up a conversation with her during her time in the examining room.

Her home on Laurel Street was only a few minutes from his office, so he decided to walk over and then come back for the buggy and head home. With Sarge at his side, he took his time along the way, enjoying the peaceful sights and smells of the approaching winter as he went.

Dusk was just settling over the town, but there was still enough light that he could see the stark tree branches, now mostly barren of their leaves, whipping against one another in the wind. From the porch of a brick, two-story home, a mother called her children inside, while a few houses down, two adolescent boys came at a run. They stopped long enough to pet Sarge, who stood at attention as if he were merely tolerating their fuss rather than soaking it up, as Daniel knew to be the case.

"You'll have to stay on the porch while I'm inside, you know," he told the dog as they climbed the front steps. "Something tells me Miss Gladys wouldn't take to the idea of having you traipse about her immaculate house with those dusty feet." The hound regarded him with an indignant stare, but when Daniel ordered him to stay, he plopped down at the end of the porch without protest.

Daniel knocked on the tall double doors twice, surprised when no one answered. He hesitated only a moment before going around to the back, thinking Miss Gladys might well be in the kitchen at this time of day, preparing her supper.

Unease stirred in him when he found the back door ajar and heard no reply when he called out. He couldn't quite reconcile the idea of Miss Gladys going into another part of the house with a door left open. Once more he knocked on the door frame, and then again. When there was still no response, he stepped inside the kitchen, looked around, and called her name.

No answer.

Too concerned now to feel like an intruder, he left the kitchen and started down the hall. After only a few steps, he saw a form sprawled at the bottom of the stairway.

"Miss Gladys!"

He hurried the rest of the way and dropped to his knees, taking the elderly spinster's hand. He was relieved to feel a strong pulse, but she still didn't respond when he said her name.

Fumbling in his medical bag, he found smelling salts and passed them carefully and briefly under the unconscious woman's nose. After a few seconds, she stirred, shaking her head slightly, and then she finally opened her eyes to look at Daniel with a bewildered expression.

"What…"

Daniel slipped an arm beneath her shoulders. "Easy, Miss Gladys. It seems you fainted."

She stared at him and then scowled. "I have never fainted in my life, young man," she muttered, her speech somewhat slurred.

With a twinge, he realized that for the first time since he'd met her, she looked her age—elderly and frail. Clothed in a simple housedress instead of the more formal attire she usually wore, and with her hair worked free of its usual elaborate style, she scarcely resembled her proper and perfectly groomed self.

"Nevertheless, I want to examine you thoroughly. I believe you did pass out," Daniel insisted. "Are you in pain at all?"

"Indeed not. I was hurrying down the stairs. I must have simply lost my balance and tripped. I'm quite all right now."

She tried to twist away, but he held on to her. "Give yourself a moment, and then I'll help you up." When she sank back with a sigh, he asked, "You said you were hurrying. Do you remember why?"

She sighed. "Of course, I remember. Someone was in the house."

Startled, Daniel repeated, "Someone was in the house?"

She reached to pat her hair but winced with the movement and quickly lowered her arm. "Yes, that's what I said. Now, I'd really like to get up. This is most uncomfortable. At least help me to the sofa."

It was Daniel's turn to sigh. "All right. But slowly."

With Daniel firmly supporting her, she managed to get up and make it into the living room—though with none of her usual grace. Once there, she resisted his attempt to help her lie down on the sofa, instead assuming her typical straight-backed position with her hands clasped neatly in her lap.

Daniel sat down beside her and reached for his case. "I'll just check your heart—"

She shook her head. "My heart is quite all right. I can assure you everything is all right. Don't take on."

He ignored her protests, and she finally relented and endured his examination, though with frequent long breaths as if to make sure he was aware of her growing impatience.

Only now did he glance around. For the first time he became aware of the somewhat altered appearance of the usually immaculate and pristine living room—the parlor, as Miss Gladys was wont to call it. Dust had collected on the lamp table nearby—not a great deal of dust, but still more than he had ever noticed on the furniture before. A few books hadn't been returned to their places on the bookcase, but were strewn on the floor, close to the fireplace, along with the contents of a bag of needlework.

Not nearly as untidy as a number of other homes he had visited, but certainly not typical of what he was accustomed to seeing in this home.

"Well, I can't see that the fall did any damage, but I expect you may be a bit sore for a few days," he finally said, closing his case. "In any event, I hope you'll be extra cautious for a time. And I want you to let me know if you experience any unusual symptoms." He paused. "By the way, any special reason you missed your last appointment?"

She gave him a blank look. "What appointment?"

"You were scheduled to come in a little over two weeks ago. Did you forget?"

She visibly bristled. "There is nothing wrong with my memory."

"No," he quickly said. "I'm sure there isn't. It's just that you seldom miss an appointment."

"I don't believe I have ever missed an appointment," she corrected him. "Including the one you're referring to. Audrey must have made a mistake on the book."

"Ah…Audrey retired, remember? You met my new assistant, Addie Rose, during your last office visit."

"Of course I remember. A very nice young lady. Much nicer, I don't mind telling you, than Audrey. Well, in any event, it really doesn't matter now, does it? You just gave me a thorough checkup and found me to be quite all right."

"That's true. But—"

"So it's almost as though I didn't miss an appointment."

Distracted now, Daniel merely gave a nod. His mind was

racing, his thoughts cluttered and disturbed. Something was very wrong, and his initial sense of where the problem might lie made him heartsick. Thoughts of Stephen's mother crowded in on him. He hadn't known the elderly widow before the dementia settled in, so as much as her condition saddened him, at least he hadn't watched her decline. But he did know Gladys Piper. He had always been impressed by her keen intellect and piercing perception, her self-confidence and the respect she perhaps unknowingly commanded.

He was more than a little worried that she might be in the initial stages of the same heartrending disorder Miss Ruth Ann suffered. He had come to admire and genuinely like this woman.

Carefully, he touched her hand. "I take your point, Miss Gladys, that this has been a kind of unscheduled examination. All the same, I'd like you to come into the office tomorrow, if you would, so we can talk more at length. I'd like to make quite certain you're still doing well."

She raised one delicate eyebrow. "Is that really quite necessary? I have a number of things planned for tomorrow."

"I won't keep you long. I promise."

She gave a deep sigh. "Very well. But I think you're being overly cautious."

Daniel gave her a smile. "You may be right. But humor me, won't you?"

She sighed again but finally tipped her head in agreement.

Relieved, he ventured his next question reluctantly—and with some measure of uncertainty. "Now, then, what did you mean when you said someone was in the house?"

The same quizzical look he'd seen earlier again crossed her features.

"You said you were hurrying down the steps because someone was in the house," he reminded her.

She frowned and then seemed to search her thoughts. "I said that?"

Again, an alarm went off in Daniel. "Why, yes. You did. And I'll admit I was concerned after finding the back door open." He paused. "That's how I got in when I arrived. Through the back door."

"I never leave my doors unlocked," she protested, her tone somewhat shrill.

Daniel tried to coax her back to the subject. "I'm sure you don't. Still, anyone can forget once in a while. But what made you think you had an intruder? Did you hear something?"

She blinked, but the worried look that had settled over her features a moment before remained intact. "I...must have." She lifted a hand in dismissal. "I can't think right now. I'm really very tired. I'm sure I'll remember all about it tomorrow when I come in."

Daniel's thoughts raced. "Why don't I just stop by before lunch?" he hurried to suggest. "That way you won't have to hitch up your buggy or come out in the cold. It's no trouble. I'm sure I'll have other calls to make as well."

To his surprise, she delayed only a moment before agreeing. "If you're sure you don't mind..."

"I don't mind at all," he said, getting to his feet.

He was reluctant to leave her alone, but there seemed to be no choice. "If you're quite sure you'll be all right now, I'd best be on my way." He paused. "If for any reason you'd need me before tomorrow—any reason at all—just have Sy Fordham next door come and get me."

She sniffed, and the familiar lift of the chin and acerbic tone he'd grown used to reappeared. "I could walk to your house before that old geezer could find his hat and coat. Besides, I am perfectly fine, and there's no reason I should need you before you stop by tomorrow."

Properly chastised, Daniel said his goodbyes and went to reclaim Sarge from his cold perch out front. In spite of the return of Miss Gladys's more prickly nature, however, he left with a heavy heart and no small measure of concern.

TWENTY-TWO

A New Idea

Her beauty filled like water the four corners of my being.
PATRICK MACDONOGH

*T*he next morning, Daniel wasted no time in describing to Addie Rose his visit with Miss Gladys.

He had spent most of the night awake with a gnawing unease about the woman, troubled as much about her future as what he suspected to be the present state of her mental health. And, admittedly, in the midst of his disquiet, he had found himself wanting to confide his concern and unease to Addie Rose.

Not only was she always an acute and attentive listener, but she could also be counted on for a sensitive and discerning response to his concerns about a patient. She seemed to have an uncanny ability to clarify his feelings and then to actually put into words the course of treatment he might want to consider for that patient.

Unlike Serena, whose attempts to show an interest in my work often fall flat, no matter how much I might appreciate her efforts...

There. He'd done it again. These erratic comparisons between

Addie Rose and Serena, unbidden though they were, never failed to rattle him, even irritate him. Addie Rose, after all, was his employee, perhaps even a friend, but Serena was—

Serena was what? The fact was that he had neither seen her nor heard from her for nearly two weeks, and after all this time he had to admit that this was just as much his fault as hers. He had known full well she'd be upset with him after his abrupt cancellation of her family's dinner invitation. But what else could he have done?

The Corcoran toddler had been in a bad way. Severe convulsions in such a young child could be deadly. How could he have lived with himself if he had put his personal plans before the treatment of a sick baby? He simply hadn't known what else to do other than cancel his plans with Serena, no matter how much her obvious anger had upset him.

"Daniel?"

He suddenly realized that his mind had wandered again, and he quickly turned his attention back to Addie Rose, who was watching him curiously.

"Didn't you tell Miss Gladys that you'd stop by this morning? Will you be going soon?"

"I plan to, yes. Would you like to go with me? The two of you seemed to hit it off really well when you first met."

"I enjoy her. And, yes, if it's all right with you, I'll go along."

"Of course, it's all right. Let's lock up and go right now. We have time before morning office hours."

Secretly glad for her company, Daniel had already started moving toward the coat closet, with Sarge leading the way.

~

Later that afternoon, between patients, he stood looking out the back window as he returned to the conversation they had begun on the way back to the office. "I thought Miss Gladys seemed a little better this morning."

Addie Rose paused and looked up from her desk, where she was sorting through charts. "But not normal," she said, stroking Sarge, who was lying close by her chair.

Daniel drew a long breath before turning back to her. "No. Not normal."

"You said she has no relatives."

"No one. There was a cousin, but I understand she died some time ago—before I moved here."

"How awful for her," Addie Rose said softly. "To be so alone."

Daniel made no reply. In truth, he sometimes caught *himself* feeling more alone than he would like, only to immediately feel shame for what even he could recognize as self-pity. After all, he had a thriving medical practice, as well as a number of good friends. Stephen and Esther Holliday. Sandy MacIver. Lawrence Hill. And he had family, though farther away than he'd like.

Even so, at times, if he wasn't careful to guard his thoughts, the pall of loneliness seemed to fall over him like a cold curtain of fog. In those moments he felt an aching sadness from being such a distance from those he cared about and those who also cared about him. At those times he had to forcibly drag himself back to the reality that was his life—and not such a bad life, at that, he quickly reminded himself.

Without warning, the afternoon sun burned through the window, catching him off guard with the sight of Addie Rose in profile. The light brushed her hair with golden arcs while accenting the blush of her skin. Daniel couldn't bring himself to look away but instead stood staring as if he'd never seen her before.

She is absolutely, incredibly beautiful. Not in a dramatic, stunning, or seductive way, but more with a quiet, winsome kind of loveliness that was all the more breathtaking for its unassuming grace.

She glanced up, and he forced himself to turn away.

"Daniel, do you think…"

But at that moment the bell over the door rang, announcing a patient's arrival. Addie Rose's voice died away, and Daniel sucked in his breath, relieved. Hopefully, she hadn't noticed his staring.

～

At the end of the day, Daniel had almost finished restocking his medical case before heading home when Addie Rose stepped into the supply room.

"Daniel, do you have a moment?"

"I do," he said, closing the clasp on the case.

"I've been thinking…"

She looked uncertain, even uneasy, and the worrisome thought flicked across his mind that perhaps she was about to resign. But why? He'd assumed that she was fairly well settled in by now, even happy with her job. Had he done something to bring this on?

Had she sensed his growing, if reluctant, attraction to her? A sick feeling washed over him. What if he had revealed even more of that attraction than he'd realized when she caught him watching her earlier in the afternoon? Good grief, was she repulsed by him?

Because of her uncommon maturity and serene nature, he tended to forget the years between them. But perhaps she was far more aware of—and sensitive to—the difference in their ages than he had ever been. He was her employer, after all, and unless he was badly mistaken, Addie Rose had been carefully sheltered and protected by her family—especially by her father.

He almost groaned aloud at his own thickheadedness. It wouldn't be the first time his feelings had got in the way of his common sense.

"I can tell you're really worried about Miss Gladys and wondering how to help her. I have an idea, but you might think I'm assuming too much. After all, she scarcely knows me, and for that matter, I have no idea how my family would react to what I'm thinking."

Daniel blinked. Confusion mixed with relief as he struggled to take in her words. Apparently, not only was his fear of losing her misplaced, but it wasn't even relevant to what she was saying.

"My feelings are mixed, of course," she went on, "but I've been wondering for some time now if I shouldn't consider making a break from my family to live on my own." She paused but then hurried on. "I love my parents—I couldn't ask for a better family, truly I couldn't—but the older I get the more difficult I'm finding it to live as the adult I am rather than as the child they still think I am. Da, especially. Honestly, in his eyes, I'm still twelve years old and need to be treated accordingly."

She stopped, her expression clearly one of frustration. "Maybe none of this makes any sense to you. From what you've told me, you've been on your own since you were a boy—"

Shaking his head, Daniel lifted a hand. "No, I hear you. And what you're saying makes perfect sense."

She drew in a steadying breath. "Well, what I'm trying to say is…do you think Miss Gladys would be interested in taking me in as a boarder? Thanks to my job, I could afford to pay her a reasonable rent—and it would mean that, at least in the evenings, there would be someone in the house to help her and look after her. And, I was thinking, as close to her home as the office is, I could even check on her during the day, perhaps go home for lunch. And it would mean Da wouldn't have to drive me in and pick me up every day, either. As it is, he has to wait nearly an hour after he gets off his shift until I'm ready to leave in the afternoon. So this would actually help him too—"

She stopped, drawing a deep breath. "If I can just make him see that. What do you think of the idea?"

Her words had spilled out in such an increasing rush that Daniel had the feeling she was trying to convince herself before talking with her dad. He had seen enough of the man to suspect that convincing him of anything other than what his mind was already set on might be a challenge, to put it lightly. And who would be more aware of that than his own daughter?

Although he couldn't help but agree with her logic, he thought it best to remain neutral for now. "It makes sense. And Miss Gladys obviously likes you a lot. But it's a big decision. How do you think your dad will feel about it?"

She attempted a smile that didn't quite work. "I expect he'll take some convincing."

Daniel thought that was probably an understatement, but he merely nodded. "Are you going to talk with him soon?"

She hesitated. "Probably. Otherwise, I'll lose my nerve. But not until I get my mother's opinion. She can usually predict Da's reaction to almost anything."

Still trying for a noncommittal tone, Daniel said, "That's probably a good idea."

She nodded and then glanced behind her. "Speaking of Da, he's probably out front by now. I'd better be going. Unless there's something else you need me to do first?"

Daniel shook his head. "We're finished for the day. I plan on being right behind you."

And that had indeed been his intention. At the time.

TWENTY-THREE

An Unexpected Invitation

If only there were more to offer her
than uncertainty and doubt.
ANONYMOUS

*D*aniel's surprise at finding Serena standing in the doorway when he started to leave propelled him into his old and awkward speechlessness.

In her fine rose-colored coat and feathered hat, she appeared her usual attractive and elegant self, but it wasn't so much her imposing appearance that stole his tongue as the awareness that she had actually sought him out after so long a period of absence—and most likely an abundant measure of annoyance with him.

"Well, I was hoping to come in from the cold," she said, glancing at the coat slung over his arm, "but you seem to be on your way out." Her tone was dry, her slightly amused expression familiar.

"Oh...no," Daniel managed, finally finding his voice. "I mean, I was about to leave, but I don't need to. I was just finished for the day and decided to head home. But there's no rush. Come in, come in!"

"You're sure?"

"Of course I'm sure. Come in." He stood back, waiting for her to enter.

Once she was inside, he took her coat. "It's good to see you." His words spilled out in a rush, betraying his surprise and a certain amount of uneasiness.

She stood watching him. "I kept thinking you might stop by the house or the school," she said, clearly expecting a response from him.

"I...wasn't sure you'd want me to."

"You mean because you stood me up." Again, the dry, somewhat amused tone.

"I certainly didn't intend it as any such thing, Serena. I just...I didn't feel I had a choice."

She breathed a long sigh. But then she smiled. "I know. You're a good doctor, Daniel. And a truly dedicated one. I suppose... there are simply times when I wish you'd take me as seriously as you do your profession."

He studied her. "I confess that most times I don't quite know how to take you."

She glanced away, and then she lifted a hand and seemed to study it. "I'm not sure I understand what you mean by that. I didn't come here to argue."

"Why did you come, Serena?" His own question surprised him, but in truth it had been niggling at him from the moment he'd seen her standing in the doorway.

She studied him. "I'm surprised you have to ask. Daniel... I was beginning to think we were serious about each other. As a couple."

Daniel was totally taken unawares. While at one time her

words might have pleased him no end, they now had the completely unexpected effect of irritating him—to the point that he didn't know how to reply.

"Have I been mistaken all this time?"

Her tone had taken on a note of bewilderment that sounded genuine, but he was still at a loss as to how to respond. Had he been the one who was mistaken? It seemed to him that almost from the time they'd begun seeing each other, she had deliberately kept him at arm's length, almost relegating him to the position of just another suitor—a good friend as well, perhaps, but to be treated lightly with no real commitment between them. Had he somehow misread her? Had he really been all that dense when it came to discerning her feelings?

"Daniel?" She stepped closer to him.

"No," he said. Yet even as he choked out the word, he felt confused, conflicted. And when she lifted her face in obvious expectancy, he still hesitated, his head swimming with the turmoil of mixed emotions.

Even when he kissed her, instead of the familiar chaos of emotions and the racing of his heart that usually struck him, he felt little but uncertainty and puzzlement.

When the kiss ended, she stepped back a little, watching him. "You're tired, aren't you?"

Unreasonably grateful for any excuse to avoid further scrutiny, Daniel nodded. "I suppose I am, yes." And suddenly, he was. "It's been hectic. A really busy time."

She continued to study him. "Who was that leaving when I pulled up? A patient?"

He frowned, but then realized she must have seen Addie Rose driving away with her father. "My new assistant."

"You have a new assistant? I didn't realize."

Feeling awkward all over again, Daniel fumbled to explain. "I hired her recently." He swallowed hard. "I had to have someone. After Audrey quit and I took on the additional patients from Owenduffy, I simply couldn't keep up." He stopped. "Especially with this recent outbreak of scarlet fever."

"You're too generous for your own good, Daniel. You simply don't have time to do everything you take on." She was still watching him closely. "That looked like a miner's wagon leaving as I came in."

"Yes. Addie Rose's father works in the mines. He picks her up after work in the afternoon."

"Your assistant is from Owenduffy?"

"That's right," he said carefully, knowing her feelings about the mining community.

She was silent for a moment, and then, "You found someone from Owenduffy with enough education to be your assistant? I'm surprised."

A touch of defensiveness rose up in him. "Not everyone in Owenduffy is illiterate, Serena. Addie Rose has a good education besides being extremely efficient in the sickroom. She's as competent as any nurse. In fact, she hopes to be a nurse eventually."

"Hmm. Ambitious. And she's very pretty as well."

He looked at her.

"I couldn't help but notice." She paused. "How old is she?"

"How old—" He shrugged. "She's in her early twenties."

She reached up to straighten his collar. "Should I be jealous?"

"Jealous?" Daniel hoped his voice didn't sound as strained as it felt. He cleared his throat. "I hardly think so."

"Good. Then I won't be," she said, tracing his chin with her finger.

This time she initiated the kiss. And this time his heart did race. So why, then, did the feeling make him uncomfortable and even leave him with a faint pang of guilt?

"Are you too tired to take me to supper?" she asked after a moment. "We could go to the inn. I know how you like Helen's chicken and dumplings."

Determined to escape the emotional uproar hammering him, Daniel quickly agreed. Perhaps spending an evening with a lovely woman—a woman who was surely much more than an infatuation, and who, for a surprising and what should be a highly welcome change, was initiating an actual date with him—would put an end to the confusion and foolishness that seemed to have possessed him of late.

"I am definitely," he said, emphasizing his words, "not so tired that I'd pass up an invitation like that."

TWENTY-FOUR

A Day of Trouble

The darkness thickened
Upon him creeping…
GEORGE WILLIAM RUSSELL (A.E.)

*D*aniel could have accepted one of a number of invitations for Thanksgiving dinner, including the one offered by Serena and her family, who were spending the day in Buckhannon at a combined gathering of relatives. By midweek, however, he had come to the reluctant realization that he was close to exhaustion and couldn't quite muster the interest or the energy needed for an out-of-town trip. Instead, he'd decided to take up the Hollidays' invitation and spend a relatively quiet day enjoying one of Esther's delicious meals and some time with the family and the new baby.

As it happened, when the day arrived, he enjoyed neither the quiet day he had hoped for nor the rest he so badly needed. A little after eleven on Thanksgiving morning, a loud and insistent knocking—immediately followed by a prolonged growl from Sarge—sent him rushing from his desk by the bedroom window to the front door. He shot up just suddenly enough to send a blast of pain arrowing down his back.

He couldn't have been more surprised to find a somber-faced Dominic Murphy standing there, his fist raised as if to knock again. "Sorry to bother you on a holiday, Doc," Murphy said, "but I'm afraid you're needed. I was sent to get you."

Daniel hushed Sarge and motioned Murphy inside. "What's happened?"

"There's been a death. You're needed to sign the certificate."

"I thought the mine was down for the day," Daniel said, puzzled.

"It's not a miner. It's a miner's wife."

Daniel stared at him. "A—who?"

"Cormac MacMahon's wife. Glenna." He paused. "Addie Rose mentioned that she'd been to your office not long ago."

The earlier pain now had lodged itself in Daniel's spine. "Glenna MacMahon?"

"Aye. She died sometime night before last, it seems."

"How? What happened?"

Murphy didn't reply right away but simply stood twisting his cap and watching Daniel. "A bad fall, according to her husband. He said she fell down the steps."

Murphy's words might have been echoing from the wind, for all the concentration Daniel could muster. He couldn't seem to get past the pain in his back or his last memory of Glenna Mac-Mahon. Her furtive look, the almost palpable fear that had emanated from her, and then her rush to get away, as if she'd made a terrible mistake in even coming to his office.

He felt he should have done something after seeing her. He should have acted on the suspicion and doubt that had lurked in a dark corner of his mind, prodding him to follow up, to do something, especially after Addie Rose told him there had been rumors about abuse.

But just what was he to do? Even Addie Rose, who knew the mining community—knew its people far better than he—had indicated there was nothing more he could have done. And yet— he could have gone to the authorities, couldn't he? In the busyness and overwork, had he simply pushed all thought of the woman out of his mind?

"Are you all right, Doc? You're that pale all of a sudden."

Murphy's voice broke through the cold weight on Daniel's chest.

He managed to nod. "I…yes. I'm all right."

"I can give you a ride over, if you want," Murphy said, still studying him with a curious look. "And bring you back."

Daniel took a deep breath and, finding his voice, replied, "No, thanks. You don't need to do that. I'll drive myself over."

But then he remembered his commitment for Thanksgiving dinner with the Hollidays. "It will be awhile, though. I'll need to make a stop first."

Murphy nodded. "All right, then, if you're sure. I'll just head on back."

"Where is she? Where do I go?"

"Oh, right," Murphy said. "She's laid out at home. Will be until sometime tomorrow. MacMahon's place is just five houses up from ours. Same side of the road." He paused. "You'll find it easy enough. There's a swing with a broken chain on the porch." He touched his cap and then turned to leave.

Daniel stood in the open doorway, mindless of the bitter wind as he watched Murphy drive away. Finally, he closed the door and walked back to the bedroom, Sarge at his side.

The chair at the desk creaked as he sank into it. He propped his elbows on the desk top, cupping his head with his hands, swallowing against the dryness of his mouth. Other than the pain that still burned in his back, he felt numb. Sarge pushed his head against his side, his usual way of attempting to comfort. At the moment, however, Daniel could find no comfort in the big dog's effort to help.

What kind of a doctor had he become? In his obsession to heal everyone who came to him, to be all things to all people, had he neglected—ignored—the oath he had taken as a young and admittedly idealistic physician when he first embarked upon the career he had dreamed of since childhood?

Even though Addie Rose had indicated there was nothing he could have done to help Glenna MacMahon other than to treat her injuries, at the very least he could have followed up on the woman, couldn't he? He'd been more than a little disturbed at the time by her suspicious cuts and bruises. How had he managed to dismiss the questions and concern her condition had triggered without at least checking on her sometime later?

Self-disgust washed over him like a slow flood. He sat there for several minutes, making no attempt to rationalize the guilt rising in him, battering him with accusation and reproach.

Finally he got up and began a sluggish walk about the house, gathering his things to leave. Sarge followed him, occasionally sniffing and pushing at him, but although mindful of his efforts, Daniel left the house alone, simply giving the dog an idle pat before telling him to stay as he locked the door.

∼

The drive to Owenduffy seemed endless. Daniel was already wishing he'd brought Sarge along for company. Alone as he was, he had too much time to think: unpleasant thoughts about his preoccupation, his patient load, and what he considered his inexcusable neglect to follow up with Glenna MacMahon.

So absorbed in his own self-reproach was he that he felt more dazed than alarmed when the first jarring blast of the mine whistle split the air. He drew the buggy to a sudden stop, his breath coming in hard, erratic spurts as his head began to clear.

The whistle continued to shriek. The sound wasn't foreign to him. There had been a few other incidents—minor ones, thankfully—and so he'd become familiar with the din. But before today he'd never been actively involved with any badly injured miners or frightened family members. Today, though, might prove to be entirely different.

Never before had he heard the whistle sound on a declared holiday. He knew it wasn't normal. And he knew it couldn't be good.

He took up his drive toward Owenduffy again, this time at a much faster speed and with a real fear churning in him. While accidents and disasters might almost seem a way of life to those outside the coal community, he'd learned enough to know that any occurrence that departed from the norm usually meant bad trouble. Surely whenever the mine whistle sounded at an off-hour, the families of Owenduffy held a collective breath, and he now found himself doing the same.

He had learned that the miners and their loved ones were strong folk, most with a solid faith and a resilience that seldom seemed to wear thin. Some might credit them with being hard, but Daniel was more inclined to think that their trials had taught them an acceptance of life as it was, combined with the ability to keep going, no matter how difficult their struggles might be.

At the moment he felt a chilling doubt about his ability to handle whatever the emergency at hand might turn out to be. But at the same time, he prayed earnestly for the stamina, the capability, and all the expertise his profession afforded him to heal and to help those affected by whatever calamity waited ahead.

There was no telling what this day might require of him. He could only pray God would make him equal to the task.

Meanwhile, the mine whistle went on screaming.

TWENTY-FIVE

AT THE MINE

The hardest thing is to wait in vain.
ANONYMOUS

By the time Daniel reached the mine, a crowd had gathered as close to the pithead as they could get. Many of the men were elderly, their caps pulled low as they talked among themselves in quiet voices. Some of the women fingered rosary beads as they kept small children in tow. Others held babies while mouthing prayers with their eyes closed. Almost every face was a mask of tension or raw fear.

Small wonder, Daniel thought. The area was a scene of unbelievable destruction. A huge chunk of earth from the side of the mountain next to the mine had been blown free by the power of an explosion. Heavy fans and cables had obviously been hurled through the air, along with untold numbers of buckets and bricks and gratings. Timbers had been torn loose and hurled outside, while railroad cars carrying coal had gone crashing into each other, splintering the mine's walls.

Smoke was everywhere. Thick and black, it poured from the

portal and settled over the entire area, burning the eyes and throats of those who stood waiting, while thick coal dust coated the very air they breathed. Hacking coughs were among the sounds that broke the silence hanging over those who watched and waited.

What a grace, Daniel thought, *that no miners were working today.* He couldn't imagine how many lives might have been saved because of the holiday.

On the heels of that thankful thought his glance landed on the mound of miners' tags that lay scattered several feet outside the portal—

He caught his breath, his heart pounding in his ears.

If the mine was down, why are the men's tags strewn about as if they'd been blown free from the board just inside the entrance—the tags of workers gone below?

Impatient for information now, he scanned the swelling crowd. His gaze landed on Dominic Murphy and then, standing nearby talking with a woman he didn't recognize, Addie Rose. Dominic's face was a dark scowl as he stood listening to Hugh Gormant, the mine super. Addie Rose appeared pale and drawn.

He threaded his way through the crowd of bystanders, nodding to Addie Rose but not stopping until he reached Dominic and the mine boss. "What happened?" he asked, his concern and impatience making his tone sharper than he'd intended.

Gormant shot him an irritated look. "Good you're here. No doubt you'll be needed."

"What's going on?" Daniel pressed. "I thought the mine was down for the day."

"It was supposed to be." Murphy's quick reply was more a snarl.

"We had a small work crew on," Gormant said. "Just a few men who volunteered."

Murphy's contemptuous expression told Daniel just how likely it was that the crew had been made up of volunteers.

"A work crew on Thanksgiving Day?" Daniel made no attempt to conceal his own skepticism. "How many?"

Gormant merely shrugged. "Seventeen men. They were up for making some extra money. There's always work to be done at a mine for those who are willing."

"So where are they? Not still below?"

"They are," Murphy said. "A cage has gone down with a couple of men to check on those working, but no one's come up yet."

At that point, Gormant walked away. Murphy exchanged a look with Daniel, and there was no mistaking the mix of worry and anger in his eyes. "To answer your question," he added, "all we know so far is that there was an explosion."

Daniel stared at him. "Do we know where? Which vein?"

Murphy ran a hand through his hair. "Nobody seems to know much, except the thinking is that it happened in the second vein." He stopped. "And as you can see, there's a great deal of smoke."

Daniel nodded. His own eyes and throat were burning from the dark black smoke thickening the air. He dug in his pocket for a handkerchief to cover his mouth as best he could.

"It's taking too long for someone to come up," Murphy said, his worried look just as noticeable in his tone of voice. "There should have been some word by now. You'd best stick around. I'm afraid we're in for a bad time of it."

"I'm not going anywhere," Daniel said.

"When we had the cave-in a few years past, the doc wouldn't go down," Murphy said, watching Daniel closely. "Said that being the only doctor in the area, he could scarcely afford to put himself at risk."

Still speaking through the handkerchief, Daniel replied, "I'll go down as soon as they'll let me." And he would, though the thought admittedly chilled him.

Murphy gave a slow nod of his head and a small, peculiar smile. "Don't be in too much of a rush. Best to find out what we can first." He looked around. "I'm going to go talk to a couple of fellows who may know more than I do. Stay close by."

Shortly after he walked away, Addie Rose came up to Daniel. "How did you get here so quickly?"

"Actually, I was almost here when I heard the explosion. I was coming to sign the MacMahon woman's death certificate. Your dad came after me." He paused. "Bad business, what happened to her."

She nodded, saying nothing for a moment. "It was strange, to say the least." Again she paused. "There's been talk. Or at least there was until this explosion happened."

"How do you mean, strange?"

She looked at him. "Well, for one thing, what was she doing outside at that time of night? In this cold?"

"That time of night? What time was it?"

"After midnight, according to her husband."

Daniel frowned. "I thought miners and their families went to bed a lot earlier than that."

"They do," said Addie Rose, her voice so quiet Daniel could scarcely hear her words.

It took Daniel a moment to respond. "So then, did her husband give any explanation for why she was up late? And outside, at that?"

He could see her mouth tighten as she glanced away. "According to one of the neighbors, her husband said that she…she often had trouble sleeping and would sometimes go outside to get some fresh air."

"That doesn't—" Daniel stopped, not finishing his thought that the husband's explanation made no sense. What woman would go out into the night so late in this kind of weather?

Unless she was trying to escape the house for some reason…

He had all he could do not to blurt out his feelings of anger and self-disgust for not following up on Glenna MacMahon after she visited his office. As it happened, he needn't have restrained himself. Not for the first time, Addie Rose seemed to read his thoughts.

"It bothers you that Glenna never came back to the office, doesn't it?"

He didn't know whether to feel relieved or awkward that, once again, she had arrowed right to the heart of his feelings. "I should have attempted to contact her. There's such a thing as being too busy—" He broke off.

She studied him, long enough that Daniel began to feel uncomfortable. At least until she finally spoke.

"Daniel." He was surprised, because she almost never used his name. She usually called him simply "Doctor." "Glenna most likely didn't come back because her husband found out that she had already come once before. If you had tried to contact her, you might well have made things worse for her."

"Do you really think so?"

She took a long breath. "Based on everything I've ever heard about the man, I do."

Daniel looked around. "I plan to talk with him before I sign the death certificate. Is he here, do you know?"

She blinked, and then she said slowly, "He's one of the men

who was working below." She paused before adding, "I've heard it said that Cormac MacMahon is always up front for making an extra wage."

A chill tracked Daniel's spine. Before he could stop the thought, he wondered now if they would ever know the truth about Glenna MacMahon's death. If her husband didn't make it out of the mine—

When he realized the assumption he was making, he felt ill and did his best to banish the thought.

"Are you all right?

Still shaken, he looked at Addie Rose as if she might have somehow sensed where his mind had gone. He struggled to catch his breath, but in that moment was spared the need to respond to her questioning look.

Someone standing close to the pithead shouted, "The cage is coming up!"

Daniel was tall enough to see over most of the crowd in front of him and close enough to hear the shout of one of the bystanders.

"No one's with them! The cage is empty except for Rooney and O'Grady!"

Daniel turned, his eyes locking with Addie Rose's stricken gaze.

TWENTY-SIX

TIME OF DESPAIR

Remembrance wakes with all her busy train...
and turns the past to pain.
OLIVER GOLDSMITH

*T*he hush that had fallen on the waiting crowd now shattered into a burgeoning swell of low cries and murmurs. More women had begun weeping with the others, while the men's voices rose in volume and intensity.

Daniel saw Dominic glance their way but then quickly turn back to Judson Gormant. Their discussion appeared to be agitated, even angry.

"Da looks as if he'd best get away from Mr. Gormant before he loses his temper," Addie Rose said, her tone worried.

"I'm waiting for Gormant to give me the word to go below," Daniel told her. "I hope he doesn't wait much longer."

She turned to him. "Oh, Daniel, no!" As if surprised by her own outburst, she touched her hand to her mouth. "It can't be safe," she said, lowering her voice. "It must be bad, with no one coming up yet."

"That's why I'm going down. Those men are going to need medical attention as soon as possible. I'm not doing anyone any good by standing around up here waiting for news."

The look of fear that cut across her face surprised him. He had to force himself not to make too much of it.

"It's too dangerous—"

"I'm sure someone who knows the way around down there will go with me."

"Yes, but—"

"I have to go, Addie Rose."

She remained silent for another moment before surprising him again by putting a hand to his arm. "You'll…be careful?"

He hesitated only briefly before giving her hand a quick squeeze. "Of course. And Addie Rose?"

Her eyes were locked on his face.

"We're likely going to be here a long time tonight. If Dominic stays, I'll make sure someone takes you home."

Something flared in her eyes. "No. I'm staying. You're going to need help."

Daniel studied her. She was probably right. By now she'd had a great deal of nursing experience and seen much that wasn't easy to take in. Even so, he was reluctant for her to witness some of the horrors he had heard could accompany a mine explosion.

"I'm staying," she said again, and there was no mistaking the resolve in her tone.

"All right. I'm going to have young Ted Carpenter bring around the buggy. If you will, go back to the office with him and gather supplies. We'll need to get together whatever we can locally and also put out a request for more help from some nearby areas. In the meantime, I'm going to stay close to Gormant and your dad so I can keep up with any news they get."

216 ～⌐ BJ HOFF

After taking her to the Carpenter lad and quickly going over a list of items they were certain to need, Daniel made his way back to the pithead to continue waiting.

～⌐

No formally trained rescue teams existed at the Owenduffy mine, only volunteers made up from among the local mine workers themselves, including a couple of foremen and fire bosses, as well as a few recently retired men. In what was considered a relatively small and unimportant mine, at least among much of the coal hierarchy, protective and necessary rescue equipment was almost entirely lacking.

Although few were experienced in rescue work—some teams were quickly formed on location for the first time—none were ignorant of the dangers they faced by entering a mine where an explosion had already occurred. Even so, they didn't hesitate to step up for the harrowing rescue search.

When the first few rescue workers came out of the mine, they brought news of two of the most common hazards that could be expected in a major explosion: toxic gasses and impact injuries. One member of the rescue crew, Stan Poleski, had endured less than five minutes of exposure to the poisonous air. He appeared weak to the point of collapse, and the other two men with him weren't in much better condition.

In addition to igniting a new wave of fear and dread—no survivors accompanied them—their preliminary report put an end to any hope Daniel had of going below to administer treatment. Judson Gormant told him that under no circumstances was he to go down into the mine.

"We need you right here," Gormant told him, his tone flat and unyielding. "You saw the shape Poleski and the others are in. Don't you even think of going below. When we start bringing survivors up, we're going to need you and any other doctor we can bring in here to be standing by. We can't take a chance on something happening to you."

Daniel didn't like it, but he grudgingly admitted to himself that Gormant was probably right. For the time being, at least, he would wait above ground.

~

They brought up the injured first, and Daniel was alarmed to see how few, at least in the beginning, had survived. Still, in spite of the small numbers arriving with each trip of the cage, he had his hands full, caring for the various injuries and doing his utmost to resuscitate those who were uninjured but overcome with smoke or black damp, the mix of nitrogen and carbon dioxide that could easily turn hazardous in large enough amounts.

Once Addie Rose and Ted Carpenter returned with the supplies Daniel had requested, he set the boy to helping some of the men clear the mine entrance of the debris from the explosion. He motioned Addie Rose to work alongside him, at the same time sending her back and forth to treat minor injuries on her own under his instructions.

Daniel was relieved, though not actually surprised, to see that even the horrific and shocking wounds didn't repel her, though there was no missing the compassion behind even her more strenuous efforts. When he did his best to stop the flow of blood from young Caleb Riley's injured arm, muttering to himself that he hoped the boy lived long enough to reach the hospital where the limb would doubtless require amputation, he noted only the slightest pause in Addie Rose's movement as she handed him another bandage. But the glaze of tears in her eyes was all too evident.

"Tell me if you need a break," he cautioned her. "I know this isn't easy."

"I'm all right," she said, wiping a none-too-steady arm across her eyes. "I just wish we could do more."

Daniel knew he was showing his own frustration when he replied, but he was too tired to mask his feelings. "We just don't have enough equipment or the right facilities. I can't do what needs to be done in all this dust and smoke and given the lack of supplies."

She lifted her head and glanced across the unconscious Riley boy. "You're saving lives, even in the worst of conditions, Daniel. Don't expect the impossible of yourself."

Surprised by the firmness of her tone, he bit back his thought that if he'd expected more from himself with the MacMahon woman, she might still be alive. He wanted to take Addie Rose's words to heart, but ever since he'd learned of Glenna's strange death, he couldn't stop questioning himself and wondering whether he could have somehow prevented that tragedy.

"Doc! We need you over here! It's Tom O'Donnell!"

Daniel was jerked out of his troubled thoughts by Davey McNamara, a young newcomer to the area and one of the workers who hadn't gone below today. By the time Daniel reached the still form of Tom O'Donnell, he sensed he was too late. Sure enough, his closer examination confirmed that O'Donnell's injuries had already claimed the middle-aged miner's life.

Shaken, for the deceased O'Donnell was a former patient and a member of his church, Daniel had to walk away from the scene and try to come to terms with the loss of the man as well as the other horrific events of the day.

Addie Rose followed him. "You knew him well?" she questioned quietly.

Daniel nodded. "Yes. He was a good man." His gaze went over the nightmarish scene only a few feet away. The stretchers where lifeless forms still lay exposed to the cold wind, awaiting removal. The wounded, moaning in pain as they begged for relief or care or, in some cases, a simple drink of water. And the families. Loved ones who stood nearby, staring in silent shock or wailing in grief.

He was thankful for the other two doctors who had been brought in from nearby communities and now worked with studied efficiency, their faces lined with concentration and, at times, frustration. A number of women worked alongside them, makeshift nurses who before today had never been exposed to even minimal wounds, much less the brutal, often sickening injuries of today's disaster.

"We've lost a number of good men this day," he murmured, more to himself.

Addie Rose's touch on his sleeve was tenuous, her tone of voice gentle when she replied. "But we would have lost even more if it hadn't been for you."

He looked at her. "It's never enough."

She frowned. "What do you mean?"

Daniel took a long breath and looked away. "In a situation like this, you learn just how inadequate you really are. You can never do enough."

For a moment, a memory he'd thought long buried rose up

in him, shaking him with almost painful clarity. The memory of another field where he—along with other doctors—scrambled to tend to countless wounded and dying soldiers. A field where pain-racked men and boys lay strewn like so much debris, brought down by the senseless destruction of war. A war between brothers and even fathers and sons. A war that to this day caused survivors to agonize over its final resolution.

But at least that destruction had given birth to something of value: the gift of freedom for an entire people. But by any stretch of the imagination, today's disaster held nothing but meaningless tragedy.

"Daniel—"

Addie Rose's voice brought him up short and called him back to the present. "We should go back."

He nodded and, taking her arm, started walking.

∽

Long after sunset, Daniel came upon the lifeless form of one of the last few explosion victims. Cormac MacMahon. So minimal was the outer damage of MacMahon's body that at first Daniel found it hard to believe the man was gone. He searched desperately for some sign of life he might have missed in his quick initial examination. But there was no mistaking the bleak reality of MacMahon's death.

With trembling hands, Daniel covered the body of the deceased. In spite of his suspicions about MacMahon, he felt a burden of regret and even sadness for the man's death, but even more, however, for that of his wife. Especially given his own personal remorse that he hadn't done more for Glenna. Whether it would have made any difference for her or not, only God knew.

But Daniel knew that at least it would have made a difference in him. As it was, he would carry a leaden measure of guilt in his heart for a long, long time.

If only... What a nagging burden those two words could bring to bear.

For several moments—until Addie Rose came in search of him—he stayed on his knees in the dirt, praying for Cormac and Glenna MacMahon, and then seeking his Savior's forgiveness... and the grace to forgive himself.

TWENTY-SEVEN

QUESTIONS

If one does not question, nothing will change.
ANONYMOUS

he days following the mine disaster seemed long and leaden. Daniel had all he could do not to give in to the weariness and depression that threatened to weigh him down. But in addition to the numerous funerals he attended, he still had office hours and patient calls to keep up with, so he did his best to maintain a schedule, and a rigorous one at that.

Thanks to Addie Rose—and he was increasingly thankful for her—his office continued to run as smoothly as ever. These days she accompanied him on patient calls more often than not, and her sense of order and serene assistance kept him from lagging behind on these as well.

But there was one element to his days that not even Addie Rose could alleviate: his anger. Anger at the greed and the callousness of the mine owners and bosses, including Judson Gormant, who had sent the men down below, away from their families, with only a minimum crew of workers and virtually no backups to scout and maintain safe working conditions. Never mind that the miners had volunteered. They'd done so because they needed the work. They did it for the money, and possibly even because they hoped to win a bit of favor with the company that employed them.

As if the company was even aware of their needs or their hopes.

If it ever occurred to Daniel that at least a part of the anger churning in him might also be related to his feelings of failure regarding Glenna MacMahon, most of the time he managed to block the thought. Or at least harbor it in the recesses of his mind.

In what little free time he managed to eke out, he had already begun to quiz Dominic and one of the other foremen about any hazardous conditions in the mine. At first the two men seemed reluctant to confide what they knew. Dominic had even gone so far as to issue a warning. "You go asking too many questions and the company finds out, you might just bring a piece of trouble down on yourself. I'd be careful who you talk to if I were you."

"You told me yourself there were more than a few hazards down below," Daniel reminded him.

"That I did, but I didn't mean you should be taking what I told you anywhere else."

"Don't worry. I'm not mentioning what I've heard or where I heard it. Just asking some questions, is all."

Dominic shot him a piercing look. "And what would you be planning to do with what you hear?"

"Maybe nothing. It depends on what I learn. But knowing the mine isn't safe makes me wonder if there might not be a way to bring about some improvements."

Dominic's glare darkened. "Listen to me, boyo. You'd do well to remember that there's no such thing as a safe coal mine. Any man among us who goes below knows only too well he might not be coming up again. That's the chance we take. It goes with the job."

"But surely there are some safety measures that could be put into effect?"

"You're thinking we haven't tried to make our jobs as safe as possible? The bosses have been approached time and again, but to push too hard means risking your job. Not a one of us can afford that."

"All the more reason it would be better for someone who's not a miner to bring certain safety issues to their attention." Daniel paused. "Someone like me."

Dominic crossed his arms over his chest and studied him.

"That might be or might not be. But as I said, I'd be careful who I talk to."

"Advice taken."

Saturday afternoon, as he reread the letter he'd just written to the company office, Daniel again thought about Dominic's warning and wondered anew what the miner might have been hinting at. His demeanor had been curiously uneasy, his tone even troubled when he'd issued his caution to Daniel. Yet he had stopped short of asking him to keep his silence.

What had been behind his peculiar warning?

Did it really matter? Daniel was determined to find some way to improve the safety conditions in the mine for those men whose backbreaking work supported their families and the community of Owenduffy. Bleak as the locale might be, it was home for numerous families, many of whom had left the countries of their birth in search of a better life for themselves and their loved ones.

At the very least, they deserved a safe working environment—one that could only be provided by their employers.

If he raised a few hackles in the process of improving the miners' conditions, so be it. Something needed to be done to help these hardworking men who risked their lives every time they went to their jobs. He had meant what he said to Dominic. It might be best if someone who wasn't a miner were to raise the safety issues instead of one of the miners, whose job might be threatened by what could be viewed as interference or even agitation.

After all, it wouldn't be the first time an Irishman stuck his finger in a stew not of his own making. The worst that could happen would be a bit of a burn.

Unless, of course, the stew boiled over.

～～

That afternoon, he hung the "Closed" sign on his office door and walked over to Miss Gladys's house. This was moving day for Addie Rose, and he intended to help however he could.

To his surprise, she had indicated that her parents, although understandably concerned at first, had finally accepted her determination to move in with the ailing spinster. As expected, Dominic had given her a hard time in the beginning, but apparently he seemed to be taking her decision in stride. At least, Addie Rose had confided, her father had ceased lecturing her about the "foolishness" of her latest move toward independence.

She was candid in admitting that she suspected her father's change in attitude was most likely due to the influence of her mother. "Mum accepted the reality that I'm no longer a child some time ago. I'm guessing that she managed to convince Da of that fact as well."

For his part, Daniel was exceedingly grateful that Miss Gladys had accepted the idea of a companion as easily as she had. He had feared that she might fight the idea, but ever since the day he'd found her passed out on the floor, badly shaken and disoriented, she had seemed much more open to his suggestions and advice.

In truth, that actually bothered him a little, this change in behavior from the determined and independent soul she had once displayed to the almost childlike demeanor she exhibited these days. Naturally, he was careful to suggest only what he sincerely believed would be in her best interests, but at times her easy acceptance still caught him off guard, and he actually missed the more feisty Miss Gladys he'd grown accustomed to.

He was pleased, though, to see that she clearly welcomed Addie Rose's arrival. She had already insisted that her new companion take advantage of the comfortably furnished, attractive bedroom across the hall from her own. Moreover, while Daniel and Addie Rose carried in and arranged her few wardrobe items and personal effects, Miss Gladys hovered nearby, occasionally offering a crocheted piece or a small decorative item "just to add a touch of color to things."

In fact, by the time they carried in the last of Addie Rose's belongings, Daniel was relieved to see that both she and Miss Gladys were clearly satisfied with their new situation. He found himself enjoying their obvious satisfaction, almost to the point that when the work was finished he felt reluctant to leave.

But when he did leave, his reluctance in no way diminished the sense of relief that accompanied him, relief that Miss Gladys would no longer be alone all the time but would now have someone in the house with her, at least in the evenings and at night. He had already learned that dusk and darkness definitely increased her disorientation, and attacks of fear seemed to strike her more often lately. Addie Rose's presence might not mean an end to those attacks, but just the presence of another person would surely help to comfort her.

As he rode home, he wondered, somewhat whimsically, if there was any situation at all that Addie Rose couldn't improve simply by being present.

The thought brought a smile, quickly followed by the somewhat discomfiting awareness of the difference her presence had made in his situation.

More to the point, the difference she had made in his life.

But what about Serena?

Indeed. What about Serena? He had neither seen nor heard from her lately. Not that it should be entirely up to Serena to get in touch. Admittedly, he should have made some gesture toward her, some effort to ease the awkwardness that seemed to hover between them these days. But if he were to be entirely truthful with himself, hadn't he purposely delayed making contact with her, uncertain as to how to go about it or how he would be received?

Or to be even more honest, did he even want to go about it?

The sudden unbidden question startled him, and he immediately tried to rationalize it, reluctant to examine it too closely. Of course he wanted to set things right with Serena. He hated this uncomfortable distance that had settled between them. After all, he was in love with her, wasn't he?

Another question he was unwilling to examine too closely.

TWENTY-EIGHT

An Unpleasant Surprise

The grey, chill day
Slips away with a frown.
JAMES STEPHENS

Daniel had never made a practice of having his evening meal at Helen's Mountain Inn. He usually indulged himself with a hefty enough lunch that by evening a light snack satisfied him just fine. Today, however, he had actually skipped lunch because of a late morning with patients, followed by an even busier afternoon.

Now that his day was finally coming to a close, he sat alone at a small table by the wall at Helen's, taking his time with the meal while making some notes on Molly Frazier, his last patient of the day. A young mother of eighteen years, she had come to the office with her infant son in hopes of getting some medication for herself after describing a series of ongoing sick headaches.

At first Daniel had suspected the fatigue and tension that could sometimes accompany the first few weeks of motherhood.

After examining her and talking with her, however, her symptoms had begun to puzzle him.

As he sat reading through his notes, something occurred to him that he hadn't grasped during the examination. He almost groaned aloud when he realized what he'd missed. While he had been looking for something more serious, the fact was that every symptom pointed to the fact that Molly Frazier needed eyeglasses!

He determined to call on her as soon as possible—hopefully tomorrow—and let her know that an eye examination would most likely confirm what he now suspected. In the meantime, he reminded himself that too often he caught himself fretting about the worst-case scenario for a patient when sometimes a simple answer was right in front of him. He couldn't help but wonder if other physicians erred in this manner on occasion.

He drew in a deep breath and passed a hand over his face, keenly feeling the weariness and fatigue of what had been a long, strenuous day. It didn't help that the headache with which he'd begun the morning seemed to have settled in place again for the evening.

Glancing around, his gaze froze on a table at the far end of the room. It took a moment for the identity of the four occupants to register, but there was no mistaking the profile of Addie Rose. Seated across from her was an attractive young girl with the same rich, fiery shade of hair and a strong resemblance to Addie Rose. In the chair beside the girl—who looked too much like Addie Rose not to be her younger sister—was Clay Holliday, Stephen and Esther's son, while at Addie Rose's side sat a nice-looking fellow with broad shoulders, a strong profile, and a thick shock of dark hair.

Daniel couldn't help but stare. Addie Rose was laughing at something the unknown man at her side had said while shaking her head as if in good-natured protest.

Daniel's throat locked, and he struggled to get a breath, but he couldn't seem to look away. Shaken, he gripped the hem of the tablecloth to steady his hand.

He was vaguely aware that it was unreasonable for him to have assumed there was no man in Addie Rose's life. Why wouldn't there be? She was young, exceedingly lovely, and no doubt would catch the interest of any number of potential suitors. It was altogether understandable that she would be romantically involved with someone. Why would he have expected anything else?

And why is that bothering me so much?

He had absolutely no business entertaining any thoughts about her personal life.

Addie Rose was his employee, nothing more. She had every right and reason to be involved with someone special.

Even if that weren't the case, there was no excuse for the angst now grating at him. After all, he had his own romantic interest, didn't he? There was no denying the fact that he spent an inordinate amount of time considering the prospect of marrying Serena.

At least there was a time when I considered it....

It occurred to him now with a stab of conscience that he couldn't actually remember the last time his thoughts had taken that turn. He'd made no attempt to see Serena since they'd had dinner together a number of evenings ago. And—more to the point—he had scarcely thought of her since then.

In truth, however, he could not make the same claim about Addie Rose.

Almost reluctantly, he turned his gaze back to her. Not for

the first time, he noticed that her hair was streaked with a sheen of its own that had nothing to do with the evening light filtering in through the windows or the candle glow wafting from the table. It was as if the sun had polished it earlier in the day, and it still retained its radiance. Her profile was delicate, yet precise and even strong. He knew well the lines of her slim shoulders, having often seen her bend to comfort a frightened child or share her own strength with an elderly grandmother in pain.

And there was no denying that more than once he had been tempted to clasp those graceful shoulders when he sensed her empathy and her longing to help a suffering patient.

Shaken, he forced himself to look away. Then, without finishing his meal, he scraped his chair back from the table and quickly crossed the room.

～

Addie Rose saw Daniel fumbling to pay his bill and then hurriedly push through the exit. Surprised that she hadn't seen him earlier, she wondered why he hadn't at least come over to their table to say hello. Perhaps he simply hadn't seen them. If he had, surely he would have stopped by. Not only to say hello to her, but as a close friend of Stephen Holliday, no doubt he also knew Clay well.

She tried to ignore the disappointment that settled in as she watched him leave. Her sister Elly nudged her just then and said her name in a low voice.

"I'm sorry?" she said, feeling her face heat.

"I asked you if that chocolate pie is as good as it looks. I think I might try some too."

"Oh. Yes, it's fine." The truth was that she had scarcely tasted the pie. Its flavor had died in her mouth as she watched Daniel leave the restaurant.

The others went on talking then, but Addie Rose found it almost impossible to concentrate. She couldn't seem to think about anything else but Daniel. Even at some distance, there had been no mistaking the fatigue lining his features or the uncommon pallor of his skin. For days now, he had seemed exhausted. Once she even ventured to suggest that he take a few hours off.

It had been no surprise when he'd simply smiled and shook his head, murmuring something about the ever-increasing patient list. If there ever was an example of a doctor being too dedicated, Daniel Kavanagh was surely it. More than once she had wondered if he ever got any real rest. She had the feeling that even after office hours—perhaps long after office hours—he continued to practice medicine, if only in his mind.

Addie Rose knew it wasn't her place to worry about him. He had certainly been a doctor long enough to know his own limitations. But she feared that knowing those limitations and heeding them didn't necessarily work together for Daniel. She sensed that he seldom thought about himself at all, much less gave any consideration to his own well-being. That being the case, there was clearly no good reason for her to spend her own energy doing so. And yet she couldn't seem to keep her thoughts off him for any length of time.

More than once she had asked herself why. And more than once she had failed to suppress an uncomfortable suspicion that her concern for her employer might be more than a reasonable interest in his well-being.

With an uneasy sigh, she forced herself to turn her attention back to the conversation taking place around the table. Even with a determined effort, she found it difficult to pick up the threads of what she'd missed and make an attempt at being part of the group.

But she had promised her dad to keep an eye on Elly and Clay, so she forced herself to focus and join in. At least her cousin Philip had a great sense of humor and kept them all laughing, so after a few minutes she managed to almost enjoy herself.

TWENTY-NINE

Darkness Falling

*The dark seems at its heaviest
when we're reaching for the light.*
ANONYMOUS

On Saturday afternoon Daniel headed out to the Hollidays'.

Esther had asked him to come and have a look at baby Anna.
Apparently, the new little one had been restless lately and not as
interested in eating as Esther would have liked.

He wasn't overly concerned about the baby because it wasn't all
that unusual for an infant's appetite to fluctuate early on, but he
understood Esther and Stephen's concern. Besides, he was eager
to spend some time with his friends. His hours had been so busy
of late that there had been precious little opportunity for a visit
with some of his favorite people, and the Hollidays were at the top
of that list. He only wished he wasn't feeling so tired and still har-
boring the same headache that had been plaguing him for three
days now. He actually felt almost dizzy from the fatigue and the
pain in his head.

Sarge roused him from his thoughts with a sharp bark, as if to remind him that they were nearing the Hollidays' farm. "Yes, I know we're almost there," Daniel said, slowing the buggy still more as they started down the lane. "You're just impatient for whatever treat Esther is saving for you."

Sarge gave another short woof of agreement as Daniel parked the wagon just outside the gate. By the time they reached the porch, Stephen was at the door, waiting with his usual vigorous handshake. It occurred to Daniel that nowhere else had he ever felt more welcome than at the Hollidays'.

Sarge was also made to feel at home here. After padding happily into the living room, he immediately dropped down beside the fireplace where an oversized log cheerfully burned.

"He'll be asleep by the time we leave the room," Daniel told Stephen.

"I don't know. Once he gets a whiff of that beef roast Esther has in the oven, he may take off for the kitchen."

Normally, Daniel's stomach would have begun to roar at the very thought of one of Esther's sumptuous meals, but for some reason today he felt nothing. He told himself that would probably change as soon as he reached the kitchen, where Stephen said they would find Esther.

"Is Anna asleep?" he asked Stephen on the way down the hall.

"She is. And if she takes her usual nap, we won't hear a sound out of her for another hour or so. She's a good little sleeper."

"Esther's been concerned about her, I know."

"Well, yes. But I think she just has the jitters because it's been so long since we've had a baby in the house. You'll check her over while you're here, though, won't you?"

"Of course. I'm looking forward to seeing her again."

Esther was just taking the roast out of the oven as they entered the kitchen. "It's about time you showed up in my kitchen, Daniel Kavanagh! I was beginning to think you'd forgotten where we lived."

"Nothing like that, Esther. And trust me, I haven't been absent because I wanted to be."

She set the roast on top of the stove and turned for a hug. The minute Daniel bent over, she reached to clasp both his shoulders, intently searching his face. "Oh, Daniel! You look so tired. And way too thin."

He grinned at her, enjoying her motherly attention. "I confess I am tired, Esther. But not too tired to tear into that good-looking roast you just took out of the oven. I'll most likely put on some extra pounds today."

"Good! Now you and Stephen pull up a chair and talk to me while I get everything else ready. Mother is visiting and having her dinner with the widows at the church today and won't be home until later. So we'll have an early meal without her. Hopefully, Anna will go on napping for a while until we're finished, and then I'll feed her."

"Why don't I help you carry everything out to the dining room table first, and then we can visit while we eat?" Stephen offered.

"I wouldn't mind. I've already set the table, so all we need to do is get the food on. Clay will be here, but a little later." She drew a long breath. "He was stopping by to see Elly first."

Daniel didn't miss the frown that creased Stephen's face, but his friend kept his silence as they carried what appeared to be enough food to feed an entire neighborhood into the other room. It bothered Daniel more than a little that by the time the various dishes were in place he still wasn't feeling hungry for Esther's impressive efforts. He had been so sure the very sight of the food would stoke his appetite.

In truth, he actually felt too tired to eat. He tried to concentrate on taking one bite after another and still join in the conversation around the table, but it was becoming more and more difficult to swallow, much less speak.

It didn't take Esther long to notice his condition and comment on it.

"Daniel, are you all right? You've hardly touched your food."

Strange. Her voice sounds as if it's coming from far away. And why does the sight of all the food on my plate seem little more than a blur?

The longer he sat there, his body began to feel extraordinarily heavy, as if weights were pulling down on his legs and arms. He looked at Esther, intent on answering her so she wouldn't think him rude. She had obviously worked most of the day on this meal, and he wouldn't hurt her feelings for anything. But the truth was, he could scarcely think or focus, much less eat, and to save him, he couldn't seem to form an answer to her question, certainly not one that might explain the inertia settling over him. He was beginning to feel as though he might collapse and fall into his food or even drop from his chair.

"Daniel! Oh, Stephen, he's passing out! Help him!"

He felt strong hands grasp him under the shoulders and then wrap him in a sturdy embrace. His face grew numb. He tried to speak but could form no words. The table seemed to move away from him. He felt as if he were being lifted, but that couldn't be. He was too big for anyone to lift. Unless Stephen—but why would Stephen be trying to lift him? And why was the room so dark? It was too early, and yet the night was definitely settling in. There was no light now, none at all…

There was nothing but darkness enfolding him, suffocating him. Nothing but darkness.

THIRTY

THE DOCTOR AS A PATIENT

Why is it effects are
greater than their causes?
OLIVER ST. JOHN GOGARTY

*V*oices. Nearby, whispering.

He heard a baby cry, then stop. Was he in his office? The exam room? He didn't think he could open his eyes. Somehow he knew it would hurt, so he tried to feel with his hands. He touched fabric, warm and smooth. Medicinal smells…so he was in his office, but something was weighing him down. His chest felt heavy. Everything about him felt heavy…his arms and legs, even his head.

"Daniel? Dr. Kavanagh? Can you hear me?"

He should know that voice. It was familiar, but his mind was numb, and it hurt. It was hard to think.

"Daniel, it's Ted. Ted Gardiner. Dr. Gardiner, from Clarksburg. Remember me? You helped me earlier this year with my surgery class at the University."

Ted Gardiner? Yes, of course, I remember him. A good doctor, and a good teacher too. But what is he doing here? His practice is in Clarksburg.

"Daniel? You need to try to wake up now. You've been sleeping for a long time."

But not long enough. He felt as though he could do with several more hours of sleep. So tired. He didn't think he had ever been so tired.

"Daniel."

A gentle touch on his shoulder. Why was Gardiner so insistent that he wake up? The man was a doctor, after all. Couldn't he tell that he needed more sleep?

"Daniel."

A different voice this time. Was that Esther? But why was she here? Was something wrong with the baby? He'd best get up and see.

"What's wrong, Esther?"

"Oh! Daniel! Thank heaven, you're awake!"

"Anna? Is it Anna? I'll have a look…"

A hand on his chest restrained him. "Whoa, Daniel—Dr. Kavanagh. I'm afraid you're not going anywhere just yet."

Ted Gardiner again. What in the world is going on?

Finally, Daniel managed to open his eyes, snapping them shut almost immediately against the light. But not before he caught a glimpse of Ted Gardiner leaning over him, while Esther and Stephen stood at the foot of the bed.

The bed! What in the world was he doing in bed? And at the Hollidays'. He struggled to sit up but immediately fell back. "What—"

Gardiner gripped his arm. "Easy, Daniel. You need to listen to me. You're all right now, but you've had a bit of trouble."

Trouble?

"What kind of trouble?"

"Do you remember passing out?"

"I passed out? But I've never passed out..."

"Well, I'm afraid you can't say that anymore. Apparently, your friend Stephen caught you or you might have been in worse shape than you are now. It seems he saved you from a tumble."

Daniel looked toward the foot of the bed to see Stephen smiling at him. "Good thing you're as light as you are, my friend, or we might both have been in some trouble."

"But—"

Gardiner had already begun to check his pulse. "Just give me a minute now, and I'll answer any questions you have." When he glanced up, he nodded. "You're doing better. Yes, a good bit better."

Bewildered, Daniel had all he could do to form a coherent question. "I actually did pass out?"

"Oh, yes. How do you feel?"

"How—" Daniel broke off. How did he feel? Confused. His mind felt as if it were enveloped in a fog. But the headache he'd been struggling with for days seemed to have eased, at least a little. That alone was a relief.

"Am I ill?" he finally managed.

"Ill?" Gardiner repeated. "Well, yes. But you'll be all right in time if you start taking care of yourself. However, you need to know that you were definitely headed for something more serious than exhaustion, although that's trouble enough."

"Exhaustion?"

"That's right. Total exhaustion. And as I'm sure you know, your heart has its limits. If you stress it beyond its endurance, it will rebel. Not getting enough rest or sleep, not eating right, in general not looking after yourself at all…I'm quite certain you're familiar with the condition we call exhaustion after all your years in medicine."

"But how—"

"How did it happen?" Ted Gardiner cracked a knowing smile. "You tell me. I understand you've been in the middle of a scarlet fever epidemic for some time now. Not to mention a local mine disaster. Tell me about the hours you've been keeping, why don't you?"

Daniel stared at him. In that moment he decided there was no way he was going to admit to another physician—especially one he respected as much as Ted Gardiner—just how neglectful he'd been of himself. As a physician, he should have known that he was only borrowing trouble.

When he didn't answer, Gardiner gave another nod, saying, "Right. Well, we've probably all been there, I expect. And eventually we have to pay the price. I can give you a tonic, and I'll certainly check on you frequently, but in the long run it's up to you. I think you know what you have to do."

Daniel knew all too well. What he didn't know was just how he could do it.

"And before you start peeling off the reasons you can't leave your practice long enough to recuperate—yes, you can. And you will. You must."

When Daniel started to object, Gardiner cut him off before he could get the words out. "Now listen. I have an assistant, a young fellow fresh out of medical school, who could actually use a little more work. I'm going to see if he'd be willing—and I'm sure he would be—to cover your practice for a few days—"

Again Daniel tried to interrupt, and again the other refused to let him. "It won't be a problem. And Nolan is a good physician—at least he's going to be, once he gets a bit more experience. It'll be good for him to take on more responsibility for a few days, more than I can give him in our practice at the present time. I've been so busy teaching I've had to cut down on my patient load, so I've been doing a number of referrals."

Daniel frowned. "You said something about a few days?"

Gardiner smiled. "Well…two weeks, Daniel. Two weeks, maybe three. At least. I can't say for certain that will be long enough. We'll have to see how you do, but I do know you'll not be a hundred percent before then. And if you need more time, I'll see to it that Nolan gives you what you need."

Daniel's mind felt as if it were sliding back to its earlier numbness. He couldn't begin to imagine not working for a day or two, much less two weeks or more. Yet something stirred within him that seemed to hint that Gardiner was right, no matter that it went against his very nature to agree with the man.

"I understand you also have a very capable nurse working for you."

He looked at Gardiner. "Addie Rose? She's not actually a nurse."

"But she's experienced with your practice and acts as your assistant?"

"Yes, but—"

"Good. Then she'll be of real help to Nolan with your routine and your patient files. She seems more than willing to help—and highly capable."

"You've…talked with Addie Rose?"

"Oh, yes. She was here earlier this morning. Apparently, once she got the news about you, she drove in and stayed until early afternoon."

"Addie Rose drove in?"

Gardiner smiled. "That's right. She said she has a new buggy of her own. And she was obviously quite pleased with it."

"Good for her. I knew she was saving for one. But… Wait. How long have I been asleep?"

Gardiner looked at him, his eyes narrowing. "You honestly don't know?"

"No. Well, for hours, I suppose—" Daniel stopped, uncertainty eating at him.

"This is Sunday, my friend. Sunday evening. You've been out since yesterday afternoon."

"Sunday?" Incredulous, Daniel looked toward the window and saw only darkness. "I've been asleep since yesterday?"

"You have indeed," replied Gardiner. "Deeply asleep. That's why Stephen sent his son into Clarksburg to find a doctor this morning. Your friends here have been very concerned, and rightly so."

Riddled with shock and confusion, Daniel could scarcely get his breath. He looked toward Esther. "Esther, I'm sorry! So sorry. I wouldn't have put you out like this for anything—"

"Oh, for goodness' sake, Daniel! As if your sleeping under our roof is putting us out after everything you've done for us and our family!" She wagged a finger at him. "I don't want to hear another word. Furthermore, you're going to stay here during your recuperation until Dr. Gardiner says you're completely well, and that's final."

"No, I can rest at home. But the baby… You were worried about Anna. I was going to check her out." He tried to pull himself up.

"That little sweetie is just fine," put in Dr. Gardiner, carefully pushing him back onto his pillows. "I've gone over her thoroughly, and she couldn't be any healthier."

Daniel looked from him to Esther. "But you've been concerned—"

She waved a hand toward her husband. "Stephen says I worry about everything where Anna's concerned. And I suppose I do. It's been such a long time since we've had a baby in the house that I can't help but hover. But Dr. Gardiner says she's thriving and that babies sometimes change their eating habits and other parts of their routine, so that's helped to put my mind at ease."

She came around to pat his arm. "Now, no more talk of your going home. You're staying right here where I can keep an eye on you. Besides," she added, "no doubt Stephen will rather like the idea of having a doctor on the premises to keep me from fussing so much over Anna."

"That sounds like an order to me," said Ted Gardiner. "If you're wondering, your Miss Addie Rose has promised to stop by each day and bring you up to date on what's happening with your patients. And I'll make sure Nolan also stays in continual contact with you."

Daniel couldn't deny to himself that he found the idea of seeing Addie Rose every day more than a little pleasing. But then another thought struck him. "Sarge! Where's Sarge?"

Again Esther touched his arm. "He's just fine, Daniel. Right now he's out on the front porch. He can stay with us too for as long as you're here. In fact, there's no reason he can't share the room with you, if you like. He's most welcome to stay indoors. We love Sarge too."

"That seems like a good idea," Ted Gardiner said. "I expect he's a bit put out by now about being separated from you. I didn't like the look in his eye when I arrived today. Where in the world did you find a dog that size anyway?"

"He's been with me since the war," Daniel explained. "And don't let him fool you. He really is all bark and no bite."

"Good to know," said Gardiner. "Given his size, I wouldn't want to think about his bite."

⁓

Late into the night, Daniel lay half dozing, listening to the comforting sounds of Sarge snoring at the side of his bed. He felt a peace that surprised him, given the unexpected change in his usual hectic routine. Unexpected, and yet not entirely unwelcome.

In truth, he supposed he was too exhausted to feel much of anything other than a quiet sense of gratitude that he had friends such as Stephen and Esther Holliday. Although it went against his basic nature to feel altogether comfortable about lying in a bed that wasn't his own, in a house that was also not his own, admittedly he was too weak to do anything else but accept his current circumstances.

That being the case, he was thankful for these two special people who were doing their best to help him feel at home, right down to allowing his faithful dog and companion to bunk in with him. And he was thankful for Ted Gardiner, who had gone out of his way to take care of him and offer his assistant on an ongoing basis.

There was no denying that he was greatly blessed, so it was only right that he be grateful and not give in to the worry and self-disgust that insisted on weaving in and out of his consciousness. Even so, he recognized the fact that he was now facing days of idleness that might have been avoided if he'd only been more careful, more perceptive about his own human weaknesses and limitations.

He realized that berating himself was futile and would be of absolutely no benefit in his recovery. Nevertheless, it was a difficult stumbling block to avoid.

When he felt the warmth and weight of Sarge's big paw on his arm, he realized his restlessness must have awakened his loyal pal. Only then did he manage to say a thankful prayer for the undeserved goodness presently surrounding him and finally wind down enough to fall asleep.

THIRTY-ONE

VISITORS

*There is no denying
that some visitors are more welcome than others.*
ANONYMOUS

Addie Rose was searching Miss Gladys's kitchen when she heard a strange noise that seemed to be coming from the pantry.

She had made it a practice, ever since moving in with the ailing spinster, to get up well ahead of Miss Gladys and prepare a good, nourishing breakfast for the two of them. Because she was running a bit late this morning, she was looking for something simple that she could put together more quickly than usual.

She stopped her search of the cabinet beside the window and turned toward the pantry, to her left. After a moment of silence, she turned back to the cabinet and pulled a bag of oatmeal down from the second shelf.

And then she heard it again. A slight rustling, like the tearing of paper, but a little louder this time. She started for the pantry but then stopped. She wasn't actually afraid of mice, she reminded herself, having encountered more than one at home on occasion. On the other hand, she wasn't overeager to meet up with one either.

She waited another second or two before going back to the counter to pick up a dishcloth, thinking she could always toss it over the creature if it darted out at her. She hesitated only a moment before approaching the pantry, pulling aside the curtain that separated the small room from the kitchen. Without warning, she remembered what Daniel had told her about Miss Gladys hearing a "strange sound" the day she fainted, and she tensed, holding her breath.

As she stood there, the rustling continued. She swallowed against a dry throat and pulled a steadying breath before taking another step.

She was met by total silence—until the floor-length drapes covering the shelves suddenly parted. Something crept from behind the drapes, hissed at her, and then ducked between her legs and went scurrying across the kitchen floor.

Addie Rose cried out, but her shock lasted only long enough for her to identify the culprit for what it was: not some menacing, brutal creature to fear, but rather a small and most likely harmless, though uninvited, animal—the likes of which she had grown up often wishing to possess as a pet but was never allowed to keep in the house: a kitten.

"Oh!" The soft exclamation escaped her as the tiny visitor stopped at the kitchen door, which Addie Rose had earlier closed to keep any noise from waking Miss Gladys.

"How in the world did you get in here?" she said, keeping her voice quiet in hopes of not frightening the little intruder, while looking around for some kind of entrance from the outside.

Seeing nothing unusual, she turned her attention back to the furry, gray-and-white spotted feline, who had resorted to charging around the kitchen floor, clearly in search of an escape route. Addie Rose stood unmoving against the wall, watching the obviously frightened kitten and feeling a nudge of pity for its unmistakable panic.

Another few moments of quiet passed in which Addie Rose continued to stand, not moving but murmuring an occasional sound of reassurance. As suddenly as it had begun racing about, the kitten stopped, crouching in the corner across from her, watching her with wary eyes.

"I'm not going to hurt you, little one," Addie Rose murmured. "But I hope you'll get over being afraid of me. I'd really like to pick you up and introduce you to Miss Gladys."

On the heels of that thought, however, she realized that Miss Gladys might not take to the idea of a feline guest making itself at home in her pantry. It might be best, at least for now, to leave things as they were.

With that thought, she made her way slowly to the door from the kitchen into the hall and eased her way out, leaving just a narrow crack so she could spy on the small intruder. The kitten stood unmoving, its back raised high, watching her go.

Outside the door, she watched through the narrow opening. It took only another moment before the little visitor—whom she had already decided to name *Sneaky*—began to slink soundlessly back to the pantry, where she disappeared behind the curtain.

Addie Rose gave herself a silent reminder to check the storage area a bit later to make certain there were no open containers that could be invaded. At the same time, her instincts hinted that, at least for the time being, it might be best to keep their uninvited occupant a secret.

⟶

On the way out to the Hollidays', Addie Rose could scarcely wait to tell Daniel about the kitten she'd discovered in the pantry. Anxious to see him, she urged her mare, Buttermilk, to pull the buggy at a quicker-than-usual pace.

She enjoyed having even a small bit of news to relay, as it was all too obvious that the days away from his practice were wearing on Daniel. She could tell he was always glad to see her and anxious to hear about her day. And if she were completely honest with herself, she was always eager to spend whatever time she could with him, although she tried not to give too much thought to the reasons why.

She felt a little guilty to be so relieved Dr. Nolan wouldn't be visiting Daniel with her today, as he usually did. Dr. Nolan was tied up with some home visits, and she'd insisted that there were forms to sign and information to gather from Daniel that required her to visit with him instead of accompanying Dr. Nolan.

She had to admit that it was a really nice thing Dr. Nolan was doing, filling in with the patients while Daniel was laid up. And he seemed to be a good doctor, more than capable, although she had sensed their patients were anxious for Daniel's return.

But the man had a flirtatious way about him that made her uneasy. On the days when she was going out to the Hollidays', he always seemed a little too quick to insist on going with her. Not only that, but he was always ready with a compliment or flattering remark in or out of the office. There was no denying that he made her uncomfortable.

Recently, Daniel had insisted that Dr. Nolan make use of his buggy while he was laid up, so now he could come and go as he wished. And he did just that, even inviting Addie Rose to leave her buggy at the office and ride with him to visit Daniel—which she had refused to do.

His freshness would have been unwelcome even if he were single. But Brad Nolan was a married man, and he and his wife were expecting their first baby soon. It was possible he simply meant to be nice to her, but Addie Rose didn't think so. In truth she avoided him as much as possible, difficult though it was as they worked together in—and sometimes out—of the office.

He wasn't the only reason she would be exceedingly glad when Daniel got back to work, but he was definitely one of the reasons. At any rate, she had precious little time to spend alone with Daniel these days, and she had to admit she was looking forward to today.

～

Daniel had made it his business to be up and sitting in a chair by the window when Addie Rose arrived. He hated this time of forced idleness and was determined to regain his strength as quickly as possible. He knew Esther worried about him, often insisting that he not push himself, but he had learned enough about the patients he'd treated over the years to realize that there was such a thing as not pushing oneself hard enough. Staying idle too long could cause even more problems than not getting enough rest.

Besides, he detested the thought of appearing ill in Addie Rose's eyes. Even though he continually made an effort to hide his growing attraction to her, he still found himself disgusted by the thought that he might appear weak or less of a man to her.

To complicate his feelings even more, not only did his interest somehow feel like a betrayal of Serena, but he feared just how Addie Rose might react if she became aware of what would most likely be his unwelcome feelings for her. Was it possible that she'd be so put off she might even resign from her position?

He could scarcely bear to even think of the possibility. Not only because he'd come to depend so greatly on her assistance, but because he had come to the point where he couldn't imagine what his life would be like if she were no longer a part of it.

As he watched her now, her head bent low over the papers she'd brought for his signature and the list of questions she had drawn up for his input, his heart seemed to swell and beat a little faster than normal. It was becoming almost impossible to ignore the feelings her nearness generated these days.

"Daniel?"

He started, realizing she had apparently asked him a question. "I'm sorry—"

"If this is tiring you—"

"No," he interrupted her. "I just…I don't seem to concentrate as well as I need to these days," he said awkwardly. "What was it?"

"I wondered if you want me to put some of your patients with more serious problems off until you're back in the office."

He tried to think. "No, I have Ted Gardiner's assurance that Brad is a fine doctor. I'm sure he can handle everything without any problem. Unless…" He paused, thinking.

"Yes?"

"Patrick McManus. With his heart condition...well, you never know just what to expect with Patrick. I should talk with Brad about him. But in case of an emergency, of course, Brad would need to see him right away. Next time he's out here, I'll fill him in on Patrick." He paused again. "And little Keely Glynne. Those fragile bones of hers can snap almost anywhere that can't always be detected right away. At the slightest sign of an ache or pain, she needs to be seen immediately."

He waited as Addie Rose made another note, appreciating her serious attention to detail almost as much as he enjoyed watching the way one wave of her hair fell over her right eye as she hovered over her pad and pencil.

But when she lifted her head and caught him staring, he quickly cleared his throat and fumbled to avoid his embarrassment. "So what's Brad like to work with?"

He noticed her hesitation and wondered about it.

"He's...the patients appear to like him. He's thorough and well organized. Obviously intelligent."

Daniel nodded. "That's my impression of him as well. He's not keeping you too busy, is he? You're able to maintain your regular working hours?"

Again, she seemed to hesitate, but her reply wasn't in any way negative. "Yes, there's no problem there. He's...he's careful about not keeping me late or expecting too much."

Again Daniel nodded. "Good. I'd want you to tell me otherwise."

She appeared to study him for a moment, but then she lowered her head and finished whatever she'd been writing

After a moment, she slowly put her pencil down and again looked at him. "So, how are you feeling by now?"

"Like I'm going to crawl out of my skin if I don't get back to work right away."

She smiled. "What's Dr. Gardiner telling you?"

"Last time he stopped by—a few days ago—he told me I need to be patient with myself," he said with another sigh. "He says I've made good progress, and I get the feeling he's close to giving me the go-ahead to get back to normal. It's been almost two weeks since all this started, after all. It had better be soon, or Esther is most likely going to send me packing out of sheer desperation. I'm probably driving her wild with my bad moods and pouting."

Still smiling, she said, "Somehow I find it difficult to imagine you pouting. And it strikes me that Esther is far more interested in making certain you have a complete recovery than in getting you out of the house."

"Trust me, I'm not the best company when I'm bored. And I am *bored.*"

"Well, I'm sure Sarge will be just as glad as you when you get home and back to normal."

At the sound of his name, the Newfoundland lifted his head to look around, and then he let out a snuffle and returned to his nap. But only until Addie Rose stood and began to gather her things. Without hesitation, the big lug then stirred himself and got to his feet, whimpering as he watched her prepare to leave.

Trying to avoid any sense of self-pity, Daniel nevertheless couldn't deny the fact that he was feeling the same keen sense of loss as his canine companion.

THIRTY-TWO

HURRIED EXITS

I turned my back
On the dream I had shaped,
And on this road before me
My face I turned.

Padraic Pearse

Late Saturday afternoon, Daniel found himself surrounded by visitors and thoroughly enjoying himself, even though the first part of the day hadn't begun all that well.

Ordinarily, a rare morning visit from Serena would have buoyed him for the rest of the day, especially because her appearance this morning had marked only the third time she'd shown up at the Hollidays' during his illness. As always, she had looked every bit the fashion plate, dressed in a soft mauve suit and feathered hat, with not a single curl escaping from her carefully sculpted hairdo. Perfection personified. He was glad he'd made the effort to get into some decent day clothes rather than lounging around in worn trousers and shirt as had been his habit all too often since he'd been confined.

It turned out that Serena's mood wasn't as perfect as her appearance. Things started out well enough, with her quick but chaste kiss and a concerned inquiry into his progress. But when he mentioned, albeit briefly, his eagerness to get back to work caring for his patients, a faint chill seemed to replace her initial concern and set an edge to her questions.

"You do realize, I hope, that you're going to need to cut back considerably on your patient load now," she said in a somewhat authoritative tone of voice.

Caught off guard, Daniel realized, too late, that his reply sounded a bit defensive. "Well, Ted seems optimistic about my making a complete recovery. He hasn't indicated any particular need for me to reduce my practice."

"You haven't been in touch with Dr. Gardiner nearly enough for him to know just how overworked you really are, Daniel. You've been doing the work of two men far too long. And this experience you've just gone through should be proof enough of that."

Normally, Daniel would have been pleased at her unusual display of concern, but not today. Perhaps he'd been shut in and bored just long enough that his reaction was more that of impatience to get back to his practice—and irritability because Ted hadn't as yet agreed that he was ready to resume his work.

"I realize I've overdone it, Serena. And I can assure you that I'll be more careful from now on. But I can tell I'm strong enough now to get back to work, and there's plenty of work waiting for me to do. As soon as Ted gives me the go-ahead, I'm more than ready to get out of this room and back to my patients."

She studied him. When she replied, her tone was cool and laced with unmistakable irritation. "This hasn't taught you anything, has it?"

Daniel didn't quite trust himself to answer her. He supposed he should have been pleased that she was worried for him, but somehow her fretting was coming across more as resentment. Where he would have expected her to know him well enough by now to understand his eagerness to get back to normal, instead she seemed bent on making him feel stubborn and even somewhat foolish.

He thought it best that he remain silent.

"I suppose you're going to go right on trying to maintain a practice for those people in Owenduffy as well as Mount Laurel."

There it was again. That reference to "those people." As though the miners and their families were somehow less than worthy of his time and attention.

Or was he simply overreacting out of impatience and irritation? He might have conceded as much except for her next words.

Her tone actually softened as she went on. "Daniel, you can't keep this up. Can't you see that what happened to you this time might well be a warning? For goodness' sake, take care of our own people! Let those miners find another doctor!"

Our own people? His head began to throb.

"It's not all that easy to find a doctor for an entire mining town, Serena. It's not as if they can just pick one up at the nearest store."

"Oh, for heaven's sake! Now you're just being obstinate. I worry about you, Daniel. And after this, I'm going to worry even more."

Her words softened his irritation. "You don't need to worry about me, Serena. I promise you, I am going to be more careful in the future. And don't forget—having Addie Rose to help out in the office has been a big help. She's turned into a wonderful assistant."

Her look hardened. "I'm sure," she said, her tone frosty as she stood and began to put her gloves on. "I need to get going. I have some shopping to do for Mother yet today."

Daniel got up from his chair. "Well…I'm glad you came by," he said awkwardly. "I always look forward to seeing you. "

She stopped what she was doing and gave him a studying look. "Do you, Daniel?"

Surprised by her question and the way she was watching him, he said, "Of course I do."

After another moment, she looked away. "You'll let me know when you get home?"

He nodded. "I will. I imagine it will be soon."

Her smile was quick and fleeting. "I'm sure you hope it will be."

He had intended to kiss her goodbye, but something in her expression made him hesitate. She offered her cheek but then moved away from him so quickly he scarcely managed to touch her. She started for the door, saying, "I'll just peek in the baby's room. I imagine that's where Esther is."

Daniel didn't make an effort to follow her. Some instinct made him hesitate and then go back to his chair.

This wasn't at all the way he'd hoped her visit would go. And yet if he were totally honest, he had to recognize the fact that he wasn't as bothered as he would have once been.

Long after she'd gone, he sat looking out the window, wondering about the change that had come over him lately. Or had they both changed? More to the point, had Serena ever felt for him what he had once felt about her?

For the first time, he made himself face the fact that, in truth, he had always had doubts about her feelings for him. He supposed that if he were to be totally, even painfully, honest with himself, he now questioned if he could have misconstrued her feelings toward him altogether. Because of the way he'd felt about her, had he simply *assumed* she felt the same?

Could he have really been that foolish?

It chilled him to admit it, but he supposed it was entirely possible. He wasn't sure what that said about him. But even though he was in his midthirties, he had had so little experience with women that it was possible that he might have invented a relationship that had never existed. And although he was certain there were a number of things he didn't know about Serena, he had known her for long enough—and well enough, he thought— to believe it was just as likely that she wouldn't recognize a genuine love relationship any more readily than he would. Especially given her sheltered background and the supposed lack of eligible, unmarried men in the area.

He was dismayed at the thought that either of them—or even both of them—might have imagined a relationship that had never existed. Yet at the same time something in the depths of his spirit insisted that it was time to face the truth.

There was another truth he knew he needed to face, but before he could give it any further thought the center of that truth— Addie Rose—arrived, followed within minutes by Ted Gardiner.

～

After visiting for a few minutes, Addie Rose went to see Esther and the baby.

"This is as good a time as any to examine you," Ted told Daniel.

"I'm feeling good."

"That's what you told me last weekend. Not in a hurry to get back to your office, are you?"

Daniel tapped his fingers on the arm of the chair. "You know I am. But I do feel well, Ted. Honestly."

"Well, let's find out just how good you are at diagnosing yourself," the other doctor said, retrieving his stethoscope from its case.

After a few more minutes, during which he conducted what could only be described as an extremely thorough checkup, Ted straightened. He proceeded to study Daniel for a long enough time that Daniel began to fidget.

"Well?" he finally pressed.

Finally, Ted smiled. "Well, I'd say you're in good shape."

Daniel broke into a smile. "So I can get back to normal?"

"Within reason. But I want you to take your time and not push too hard. If I don't miss my guess, you could be your own worst patient because you're *not* patient. At least, not with yourself. You need to be careful, Daniel, and treat yourself the way you'd advise one of your patients. I don't have to give you a list of instructions on how to take care of yourself—you already know the procedure. Follow it. Take time to eat right and get plenty of rest. You may not think you need it, but you do." He paused. "If you think it would help, I can loan you Brad for a few more days."

Without hesitating, Daniel shook his head and got to his feet. "No. I hear you, and I'll do as you say. Believe me, I have no desire to go through this again."

They shook hands. "I'll just go and have a look at that baby and give Addie Rose a repeat of my orders for you. I'm putting her in charge of making sure you obey them."

He turned to leave but stopped when Stephen came rushing into the room.

"Good news, Stephen. You'll be rid of me—"

But he didn't get to finish his sentence. Stephen, red-faced and clearly out of breath interrupted him. "Doc Gardiner! Thank the Lord you're still here! They need your help in town!"

"What's wrong?" asked Ted.

"It's the carousel! There's a fire—a bad one! And people are all over the place! Today was free admission day for the children!"

A sick feeling washed over Daniel. This was a day that brought almost every child in town to the carousel, along with most of the parents, who were intent on keeping watch over them.

"The carousel?"

Daniel quickly explained, and then he turned back to Stephen. "You said the fire's bad?"

Both Addie Rose and Esther, who apparently had heard Stephen's shouting, appeared in the doorway, Esther with the baby in her arms.

"Real bad," said Stephen. "It looks as though it might bring the entire carousel down and spread to some of the nearby buildings. Worse, though, it started while children were waiting in line with their parents for their turn."

Stephen turned to Ted. "For certain, they're going to need medical attention—and they're going to need it right away!"

"Stephen, where's Clay?" Esther put in.

"I left him at the carousel. They need all the help they can muster to get that fire out."

The doctor was already moving toward the door. "I'll get my coat, but someone needs to show me the way."

"I'll go with you," Stephen said.

Daniel didn't have to think about it. "I'm going too. Esther, where's my coat?"

"It's there, with your other things in the closet. Your medical bag is still in there too. But, Daniel, surely you aren't going! You're not—"

"Ted says I'm fine," Daniel said, heading for the closet. "I'm going."

"So am I," Addie Rose said, giving Esther a quick squeeze on the shoulder and the baby a peck on the cheek before moving toward the door.

"Well, all right. But all of you come back here later. I'll have food fixed." She looked at Stephen. "Go on, then! I know you think you have to go. But be careful! And keep an eye on Clay."

He nodded, hesitating only long enough for a quick kiss for her and the baby.

Outside, Daniel remembered that Brad Nolan still had his buggy. "I'll need a ride—"

"You can go with me," Addie Rose said.

Still pushing an arm into his coat, Daniel set his bag in the back of her buggy with his free hand and climbed up onto the bench.

"You're sure you're all right to do this?" Addie Rose queried as they started off.

"I'm sure."

Even so, he began praying at that moment that he could handle whatever was ahead.

THIRTY-THREE

NIGHT OF FIRE

*These are the times when we are faced
with a not-so-welcome homecoming.*
ANONYMOUS

The scene at the carousel could have been stripped from somebody's nightmare.

Panicky parents stormed the fence, trying to get near the gate, but most were being held back by the sheriff and Jamie MacPhee, along with three helpers, including Clay. A few unattended children went hurtling into the crowd of adults, while others stumbled and, rather than trying to make their way out of the gate, ran in different directions, seemingly oblivious to where they were going.

Thick black clouds of smoke snaked upward and coiled toward the fence as the fire gained momentum. Daniel could feel the heat as they drew closer. Before they even reached the carousel, his eyes and throat began to burn. He dug into his pocket for a handkerchief and masked his face as best as he could, while Stephen and Ted followed suit.

Lawrence Hill, who was headed toward the burning carousel from the newspaper building, spied them and stopped, moving in beside Daniel. "Good to see you up and about again. Though this is a sad welcome home for you."

"How did this happen, does anyone know?" Daniel asked him.

Lawrence shook his head. "Lots of folks wondering about that, but no one seems to know. If I were to hazard a guess, I'd be tempted to point the finger at a group of older boys I saw building a bonfire behind the maintenance building. Other folks saw them there earlier too, but they disappeared real fast once the fire started."

As they drew closer, the sheriff said something to Jamie and then made his way toward Daniel and the others. "Boy, am I glad to see you, Doc! We already have some injured! I hope you're fit to work!"

"I am, Lon." He quickly introduced Ted Gardiner, and the sheriff's face lit still more.

"Two doctors? Great! And we'll likely need both of you. Right now we're trying to figure out where to put the injured. Somebody suggested the schoolhouse since it's so close. But I'm not sure that's a good idea."

"Too close, it seems to me," said Lawrence. "With this wind, that fire has a good chance of spreading. I don't like to think it, but the schoolhouse might go too." He paused and then said, "Why not use the newspaper building? I have plenty of room in back. And we're close enough that it won't be a problem to move folks there."

"That's all right with you?" the sheriff asked.

Lawrence nodded. "I think that might be your best option.

The injured need to be placed into some kind of shelter as soon as possible."

The sheriff looked at Daniel, who nodded his agreement, saying, "Sounds like a good plan to me. And I think Lawrence is right. The sooner the better."

~

While Daniel and Ted cleared the back of the building, Addie Rose drove to Daniel's office to load the buggy with medicines and other supplies. When she returned, they set up a makeshift working area.

Once that was done, Daniel went back outside. By now the fire was out of control. His eyes burned, and he felt his lungs struggling for air as he started for the flaming carousel. He passed a number of adults herding children away from the blaze and saw Stephen and Clay guiding folks past the fence that circled the carousel. He glanced behind him to the newspaper building, where Lawrence stood at the door beckoning inside a number of people who seemed dazed and in search of a place to go.

By now Daniel was all too aware of his recent bout with exhaustion. He felt as though a fist were pounding at his heart, and he was gasping for air as much from exertion as from the smoke billowing around him. He knew he'd have to get back inside quickly. Otherwise, instead of taking care of fire victims, he'd be the one requiring attention. He caught one more glimpse of the blaze that was fast turning into an inferno before turning and hurrying back.

Within minutes, Clay and Jamie appeared at the office leading a small boy and a woman who identified herself as the child's mother. They were soon followed by Stephen with a man and a little girl Daniel recognized. Adam Gilroy was a widower who had been in Daniel's office more than once with his daughter, seven-year-old Sally. The child seemed unable to get through even an ordinary cold without difficulty breathing. At the moment, she was clearly gasping for breath.

Ted took over the care of the little boy while Daniel saw to Sally.

And so it went. An ever-increasing number of patients, most with breathing problems brought on by the smoke, came through the door while Daniel and Ted did their best to treat them.

Addie Rose kept their supplies ready for use and scrambled to make sure they had whatever they needed. At one point, Daniel asked her where Brad was. "He went home," she said. "Apparently, their baby is on the way. And that reminds me. His brother came for him, so he left your buggy at the office. Mr. Holliday and Clay said they'd take it and your horse back to their house tonight."

For a moment Daniel wondered at her tone of voice, which seemed unusually chilly, but his attention was quickly diverted by more patients coming into the office. He was so focused and intent on treating their injuries that he soon lost all track of time. Although he could see from the window that it was growing dark, the flames from the fire cast an erratic, sinister light over their surroundings, so he had no real idea of what time it actually was.

When he finally caught his breath and glanced up from his treatment of little Eamon Fahey, he was surprised to see that the number of waiting patients had dwindled considerably. And a few minutes later, when the sheriff walked in and announced that the volunteer firemen had finally gotten the blaze under control, Daniel drew a long breath of relief. At that point he began to feel extremely thankful that most of the parents and their children seemed to have escaped the worst of the injuries that could have occurred.

That thought brought with it the memory of one of Evan Whittaker's common remarks in the midst of trouble: "No matter how bad a situation might be, we need to always consider how much worse it might have been…and give thanks."

Even now, tired as he was and aware that there were still a number of injuries awaiting treatment, Daniel could recognize the wisdom of his stepfather's words. All he had to do was consider the possible destruction and even loss of life the carousel fire might have prompted, and he could do no less than thank God that it hadn't been worse.

～

Ted had left for home, and Daniel was tending to his final patient when Serena walked into the treatment area. Other than a couple of minor smudges on her forehead and one lock of hair that had escaped above her ear, she appeared as neat as usual. Her features, however, were anything but composed.

Daniel motioned for her to wait a moment while he finished bandaging the cut on young Lena Walsh's arm and sent her on her way with her older sister. At the same time, he saw Addie Rose start to leave the room and head for the front office. She said nothing, but she paused when Daniel motioned for her to wait.

"I'll help you clean up in here," she said, glancing toward Serena and then back at Daniel. "When you're ready."

"No, you go on home. You've done enough. I'll go back to the

Hollidays' with Stephen until tomorrow. I'm too tired to deal with anything else tonight. In the morning I'll collect my things and get Sarge and go home."

She hesitated for another moment before finally saying, "You're sure? Are you all right?"

Daniel nodded. "I just need some rest. And so do you. You go on now."

"All right. Da was here helping with the firemen. He's gone now, but he said to tell you if you need anything—anything at all—you're to let him know."

"That's good of him. You go ahead now."

Keenly aware that Serena was watching them, Daniel nevertheless waited until Addie Rose was out the door and on her way to her buggy before turning back. He noticed again that Serena appeared noticeably distressed, and only then did he remember the possible danger to the schoolhouse.

He went to her. "How long have you been here?"

"Long enough to see the school burn." Her voice was tight with strain, her face pale and lined.

Daniel reached for her hands. "Oh, Serena. I'm so sorry!"

She nodded but didn't look at him.

"Is it a total loss?"

Again she gave a nod, finally lifting her face to him. "Everything's gone except the stove." She gave a short burst of a bitter laugh. "Imagine that—everything burns except the stove."

Daniel tried to pull her to him but dropped back when she resisted his embrace.

Unsure how to offer comfort, he stood motionless, watching her.

Finally she glanced around and then began to rub her arms. "I'm going home now," she said, her voice wooden. "There's nothing I can do here."

Again, Daniel made a move toward her. And again she stepped back. Daniel remembered then that he was undoubtedly a wreck, given the smoke, the wounds, and the medicine he'd been exposed to. Well, there was nothing to do for that now. Besides, somehow he sensed that his appearance had little if anything to do with her resistance.

"I didn't realize you were back in town until Stephen told me," she said, her voice still dull and unfeeling.

"I wasn't. Not until Stephen came home with the news about the fire. Ted Gardiner was there too—in fact, he'd just told me this afternoon that I could go home."

"Well, it's a good thing there were two doctors in town," she said, her tone now dismissive. "But more exhaustion and smoke inhalation aren't going to help you get well."

"I am well," he reminded her, too tired to keep the impatience out of his voice. "And I wasn't about to sit by and do nothing with all this going on."

"Of course not. I doubt that you've ever in your life thought of yourself before others, Daniel." She stopped. "Well, I just wanted to come by and see how you're doing." Again she paused. "I'm glad you've recovered. And I'm sure you're glad to get back to work."

"Yes, I am. But I wish it were under different circumstances."

She nodded. "I need to go now. My parents will be worried. We'll...talk later."

In the distance, Daniel saw Lawrence making his way from the debris of the carousel to the newspaper building. Daniel started to move away from the door, but then he stopped and, unmindful of the cold, continued to watch Serena leave.

As she pulled away in her buggy, he felt a strange cloud of sorrow fall over him. In some inexplicable way, it seemed as if tonight marked the beginning of a goodbye.

THIRTY-FOUR

Coming Home

To thee I'll return, overburdened with care;
The heart's dearest solace will smile on me there.
JOHN HOWARD PAYNE

W hen Daniel stepped into the hallway of his home the next day, he was surprised at the memories and thankfulness that washed over him. It wasn't as if he'd been gone that long, after all. Yet somehow it seemed like forever. Perhaps because so much had happened since he'd last stepped through his front door.

Sarge bounded in ahead of him with enthusiasm, of course, as if he too had greatly missed their familiar surroundings. But after only a few moments, he came loping into the kitchen to find Daniel.

And a snack.

"Yes, you big lug, I'm glad to be home too."

Daniel took the time to find one of the bones he kept stored in the pantry and placed it at Sarge's feet. "Have at it," he told his companion. "We'll get you some real food later."

In the bedroom, he looked around and then sorted through his mail and hung up his few remaining clothes that were still clean. He spent the rest of the afternoon cleaning himself up a bit, checking on things around the house, and entertaining Sarge, who had been left to his own devices for quite long enough.

Later he and the Newfie went for a walk. They made their way to the remains of the schoolhouse first. He found the site even more depressing in the stark daylight than when he'd viewed it the night before. It no longer resembled the squat, cheerful building that had provided the learning center for more than two generations of Mount Laurel children. Today it simply appeared to be a place of charred, abandoned rubble.

How long would their youth have to go without a place to gather together, to grow and learn? And how upsetting must this be to Serena, losing this place where she had spent her past few years doing a work she loved with the children she loved and who loved her?

After a few minutes, they went on to the square where the carousel had once played its music and entertained both residents and visitors. The lingering smoke and charred wood and metal made for a thick, irritating stench that had Daniel coughing and his eyes burning in only seconds. Even more painful, though, were the poignant memories of the cheerful music and excited laughter of children, families, and friends at the park. Their meeting place would be greatly missed.

Even Sarge seemed sensitive to the desolate mood that hung over the site. He circled Daniel restlessly, uttering subdued whimpers as if questioning what they were doing there.

The heaviness of the atmosphere soon began to weigh them both down, and Daniel delayed leaving no longer. As they walked away, he felt a sudden wave of longing for Addie Rose's presence, her steady cheerfulness and optimism. It buoyed him to think about tomorrow, when he'd be back in the office with her and her brightness that somehow managed to lift his spirits, even on the most difficult days.

He was tempted to stop and visit her and Miss Gladys, but he decided he needed to be sensitive to her likely need for some rest after the long hours she had put in yesterday.

Probably the last thing she needed right now was company. Feeling somewhat lost and at loose ends, he finally turned toward home, reluctantly facing a solitary evening.

Sarge chuffed just then and tried to pull ahead of him. "Well, not altogether a solitary evening," Daniel muttered to the Newfie. "I suppose you're pretty good company most of the time."

Sarge made a short puff of agreement before picking up his pace as if to urge Daniel on.

THIRTY-FIVE

WORDS SPOKEN TOO QUICKLY

What's left unsaid says it all.
ANONYMOUS

*S*hortly before noon the next day, as Daniel and Addie Rose were readying the examining room for the next patient, he mumbled something about feeling as if he'd been gone for months rather than merely a few weeks. It seemed as though they had seen twice the number of patients as was usual in a full day.

"You were missed. Can you tell?" Addie Rose said dryly.

"But it wasn't as if you didn't have another doctor here. Brad indicated he was keeping up with the patients well enough."

After tucking a clean sheet into place on the examining table, she straightened and turned toward him. "I probably shouldn't say this, but Dr. Nolan had a way of...overstating things sometimes." She paused. "As far as keeping up with the patients—well, a few of the ones I met outside the office mentioned that they were waiting for you to get back before coming in again."

Daniel looked at her. "That surprises me. I was under the impression that he was doing a good job."

"He's a good enough doctor, I'm sure," she hurried to say. "I just meant that he might not be quite as...exceptional as he seems to think."

Unexpectedly, she flushed and quickly added, "I'm sorry. I shouldn't have said what I did. I just meant—well, our patients really missed you, that's all."

"No, you have a right to your opinion about anything that takes place in this office," Daniel said, meaning exactly that and wanting to reassure her. At the same time, he chose his next words carefully. "I expect if Brad seemed a little...self-important, it might have been because he was trying to reassure himself. When you're new in your work, it's sometimes easy to exchange insecurity for overconfidence."

"I'm sure that's what it was," she murmured, quickly turning away.

As Daniel watched, she began scrubbing the sink almost furiously, as if it were coated with grime. Puzzled by this unusual behavior—Addie Rose was usually the soul of steadiness and composure—Daniel studied her for another moment.

There was no time for speculation, though. They needed to get on with the next patient. Even so, as the day went on, he found himself occasionally wondering about her uncharacteristic actions.

∽

Later, Addie Rose could have slapped herself for saying what she did to Daniel about Dr. Nolan. The way Nolan looked at her was upsetting, but no doubt Daniel found her words surprising and possibly even rude. She couldn't expect him to understand. She wasn't sure she understood, other than the fact that she supposed Dr. Nolan's freshness with her had engendered a poor opinion of the man in general.

Still, if she really thought things through, her dislike for him was most likely unreasonable. Yes, he was something of an egoist, and from what she had observed, the patients didn't warm to him as they had Daniel.

But why would they? Nolan was only temporary. And besides, Daniel had a natural warmth and concern about him that the younger doctor didn't. She had never sensed the genuine attention and personal patient interest from Brad Nolan that Daniel seemed to find so easy to offer.

She came to the conclusion that she disliked Dr. Nolan so intensely because of the unwanted advances he had made toward her. The fact that he had behaved in this way when his wife was carrying their baby somehow made it seem even worse. But Daniel didn't know about any of that, nor would she want him to. Dr. Nolan had filled in for him when it was needed, and there was no reason to tarnish his reputation. Still, she had skirted around the real reason for her dislike of Dr. Nolan, instead giving vent to things that were relatively minor—at least in comparison to the real reason he troubled her.

She had seen the puzzlement and confusion in Daniel's eyes, and she hated that her pettiness had caused it. The idea that he might think less of her—or Dr. Nolan—because of her actions today was painful to the extreme. She had spoken out impulsively and unnecessarily, and she would need to be more careful in the future that it didn't happen again.

～

Even long after he reached home, Daniel was still mulling over Addie Rose's puzzling behavior during the day. She had grown steadily more silent and remote after making her few less than complimentary remarks about Brad.

He found that strange. Nothing she had said was particularly harsh, but the fact that Addie Rose had made any sort of negative comment had surprised him. It simply wasn't like her. But her withdrawn behavior afterward was what really puzzled him. Maybe he was making too much of it, but he couldn't help but wonder if there were more to it than her somewhat thin explanation.

In any event, it probably shouldn't concern him as much as it had. Now that he was back to his practice, it wasn't likely they would have any future contact with Nolan, so he needed to let it rest.

Later that night, though, as he tried to concentrate on a journal he'd been reading, he realized that putting any questions about Addie Rose or Brad out of his mind might be easier said than done. His thoughts continued to wander in their direction.

Impatient with his restlessness, he turned out the light and resolved to go to sleep. Unfortunately, that seemed to be a lost cause as well. Instead, he couldn't stop thinking about Serena.

What would she do now? As far as he knew, the only work she had ever undertaken was in the classroom. Her parents seemed fairly well to do, so she probably didn't need a job. But he knew Serena well enough to know that she had an independent spirit and wouldn't likely be content to depend on her parents' support indefinitely.

She had once indicated that her main reason for living with them this long was that her father's health wasn't good, and she wanted to be there for her mother. Somehow he couldn't see her remaining idle for too long.

Of course, the town couldn't remain without a school. They would have to find a way to build a new facility. But that would mean raising funds and erecting a building. All that would take time. Maybe they could find a temporary location in the meantime. For the children's sake, and for Serena's as well, he hoped so. He determined to talk with some of his friends in the business world—men like Lawrence and others—as soon as possible to get their ideas.

After tossing and turning for another half hour, he forced himself to shut off his tangled thoughts and try to get some sleep.

On the floor beside his bed, Sarge exhaled a disgruntled sigh that signaled his agreement.

THIRTY-SIX

DELIVER US FROM EVIL

*God, protect me from anything
that wasn't sent by You.*
ANONYMOUS

A week before Christmas, Addie Rose was on her knees at the bottom drawer of the file cabinet behind the reception counter when the outside door opened. By the time she stood up, Brad Nolan was on the other side of the counter.

Surprised, and none too pleased to see him there, she could scarcely manage a civil greeting. "Dr. Nolan?"

He gave her a broad smile. "Oh, come on, Addie Rose. Surely you know me well enough by now to call me Brad."

She made no reply other than to fix a questioning look on him. "Is Daniel here?"

She hesitated and then shook her head, saying, "No. Not right now."

"Out on calls?"

"Yes. He should be back anytime now."

He glanced at his pocket watch. "I thought you usually went with him on patient calls."

"I do. But we've been busy lately, so I stayed in this afternoon to catch up on some things."

"Well, I can get what I need without bothering him. I left in such a hurry last week that I forgot my appointment book and my fountain pen. Dr. Gardiner wasn't all that busy today, so I thought I'd drive up and retrieve them while I had a free afternoon." He paused. "I'm sure they're in Daniel's office."

"I haven't seen them, but no doubt that's where they are." When he made no move to go into the office but simply stood there, watching her, she began to feel uneasy. "So, how's the new baby? And your wife?"

Still smiling, he leaned his arms on the counter. "They're doing just fine. And how about yourself? You seem to be staying busy."

"Yes. And I probably should get back to work. Why don't you go on into the office and see about your things?"

"I'll do that. Shouldn't take more than a minute."

Relieved, she watched him go. Instead of returning to the file cabinet, though, she remained standing, rifling through some papers on the reception desk, at the same time wishing Daniel would get back soon.

When Nolan didn't appear after several minutes, she went to the door of the office and looked in. He glanced up from Daniel's desk, saying, "I can't seem to find them."

"Try the top left drawer," she suggested. "He might have put them in there to keep them safe for now."

As she watched, he opened the drawer, looked, and then shook his head. "No. Not there." He scanned the top of the desk again. "Any idea where else they might be? I don't want to go rummaging through his things with him not here. Would you mind having a look?"

Addie Rose hesitated, but she stepped inside and went around the desk to search through the other drawers. She hadn't realized that he'd stepped behind her until she felt his arms go around her waist.

She whirled around. A mistake, because he easily pulled her closer and tightened his grasp on her.

"No! Stop it!" She twisted, trying to pull herself free, but he held her fast.

He brought his face closer to hers then, murmuring, "I've been wanting to do this ever since I met you."

Terror, then fury shot through her as she again tried to twist away from him, but he wouldn't budge. "Let go of me!"

"Come on now, Addie Rose. You don't really think I came all the way up here just to get an appointment book and a fountain pen, do you? I thought you were a lot brighter than that."

Nausea threatened to overcome her at that point, and on instinct she lashed out and slapped him as hard as she could.

He reared back but didn't loosen his grip on her. Instead, he grasped her arms and shook her, hard. "No more of that!" His voice had turned to a snarl. "You can't tell me you and *Dr. Dan* are strictly business when you're here alone together. I've seen the way he looks at you, and—"

"Let go of her. *Now!*"

At the sound of Daniel's voice, Nolan pushed Addie Rose away with such force she almost fell. Overcome and trembling with both shame and relief at the same time, she grasped the corner of the desk for support.

"Now, Dr. Kavanagh," Nolan began, raising his arms in a

gesture of surrender as he started around the desk. "Just give me a minute, and I'll explain."

Daniel walked the rest of the way into the room and stopped directly in front of Nolan. He dwarfed the other man, who stopped moving and turned pale at the sight of him.

Addie Rose had seen Daniel truly angry only once that she could remember—the day of the mine disaster. But the look in his eyes that day in no way even resembled the rage that flamed in them at this moment. And his voice when he finally spoke was so thick with the tremor of disgust and anger that, had she not been looking directly at him, she might not have even recognized him.

"You can do your explaining to Ted Gardiner," Daniel said. "But keep in mind that I'll be talking with him as well. Now get out."

"Dr. Kavanagh—"

"I said get out!"

Nolan practically ran from the room.

Only after they heard the door slam shut did Daniel turn to Addie Rose. In that moment his expression faded from fury to a look of sad regret.

~

He started toward her but stopped when he took in her appearance. She stood, not looking at him, her shoulders hunched, her arms hugging herself. Then, despite the resistance toward him that he could feel in her, he gently led her to the small office sofa and helped her sit down. He lowered himself to sit beside her, but not too close.

"I'm so sorry, Addie Rose," he said quietly.

She looked up at him as if his words had startled her. "No. There's no reason for you to be sorry. You couldn't know—"

He put a finger gently to her lips. "But I should have known. I should have realized…it wasn't like you, not like you at all, to feel the way you obviously did about another person. It just didn't occur to me…he was here such a short time—" He stopped. "Was this the first time he'd been that way with you?"

"Yes!" she said quickly. "Oh, he'd made a few remarks, and there was something about the way he looked at me…"

She visibly shuddered and Daniel reached to steady her, but he stopped before making contact. "I'm so sorry," he said again.

"Please, don't be. I'd hate it if you felt bad for something you couldn't know about, and couldn't do anything about even if you had known."

"Oh, I could have done something about it, all right, and I would have. I wish you'd told me—"

Now she put a hand to his arm, and he quickly covered it with his hand.

"I know you would have. And that's why I didn't tell you. It wasn't as if he'd actually tried anything before today. He hadn't said anything, not exactly. And I knew Dr. Gardiner trusted him to fill in for you, a least part-time. I simply didn't feel right saying anything."

"But you have such an acute sense of awareness about people. I would have trusted your suspicions."

Again she started to protest, but Daniel stopped her. "You don't have to explain anything, Addie Rose. I just wish none of this had happened, but you're certainly not responsible for any of it. And please remember that I do trust your judgment. Completely."

"Thank you. That means a lot to me."

And you mean a lot to me...

He wished he could tell her how much. But until today he hadn't been honest enough with himself to realize just what she did mean to him. At this moment, with his heart aching as he witnessed the raw pain in her, he finally realized he couldn't deny it any longer. And yet he would have to. It wouldn't be right to bare his soul to her. Not yet. At least not until after he'd had a chance to talk with Serena.

And more and more he was feeling as though that needed to happen soon. Very soon.

THIRTY-SEVEN

Miss Gladys Meets the New Houseguest

*Fond Memory brings the light
Of other days around me.*
THOMAS MOORE

Late that night, Daniel decided he needed some time to think before having the conversation with Serena that he knew he needed to have. He had no intention of delaying that talk. He simply needed to clear his head first.

Before then, though, he felt a need to let Ted Gardiner know about the situation with Brad Nolan. Just the idea of broaching the subject made him uneasy. He had no desire to come across as a talebearer with a man he so highly respected. But on the other hand, it made him uncomfortable to think Ted might be completely in the dark regarding Brad's character. Besides, in order to preserve his own reputation and standing with Ted, there was always the possibility that Brad might try to tarnish Addie Rose's character by lying about what had taken place yesterday. Even the thought made Daniel furious.

He felt a distinct need to do something to protect her, but he wasn't quite sure just how to go about it. He could go to Clarksburg and meet with Ted, but there was every likelihood that Brad would be in the office at the same time. They were working together, after all.

No, he had no stomach to even imagine the ugly scene that could occur under those circumstances. He finally decided it was best to write a letter to Ted and, without going into detail, at least suggest there had been a problem and it might be good to keep a watchful eye on his young assistant.

He faced a busy morning with a full patient load the next day, so he proceeded to write the letter before going to bed.

～

The next morning, after going to the post office and sending off the letter to Ted Gardiner, Daniel began the next part of his day by stopping by to see Miss Gladys.

It was early for a patient call, but he wanted to take this time for at least a brief visit. He couldn't help but hope that Addie Rose would still be at the house. Even though he would see her at the office, he was impatient to make certain she was doing all right after yesterday's ordeal.

As it happened, she and Miss Gladys were still at the breakfast table when he arrived. He appreciated the fact that they both seemed glad to see him and eager to make him welcome. And he appreciated even more how well Addie Rose appeared to be handling the ordeal she had just been through. She fussed over him almost as much as Miss Gladys did, plying him with a cup of coffee and some glazed sweet bread.

"If this is how you two eat every morning," he said as he sat down to the table, "I just may have to stop by early in the day more often."

Miss Gladys took pains to follow his instructions as to how much sugar and cream to add to his coffee.

"I hope you're feeling as well as you look, Miss Gladys," he said, stirring his coffee.

"I feel very well, thank you," she said, touching the napkin at her throat as if to make certain it was still in place. "But it seems to me you're looking somewhat tired, young man. You do know what they say, I expect: Doctor, heal thyself."

Daniel smiled, pleased to hear her address him as "young man" again. It had been a while since she'd employed what he'd come to recognize as an endearment.

He glanced across the table to see Addie Rose smiling as he replied, "Yes, ma'am."

He was so pleased to see this dear lady, whom he had long liked and respected, doing so well. He knew one of the traits of dementia patients, at least in the beginning of the illness, was a kind of "in and out" behavior when it was sometimes difficult to tell anything was amiss, along with other times when it was all too obvious there was a problem. He'd had a feeling that Addie Rose would be good for Miss Gladys, and from what he was seeing this morning, he thought perhaps she might even be responsible, at least to some extent, for the marked improvement he sensed in her condition.

He was enjoying himself and the company so much he almost hated to get on with his day. But their first appointment would soon be arriving at the office, so he reluctantly stood up and said his goodbyes.

"Addie Rose, you could ride with me on the way in, if you like, instead of driving yourself."

"I'd actually thought of walking this morning," she said as she stood and began clearing the table.

"I know you like your walks," Daniel said, "but it's really cold out there."

"Well…"

"Addie Rose, you don't need to be catching your death," Miss Gladys warned in a stern tone of voice. "I'll clear the dishes. You go on with your young man now."

Addie Rose stopped dead, blushing faintly as she looked at Daniel, who couldn't resist grinning at her.

"I think you should listen to Miss Gladys, Addie Rose," he said, his tone light.

"Well…"

At that moment, the door to the pantry thumped open, and a tiny kitten emerged with a surprisingly loud meow.

Addie Rose's hand went over her mouth, and Miss Gladys popped up from her chair as if she'd been struck.

"What in the world!" Miss Gladys cried out. "Good heavens, it's a cat!"

Daniel had all he could do not to laugh at the stricken look on Addie Rose's face and the shock that sparked in the eyes of Miss Gladys. Another glance, however, at Addie Rose made him suspect that she wasn't so much surprised as guilt-ridden. So this was the little visitor she'd told him about not long ago.

Clearly, she hadn't yet advised Miss Gladys of their new lodger.

~

Addie Rose's mind raced as she went to Miss Gladys and prompted her to sit down. "I can explain," she said, trying to clear her throat.

But before she could say another word, the kitten made its way to Miss Gladys and stood staring up at her. Then, totally without warning, she jumped from the floor onto her lap.

Addie Rose groaned. This was definitely not the way she had planned to break the news about their new houseguest. But it was what it was, so she struggled for some measure of control and said, "Miss Gladys, this is Sneaky."

Miss Gladys looked up at her, frowning. "So it seems. You knew about this?"

"No. I mean…that's her name," Addie Rose stammered. "I named her Sneaky."

But Miss Gladys was scarcely listening. Her hand had gone to the kitten's back, just a touch at first, and then a stroke or two. Finally, she began petting her as if it were the most natural thing in the world for her to do. For its part, the kitten was purring loudly enough that she could probably be heard in the next room.

Addie Rose looked at Daniel, trying to signal for help, but he stood stroking his chin, clearly enjoying the scene in front of him.

Meanwhile, Sneaky looked up at her with a decidedly smug expression on her tiny face.

Quickly, Addie Rose moved to free Miss Gladys from Sneaky's claws before she could tear her morning dress. "Here, I'll take her…"

But Miss Gladys apparently had other ideas. She placed her hand between the kitten and Addie Rose's reach, saying, "No, let her be. She seems frightened."

Frightened? It seemed to Addie Rose that the devious little feline was anything but frightened.

"But I need to leave for work. I'll just put her in the pantry and make sure the door's secure this time. I'm really sorry about this. I had hoped to tell you about her before—"

"Oh, for goodness' sake, Addie Rose! I'm perfectly capable of taking care of a kitten without a guardian! You just go ahead to the office with Daniel and don't keep your patients waiting." She paused and then added, "Sneaky and I will be quite all right without you to supervise."

Daniel finally spoke up. "She's right, Addie Rose," he said, his expression deceptively bland. "It seems that Miss Gladys has everything under control. Why don't you just get your coat, and we'll be on our way?"

Outside, Addie Rose practically snarled at him on the way to the buggy. "You were a big help."

His mischievous grin reappeared. "I try."

"Are you sure it's safe to leave her alone like that?"

"She's not alone," Daniel pointed out. "She's been staying alone, after all, when you're at work." He waited. "I think she's in good hands…er, paws."

Addie Rose glared at him. "You'd better be right."

He looked at her. "You know I wouldn't take chances with Miss Gladys. Besides, you can go home at noon and check on her."

"Oh, I intend to."

"Yes, I know."

She shot a suspicious look at him, but when he said nothing more, she finally settled onto the seat and sighed as they drove away.

THIRTY-EIGHT

A FAREWELL FROM SERENA

This heart, fill'd with fondness,
Is wounded and weary.
WALSH'S IRISH POPULAR SONGS

In a week it would be Christmas, and Daniel was still trying to figure out what to do about two final gifts he planned to buy: one for Serena and another for Addie Rose.

He was strongly wishing now that he'd had the talk with Serena—the one he knew he couldn't avoid—days ago. But he just had not been able to know how to even instigate a conversation with her at this point. He knew she had to be depressed and no doubt at odds about the loss of the schoolhouse. It seemed a petty idea to face her with such a heavy subject as he'd planned to approach. But it was becoming more and more difficult to keep his feelings for Addie Rose silent, and he just didn't feel right about voicing them with matters at such a standstill with Serena.

It would soon be evening—he could see from his office window that dusk was fast approaching—and he was still in the office. Addie Rose had gone home some time ago, after they'd seen their last patient, but his state of mind had kept him rooted to his chair, trying to decide what to do.

He was about to give up and head home. Sarge had been pacing in the reception area for a good half hour or more. He was probably hungry and wanting his supper. It wasn't fair to make him wait because of his own lack of initiative and foul mood.

Daniel actually jumped when he heard the outside door open. Sarge barked but immediately went quiet. Thinking it was either an emergency or that Addie Rose had forgotten something and returned for it, he got up and quickly headed for the waiting room.

No more had he stepped into the reception area than he stopped, catching a quick breath at the sight of Serena, standing just inside the door. She looked her usual perfectly groomed self, but she was pale, and her eyes were shadowed.

"Well, this is a nice surprise," he said. And it *was* a surprise, although he felt a bit uneasy about whatever might have prompted it.

"I wasn't sure you'd still be here until I saw the light from your office window," she said, removing her gloves. "Working late?"

"A little. I was actually thinking of stopping by to see how you're doing, but I didn't know if you would want company."

She stood where she was, watching him for a moment. "Do you have time to talk? I won't keep you long."

"Of course I have time. Let's go in my office. Let me take your coat. How are your mother and dad? I haven't seen them for a while." He was making idle small talk, but there was something different about her, something peculiar.

"No, I can't stay. Right here is fine."

He studied her. "Is something wrong, Serena?"

"No." She glanced away and then turned back to him. "Well, not wrong, but I need to tell you something, and I'm not sure how to go about it."

That statement put Daniel on alert. Serena was seldom, if ever, unsure of herself or at a loss for words. "Oh?"

"I might just as well tell you." She drew in a noticeably long breath. "I'm leaving, Daniel."

He stared at her, not comprehending. "Leaving?"

"Yes. Leaving Mount Laurel. A few days after Christmas, we'll be moving to Buckhannon."

This was the last thing Daniel would have expected to hear. It had the effect of leaving him nearly speechless. "But...why?"

Again she avoided meeting his eyes. "We do have family there, you know."

"Yes, I know, but you've lived here for years."

"We've lived here for years," she said, seeming to pronounce each word distinctly and with great care, "because of my job with the school. And as it happens, we're leaving for the same reason."

She went on to explain. "Clearly, it's going to be some time before we'll have a school building again. In the meantime, there's been an opening in the Buckhannon district—a rather recent opening—for an elementary teacher. I've accepted the position."

Only then did she meet his gaze again. "They offered me the job a few weeks ago, and I turned them down. But after the fire—" She left her words hang with a shrug. "I found out they were still looking for someone to fill the position. It just seems to be the best thing for me to do."

"I...don't know what to say."

"I'm sorry. I know you couldn't have expected this, but I didn't want to say anything until I was sure." She sighed. "It's a good move for me, Daniel. And for my parents. This will reunite them with our relatives there, and because they'll have family close by, I believe it will free me to have a little more independence than I've had here."

"It's just so sudden—"

"Yes, I know. I don't suppose…" She stopped, as if uncertain whether or not to go on.

"What?" he prompted.

"I don't suppose," she said, raising her head to face him directly, "you'd be open to also making a move?"

He delayed so long she gave a sad smile. "I didn't think so," she said quietly.

"Serena—"

She lifted a hand to stop him. "I know. And I understand. It was just a thought, but I was fairly certain you wouldn't even consider it."

Daniel had never had so many mixed emotions roaring through him at the same time. In truth, he didn't know *how* he felt, other than being suddenly mired in total surprise and confusion.

But there was one thing he knew beyond all doubt. His home was here. His patients were here. His very life was here. And Addie Rose was here. But even if he were actually in love with Serena, as he'd once believed himself to be, he would have the fight of his life trying to convince himself to leave Mount Laurel.

She nodded, as if she could read his thoughts. "It's all right, Daniel. I know. I think we've both been questioning our…relationship…for some time now. You don't have to explain anything to me. I've had my doubts too."

"I'm sorry," he fumbled for the right response, though he didn't even know what the right response was. "I really am sorry."

"Please don't apologize. We probably would have come to this at some point—this need to be honest with each other—even if I hadn't decided to move away. We're friends. Good friends. Let's leave it at that, why don't we?"

Daniel could feel a heavy sorrow, and yet also a vague sense of relief, building inside him. He knew she was right.

"I'll miss you, Serena," he said quietly, reaching for her hand.

He saw an uncharacteristic glaze of tears form in her eyes. "And I'll miss you. Well, I need to go now." She paused. "You have a blessed Christmas, Daniel."

She gave Sarge an affectionate pat on the head, and then she was gone.

As he watched her leave, Daniel felt his own eyes begin to mist. He knew an important part of his life had just ended, and the knowing brought a heavy blow of pain. But at the same time he also knew that Serena was making the right move for her life.

And now he was faced with the need to make the right move for his own life.

EPILOGUE

I bring you with reverent hands
The books of my numberless dreams.
W.B. YEATS

*B*efore dark on Christmas Eve, Daniel summoned up all the nerve he hoped he possessed and drove over to Miss Gladys's house.

He knocked firmly on the door and waited. When no one answered, he knocked again. Finally, the door opened on Addie Rose, a vision in a rose-colored dress topped by a white, stiffly starched apron.

For a moment he lost his ability to speak. After he finally recovered, he said, with deceptive calm, "Merry Christmas."

Although her smile met her eyes, she was clearly surprised to see him. "Daniel! Please tell me you didn't work today."

"I didn't work today. Actually, I went shopping."

Now she looked genuinely puzzled. "Then—"

"What am I doing here? I come bearing gifts. May I come in? Or am I interrupting anything?"

"Of course you can come in! And you're not interrupting a

thing. Miss Gladys is entertaining Sneaky, and I'm just finishing up in the kitchen."

Inside, he wiped his feet and let her take his overcoat, while he held on to the large sack he carried in with him.

"Where's Sarge?"

"He's at home, waiting for his present."

"And what is he getting for Christmas?"

"The biggest beef bone in Mount Laurel."

She led him on to the living room, where Miss Gladys was ensconced in her favorite rocking chair with Sneaky half asleep on her lap.

"Miss Gladys, Merry Christmas to you—" he glanced at the sleepy kitten—"and yours."

She continued to stroke the kitten's head. "And to you, Daniel. I thought you were going to the Hollidays' this evening."

"Tomorrow," he said. "Today I went to the noon service at church. Since then I've just been getting ready for Christmas."

"And what does a bachelor do to get ready for Christmas?"

Daniel watched as Addie Rose went to stand behind her.

"Why, he shops, of course," Daniel said as he dug into the sack he'd carried in from the buggy and handed her a brightly wrapped gift.

"Oh my goodness! This is for me?"

"For you and your little friend there," he said, pointing to the kitten, whose eyes were now completely closed. "Open it, why don't you?"

Wide-eyed, she lit into the package and retrieved a delicate, peach-tinted vase on which was painted a detailed picture of a kitten flying a kite in a meadow. Both she and Addie Rose gasped in unison.

Daniel was surprised to see tears gather in the eyes of the elderly spinster as she carefully turned the vase around and around, admiring it. "Look, Sneaky! That could be you!" she exclaimed. The kitten opened one eye and then immediately closed it.

"Daniel, that is just beautiful!" said Addie Rose.

"And here's yours," he said, again reaching into the bag and handing her a small but intricately molded figurine, fashioned as an angel in prayer.

She looked at him, eyes shining. "I love it," she said quietly. "It's just beautiful."

And so are you…

He studied her until she blushed, at which point he said, "I need to steal your housemate for a couple of minutes, Miss Gladys. Do you mind?"

Clearly distracted by the vase and by the kitten on her lap, she shook her head, smiling.

"Addie Rose," he said, gesturing to her. "To the kitchen, please."

She hesitated but then carefully placed her angel on the mantel and followed him.

"What are you up to now?" she said, keeping her voice low when they reached the kitchen.

With his hand in his pocket, Daniel looked at her and suddenly felt nervous. "You remember two nights ago when I told you how I feel about you?"

The same night they had shared their first kiss…

"Well, of course I remember! A woman doesn't forget a moment like that," she said teasingly. "What? Have you changed your mind already?"

As she watched, he fumbled in his pocket for the small package he'd placed there earlier. "I'll never change my mind about loving you, Addie Rose. This is to confirm what I told you the other night."

With that he handed her the package. She looked at him and then opened the package that held the seal of the promise he'd recently made to her: a sapphire-and-diamond engagement ring.

"Oh, Daniel," she whispered. "It's just…"

"It's a promise," he finished for her, reaching for and retrieving the ring, and then placing it on her finger.

"For all our tomorrows," he said, close to choking on the words.

"Yes."

"Yes what?"

"Isn't this a proposal?"

"It is that."

"Then…*yes.*"

"I'll have my Christmas present now, please," he said, bending over to kiss her for only the second time since they'd met.

"Yes," she said again.

DISCUSSION QUESTIONS

1. Have you ever found something good to come out of something you feared would be unpleasant or extremely difficult? For example, Daniel reluctantly promised to take Ben Holliday's personal effects back to Mount Laurel. Unexpectedly, he not only made a new life there, but he also found a second family. Has anything like that ever happened to you? Has something you were dreading turned out to be a blessing?

2. Why do you think Daniel was so fond of Miss Gladys, even though at times she could be difficult and distant?

3. Were you surprised by the poverty in the company town of Owenduffy? What do you think accounted for it?

4. Why do you think the coal company management deliberately tried to maintain a strict separation from the more prosperous farming and business community close by? For example, at one time Daniel was even warned that his medical skills and experience would be unwelcome by the mining management.

5. What was your early impression of Dominic Murphy? Did you change your mind about him as the story continued?

6. Daniel was confused and even puzzled by his feelings for Serena. What do you believe accounted for his uncertainty?

7. Certain Mount Laurel residents seemed to resent the mining community. For example, Daniel's receptionist, Audrey, and also Serena, as well as others, made it obvious that they believed he shouldn't treat the residents of Owenduffy at all. What do you think accounted for this kind of hostility? Do you believe it was more than simple prejudice? Perhaps even an underlying kind of fear?

8. Even though he was infatuated, possibly even in love, with Serena, what particular attitude on her part troubled, even irritated Daniel?

9. Addie Rose tended to be somewhat abrasive during her early encounters with Daniel. What do you think she finally recognized in him that changed her initial feelings to admiration and, ultimately, love? Obviously, more than mere physical attraction accounted for Daniel's growing affection toward Addie Rose. What attributes in her do you believe contributed to the change in his feelings?

10. What specific episode in the story confronted Daniel with the need to ask God for forgiveness…and to enable him to forgive *himself*?

About the Author

BJ Hoff's bestselling historical novels continue to cross the boundaries of religion, language, and culture to capture a worldwide reading audience. Her books include *Song of Erin* and *American Anthem* and such popular series as The Riverhaven Years, The Mountain Song Legacy, and The Emerald Ballad.

Hoff's stories, although set in the past, are always relevant to the present. Whether her characters move about in small country towns or metropolitan areas, reside in Amish settlements or in coal company houses, she creates communities where people can form relationships, raise families, pursue their faith, and experience the mountains and valleys of life. BJ and her husband make their home in Ohio.

You can connect with BJ at
www.facebook.com/AuthorBJHoff
or
www.BJHoff.com

To learn more about Harvest House books and
to read sample chapters, visit our website:

www.harvesthousepublishers.com

HARVEST HOUSE PUBLISHERS
EUGENE, OREGON